THE PRAYER OF THE BONE

THE PRAYER
OF THE BONE

PAUL BRYERS

BLOOMSBURY

Published by Bloomsbury Publishing, New York and London.
Distributed to the trade by St. Martin's Press

A CIP catalogue record for this book
is available from the Library of Congress

ISBN 1-58234-075-7

First published in Great Britain 1998 by Bloomsbury Publishing Plc.,
and in the U.S. 1999 by Bloomsbury USA

First U.S. Paperback Edition 2000
10 9 8 7 6 5 4 3 2 1

Typeset by Hewer Text Ltd, Scotland
Printed in the United States of America by
R.R. Donnelley & Sons Company, Harrisonburg, Virginia

The backward look behind the assurance
Of recorded history, the backward half-look
Over the shoulder, towards the primitive terror.

From 'The Dry Salvages', *Four Quartets* by T.S. Eliot

I. EARLY SNOW

I

The first time he ever went there, before he knew the history of the place, he thought of bones. A cliff of bones.

It was suggested by a number of things: the derelict cannery with its lingering smell of dead fish, the bleached antlers of driftwood on the shore, the network of trenches cut across the headland like a mass grave and most of all by the birch trees that grew along the edge of the cliff, stripped entirely of their leaves this late in the fall and more white than silver, whiter even than the snow. And, of course, there was the body.

She lay on her back, a single eye open to the sky, and the snow formed a kindly gauze over the ruin of her face.

She had worked in the evenings at one of the inns down by the harbour and most of the men in the grieving group on the cliffs had known her. You'd go in there just to look at her, one of them said.

They stood hunch-shouldered each in his own little spout of breath with the snow swirling at their feet. He thought of the cows on his grandparents' farm, steaming in the harsh tungsten light of the milking shed. Something helpless in them, something resigned. But there was anger, too.

'Where's the child?' His mouth worked stiffly in the frozen air. 'Do we know who's with the child?'

No one answered but he saw the brief exchange of glances, as if it was an odd question to ask with so many others unanswered. Probably it was. He felt a need to prove himself, to show he'd experienced more gruesome killings than this, and it irritated him, this seeming lack of confidence in himself. Besides, he had seen nothing like this.

'Looks like she was slashed,' he said. Then, feeling the silence falling around him with the snow, 'repeatedly.'

But even as he spoke he noticed a curious regularity in the wounds, as if she'd been *raked*.

'Only time I seen a thing like this was up in Montana,' said one of the men. 'And that was a bear.'

There was no response and he shrugged.

'Only we don't get no grizzlies in Maine,' the man said, foolishly, and the others looked away, embarrassed.

They'd found a shoulder bag near the body with her name and address neatly printed on the L.L. Bean label fixed to the strap.

Just to make it easy for them.

'Who found her?' Calhoun asked Jensen, the police chief from Bridport who'd called him out. They must be right on the edge of city limits, he thought, if not over. He'd seen one of the sheriff's cars among the small fleet of vehicles that had already arrived but Jensen seemed to be taking charge of things. He pointed down the track to the little gathering outside the derelict cannery.

'Two of them. Dr Wendicott, she's the team leader or whatever, and one of her students. They were on their way up to the dig.'

The dig. Calhoun took it in, trying to fix the geography in his mind as it was now, in its thin covering of snow, before Jensen's men started trampling all over it.

This entire area of the headland was scarred with a series of excavations about four or five feet deep, running back more or less at right angles to the cliff and exposing the red granite foundations of the old buildings – or walls, or whatever they were.

The body had been found at the foot of a solitary birch tree, about halfway between these trenches and the edge of the forest. If the killer had left any tracks, they were under the snow.

What was she doing here on such a night?

She'd been working here since early summer, they said, so she would know her way around.

Perhaps she'd left something here and come back to find it.

But there was no sign of a flashlight. And why not wait for morning?

He walked along one of the trenches towards the edge of the cliff. The tide was out and he could smell the seaweed off the shore. The sky seemed to he lifting slightly. Calhoun could just

4

make out the darker shade of grey that was the New Brunswick coastline across the bay. And then he saw the boat.

She was lying in the mouth of the cove, a schooner of such elegant lines, such obvious pedigree she could only be here by mistake, or else a deliberate statement, like something in a glossy advert that juxtaposes the object of desire against the bleakest of landscapes to highlight its grace and beauty. Calhoun was so startled by the vessel itself he did not at first notice the figure on the deck, a white, hooded form seated on a hatch cover, gazing out to sea. It was so still it might have been a dummy, or a snowman, and then the head turned and he knew he'd been spotted, standing on the cliff's edge, and was being watched from under the hood. He waited a moment to see if the creature would acknowledge him with a wave or some movement away from under his scrutiny but it was Calhoun who finally moved away, back to the body in the clearing.

The deputy medical examiner had arrived at last, with grumbling apologies for the delay, blaming it on the snow, an elderly man with an air of bored, seen-it-all-before assurance that Calhoun reckoned had to be assumed unless there were killings up here no one had told him about. To Calhoun's knowledge there hadn't been a violent death in Russell County for twenty years or more.

He went very quiet when he saw the face, though.

'What do you reckon?' Jensen said. 'I mean, an axe, a shovel or what?'

The ME didn't seem to hear, or else didn't bother to answer.

'D'you think we could get something over it,' he said. 'Keep this snow off of her. And me.'

Jensen looked a little lost. He was new to the job, and Calhoun had no information on him except that he'd done six weeks basic training at the Police Academy in Augusta, which gave him a head start on the last chief. It was an open secret that Marty Hendricks had been so ignorant of the law he thought a case was closed when the insurance paid up. Jensen was keen. He was like a large puppy dog, eager to impress, but with so many masters he didn't know whose stick to run after.

'What's with the schooner?' Calhoun asked him, quietly, while his men were trying to fix up some plastic sheeting in the trees.

5

'The schooner?'

Jensen repeated the word as if it was entirely unfamiliar to him, a technical term he hadn't picked up at the Academy and might lose him a few marks in the ongoing assessment.

'There's a boat down there in the cove,' Calhoun told him. 'D'you know whose it is?'

But Jensen didn't know whose it was. Didn't even know it was there.

'D'you want me to find out?' he asked.

'Might be an idea,' Calhoun said, but his attention was on the ME now as he knelt down beside the body. He was removing some of the snow from the face with a small brush and Calhoun saw the first jagged hole appear in the mess of flesh and bone at the angle of her jaw.

II

There were ten wounds, Fentiman said, in two distinct patterns, one crossing her face diagonally from just above her left ear to her nose, the other running along the edge of her jaw and into her throat. There were fractures to the lower mandible and the cranium and both the carotid and the temporal arteries had been severed.

He thought it was a bear but they wouldn't know for sure, he said, until after the autopsy.

Calhoun watched as they zipped her into the body bag. He was strangely reluctant to let her go.

'And this is where she was killed?'

'I believe so. With her back to the tree.'

'How do you know that?'

'Angle of the wounds to the jaw, mainly. Also, there's a slight contusion on the back of her head and some bark caught in the hair.'

'So you're saying she was standing throughout the attack?'

'That is what I am saying, yes.' Fentiman had a way of answering questions – at least, when Calhoun asked them – that indicated he thought the questioner was a moron. Calhoun was inclined to think of this as a cover for his own uncertainty.

'You don't find that extraordinary?'

'In what way?'

'Well, that she was slashed repeatedly across the face, hit hard enough to fracture her jaw and her skull, and remained in an upright position.'

'I didn't say she was slashed repeatedly. A bear has five claws. I believe that only two blows were struck. One to the face, one to the jaw. One, two. Possibly the first blow knocked her against the tree. I assume she was in the process of sliding down the tree when she was struck by the second blow and knocked to where you subsequently found her.'

'Time of death?'

'In this weather? You've got to be joking.'

Dr Wendicott was tall for a woman, maybe five foot eight or nine, with strong, almost Slavonic features, an impression heightened by the Russian-style fur hat she wore. She might be thought beautiful in a more forgiving light, despite a slight disfigurement: a scar running down from the side of her nose to her upper lip, tugging it up a little at one corner. She was in her late thirties, Calhoun thought, perhaps a little younger, it was hard to tell with the cold pinching her cheeks and making her eyes water. Or maybe that was grief. Calhoun asked if there was somewhere they could go out of the weather and she took them into a room on the ground floor of the old cannery that they used as an office.

It wasn't much improvement on the outside. There was an old wood stove but it wasn't lit. A heap of apple wood stood beside it ready for burning. The walls looked damp. Dr Wendicott sat herself at one of the desks, shoulders hunched and her arms folded hard across her chest with her hands tucked under her armpits. Jensen sat at one of the others with his notebook out. Calhoun stayed standing, doing a little shuffling dance on the wooden floor to kick some life back into his feet. So far as he knew, this place hadn't been used for years, not as a fish cannery, but they obviously had power. There were computers on the desks and a photocopier. The walls were covered with maps and photographs of the site. Also some of the team working on the dig, taken over the summer. Young men and women in shorts and T-shirts, happy-smiling in the sunshine. Calhoun looked more closely.

'She's the one in the red baseball cap.' Her voice was as bleak as the room.

'Did you know her well?'

'Not very.' He turned to look at her, wondering if that was it. She sighed and started again. 'I hardly spoke to her really. Charlie knew her better.'

'Charlie?'

'Charlotte. Charlotte Becker. She was with me when we . . . found the body. She's one of my graduate students.'

8

'And what was Miss Ross?'

'One of the field assistants. Recruited locally. We have three or four local people helping us with the field work.'

She didn't look at him directly but stared at the desk in front of her, hunched inside her leather parka, a stiffness in her features that might have been from the cold. She still wore her hat but the few strands of hair he could see were a pale blonde.

'So when did you last see her alive?'

'Yesterday. Up on the site. We were working till about four o'clock in the afternoon. Till we started to lose the light. Then she went . . .' She stopped abruptly and put a hand up to her forehead, pressing with her fingers as if to keep the thought shut in there, unspoken.

'Excuse me?'

'Her little girl. She went to pick up her little girl.'

It was the first sign of emotion.

Calhoun's voice became softer, more careful.

'How old is she?'

'Nine or ten, I'm not sure exactly.'

'Do you know where she is now?'

'No. No, I don't. She . . . they had accommodation in the town. An inn, I think.'

Calhoun nodded. The address was on the label of her bag. The Old Barrack House, Bridport. She slid open a drawer in the desk and pulled out a file.

'This is the form she filled in when we gave her the job.'

He studied it briefly. Age twenty-eight. Single, one child, a daughter, Freya. Next of kin given as her sister, Jessica Ross, with an address in Oxford, England.

'What's this place like at night?' he asked her. 'I mean, is it lit up or anything?'

'We have a light on the forecourt where we leave the vehicles.'

'Nothing on the site itself?'

'No.'

'And you have no idea why she came back, after dark?'

He thought he saw something in her eyes, a flicker of . . . caution? Or even anger. But then she shook her head.

He asked about the dig but what she told him was of purely academic interest: the site of an old colonial fort, built by the

French, taken by the British and destroyed by the Indians. The forest had grown back over the ruins and kept them hidden for hundreds of years. Then, a couple of summers back, a party of picnickers had unearthed human remains.

'It's probably the most important early colonial settlement we've ever found in Maine,' she said. 'We were very excited.'

She made a small, almost apologetic move with her hands, as if it was an inappropriate comment in the circumstances, but he pressed her for details. They'd done some preliminary work shortly after the discovery, she said, and started in earnest last spring. Since then, four of them had been up here on a more or less permanent basis: herself, her colleague, Pete Jarvis, and the two graduate students, Charlie and Laura. She lived in her own camper and the others in rented trailers, one for Dr Jarvis, the other shared by the two young women. Then there were the field assistants and over the summer up to thirty students from the university, camping out in tents on the headland. They'd marked out the site in a grid and uncovered about a third of it, so far, removing over a thousand artefacts.

'And you went up there this morning,' he said, 'in the snow.'

'Yes . . .' a moment's hesitation, and again that flicker of what might be caution . . . 'We knew we wouldn't be able to do any work. We just wanted to look, see what difference the snow made. I guess we knew we were finished for the season, really.'

'And that's when you found her.'

'Yes.'

'And you knew who it was.'

'Not at first. How could we?'

Calhoun said nothing. She was staring at him now, almost angrily.

'What can have done that?'

'What', he noted, not 'who'.

'We don't know yet,' he said. 'So when did you realise it was Miss Ross?'

'Only after we'd called the police. We were just standing outside here and Charlie said, it was Maddie, wasn't it?'

'Maddie?'

'That's what we called her. Short for Madeleine.'

'And what made her think that?'

'I don't know. Perhaps it was her clothes . . . And then we saw the car.'

'The car?'

'Her car. An old VW, you know, a Beetle.'

Calhoun looked at Jensen and Jensen looked stricken.

'Where is this car?' he said carefully.

It was on the far side of the cannery, pointing back towards the highway, a red Beetle convertible, shrouded with snow. It had clearly been there all night.

Calhoun tried the door. It wasn't locked. Candy wrappers, magazines and road maps littered the floor and upholstery. And there was a doll on the back seat, in Indian costume. The interior smelt of something vaguely familiar, like musk. The perfume she used? Then he saw the bundle of sweet grass fixed above the door, like the ones they sold at the Indian store on the reservation. He withdrew his head and carefully closed the door.

'Did she usually leave it unlocked?'

'She could be a bit vague at times,' Dr Wendicott said.

You didn't like her, Calhoun thought. Just because she was 'a bit vague at times', or was there another reason?

'Quite often she couldn't get it to start,' she said. 'That's why she left it here, facing down the slope.'

Calhoun looked down the narrow strip of road. The police vehicles had ploughed up the snow and it formed a stark, straight break through the forest to where it met the highway about half a mile inland.

'So she came back at night and she left her car at the back here, pointing downhill in case it wouldn't start again, and she walked along the side of the cannery, past the three trailers and on up the track to the dig. And none of you saw her.'

He was thinking aloud, really, but she answered him all the same.

'It wasn't the kind of night to be about,' she said.

III

'I'm a witch, I'm a witch, I'm a wicked, wicked witch.'

Shrill, piping voice, waving her cardboard broomstick from the side of the road and Jessica, miming terror, pedalling her bicycle a little faster along the side of the park. Witches and warlocks, ghosts, a skeleton and a dancing devil. Baby ghouls with mummy ghoul shepherding them along the pavement, practising their apprentice wails. Hallowe'en, sugared and candied, tamed of its terrors. Not like it used to be.

Jessica, in a rare mood of nostalgia for her own haunted childhood, trudging the treadmill wheels of her bike through the thin gruel of fog, in through the gaunt gates of Lady Margaret Hall and across the quad and the lights blazing in the windows. Home. Such as it is.

She carries her basket of books up the stair to her room. A room of one's own, cosy with books, a few family photographs, the Tuscan tiles on the wall, the water-colours of Venice . . . All she has ever wanted. She sits on the bed, smoothes the white counterpane with the flat of her hands, trying to recapture the content that was there at the beginning. But it has gone, seeped away with the dank autumn days.

With the light on, it is suddenly night outside. She has to press her nose against the window to see anything at all, and then across the lawns she can make out the tops of the trees along the river, floating eerily above the bank of fog.

A wave of desolation so strong she recoils, breathless, a shiver that turns into a shrug, sloughing off this mood that is dangerously close to self-pity, that reminds her of her first months at boarding school before she butched up, learned how to survive if not enjoy.

Oxford can be a lonely place. Jessica has no real friends here, nobody she has known for more than six weeks. She moves in that uneasy territory between love of her own company and acute loneliness. Tonight she feels herself veering perilously close to the lonely. But does that matter? There is a part of her that insists she must train for loneliness, harden herself, eradicate this weakness in her. She does not know what part of her heredity this comes from but she values it as a necessary life skill. The other, gregarious Jessica, craves company, distraction, conversation . . .

But there are techniques for dealing with this.

Briskly unpacking the books she has brought back from the library. Freud's *Totem and Taboo*, *Witchcraft and Witch Trials* by L'Estrange and the one she's been waiting for since the start of Michaelmas term: John Taylor's *Witchcraft Delusion in Colonial Connecticut*.

Good Hallowe'en reading.

The postcard drops out on to the floor and she stoops to retrieve it, glancing at the picture with casual interest. A small child leading a large bear along the bank of a river, a rear view, the two figures walking off into a faint mist. The child looks Victorian, a squat little figure, almost dwarf-like, dressed in a blue frock with little white pantaloons and a pale straw hat, and she holds the bear by the shaggy hair of its neck. The animal appears docile, trotting along beside her on all fours like a huge brown dog. A bit weird but not particularly scary. No reason for that writhing snake of apprehension that coils up Jessica's spine and expires, trembling, in the back of her neck. Then she notices the trees. There is a line of pollarded willows along the bank of the river and the nearest of them, the one the figures have just passed, seems to be waving its lopped-off branches as if to attract their attention. And, peering more closely, Jessica can just make out the lines of a face, etched in the trunk, contorted into a caricature of extreme alarm.

She turns the card over but there is no message. The book it fell out of is Goldsmid's *Confessions of Witches Under Torture*.

And then, for no particular reason, she thinks of snow, the first time she ever saw snow . . .

They were in Kashmir, in the foothills of the Himalayas; an old hill station from the days of the Raj which the government was trying to turn into a ski resort without much success. It was very cold. There was hardly any heating in the hotel and when they asked for hot-water bottles, the night porter first looked puzzled and then brought them two little teapots filled with boiling water. Their father put the teapots under the bedclothes to see if they'd work but the steam from the spouts made the sheets wet. The girls thought this was so funny – having teapots for hot-water bottles – they couldn't get to sleep. They hugged each other under the blankets, giggling and shivering.

It snowed during the night and they looked out of the window on to a landscape remarkably like the Christmas cards they were sent from the place their father still called home, except for the giant peaks of the Himalayas marching across the horizon. He took them outside to build a snowman and they had a snowball fight just like the children in the pictures. But it wasn't as cosy as the Christmas cards with the snow-covered cottages and churches and coaching inns. It wasn't so safe.

Their father said there were bears in the mountains. He said they chased the skiers and sometimes caught them and ate them, which was why hardly anyone ever skied all the time they were there. Except him. He said he could out-ski a bear any day of the week. Years later, she was surprised to find that Maddie had believed this story. Still did, in fact, though she was a young woman then. 'Of course it wasn't true,' Jessica told her, but because she had this need always to explain things, even the absurd, even the inexplicable, she added: 'Bears hibernate in winter.'

And they both laughed.

'I used to be so scared,' Maddie said. 'Thinking about the bears eating our daddy.'

Their father was a shaman. Princes and governments paid him large sums of money to advise them. He cast spells to cure the ills not just of individuals but of whole societies. He foretold the future. He dispensed harsh medicines. He did not tell people he was a shaman or they would not have trusted him. They would not have taken his medicine. He told them he was an economist. Then they were prepared to do everything he told them, especially if they paid a high price for his wisdom and their people more.

But he told the girls what he really was.

14

'I'm a wizard,' he told them. 'It's all done by magic.'

He was the Great Wizard of the West.

He looked like a wizard. He was tall and bearded with thick, fierce eyebrows and piercing blue eyes and a strong, wise face.

Sometimes when he was in the privacy of his own home or hotel room he wore a caftan of many colours and burned incense and told them stories. They sat round him, the two little girls, and listened to his stories and watched him with their big brown eyes through the curling smoke of the incense.

He spent much of his time travelling in India and the Far East, and after their mother died he kept them with him. They liked that. It was their best time. A magic time. When they were older he sent them to boarding school in England and that was not so good. Jessica made the best of it but Maddie was more unhappy than she was, more angry and less able to adapt. The first time she was expelled their father was inclined to be tolerant. Maybe the school was too strict, too keen on discipline. It suited Jessica, but not Madeleine, who was more independent, more like her father. So he sent her to a school that was less structured, more liberal. 'You have to let her go her own way,' he told Jessica, as if it was her fault. But a year or so later, when she was expelled a second time, he let her go to Hell.

He was back in England then, expounding his theories. He wrote them all down in a book and became very rich and quite famous. He convinced many people, but not the girls. By then, they were no longer proud of him, their secret shaman of a father. By then, they had become quite cynical of him. 'The old charlatan,' Maddie called him. She no longer believed he could cure the ills of the world; she believed he caused them.

She would begin many of her sentences with the words, 'It's people like *him* . . .'

But Maddie was a rebel, an outcast. Maddie was a Donga, one of the tribe of Dongas who lived in tree huts in forests that were in the way of Progress and who tried to resist it.

My father is a shaman and my sister a Donga, Jessica would think. She carried the thought around with her, repeating it in her head like an incantation to ward off the evil eye, the ridiculous, the absurd, to keep her sane and normal. She was determined to be normal. She worked very hard at being normal.

IV

They'd carted the body off for the autopsy leaving a dark patch in the snow. It was strangely more sinister than seeing her lying there, that small violent tear in the fabric of the landscape.

Jensen came up to him. He'd spoken to Hannah Crew, the woman who ran the Old Barrack House. Madeleine Ross had worked there most evenings, serving at table, but Thursday she had a night off.

'She went out at about seven o'clock,' Jensen said. 'Said she was meeting some friends from the dig. Hannah put the little girl to bed.'

'She wasn't worried when she didn't come home?'

'Apparently she sleeps in one of the cabins round the back. Hannah had the little girl in with her for the night. In the morning she ran her in to school.'

There was something not quite right about all of that, but Calhoun let it go for the time being. Jensen said Hannah was prepared to break the news to the child if no one else was.

Calhoun looked back at the camper and the two trailers parked in the shelter of the cannery and wondered about the sleeping arrangements and whether Madeleine Ross had any part in them. So far as he knew there was only one man living there, but that was not necessarily conclusive.

However, there didn't seem to be any other reason for her to be out on the headland late at night, unless there was something she came back to find, something she couldn't take away earlier. She wouldn't be the first person to steal things from a dig. *We've found over a thousand artefacts*, Dr Wendicott had said. What kind of artefacts? He should have asked.

'Where the hell did *he* come from?' Jensen said.

Calhoun turned and saw the figure walking towards them along the edge of the cliff, head down, hands in the pockets of his white parka. When he was a few yards away he stopped and looked from one to the other and asked who was in charge here. As if he owns the place, Calhoun thought.

'Who wants to know?' Jensen asked, more truculently than he needed to.

'My name's Innis Graham,' the man said, and he pointed his face towards the sea. 'That's my boat down there.'

But Calhoun didn't look at his boat, he stayed looking at Innis and Innis saw how he looked at him and his eyebrows lifted in a way Calhoun remembered very well. The way he'd looked even then, as a child, when someone presumed to question him or to treat him in a way that he did not consider well-mannered or respectful. He wore a beard, like most men from Down East who went out to sea in boats, but you could still see the boy in him. But Calhoun would not have recognised him without the name.

'Innis Graham,' Calhoun repeated. It was not a question.

The eyebrows contracted. He looked uncertain.

'Do I know you?'

'It was some time ago,' Calhoun said.

He must have been eleven when they first met – and thirteen or fourteen when he last saw him. Just three summers, but by a strange trick of memory and imagination they had expanded with the years so that they seemed to fill his entire childhood. Endless summers, sailing Innis Graham's dinghy round the islands in the bay, eating the picnic lunches the woman he called Cook prepared for them in the mornings.

He'd grown tall – two or three inches taller than Calhoun – and leaner, rangier. He wore his hair long and his face was tanned even this late in the year.

And there was a mark that might be a bruise just below his left eye.

'Michael? Is it? Michael Calhoun?'

No one ever called him Michael, not now. Everyone called him Cal. But his mother used to call him Michael sometimes, when she was pissed off with him or when she wanted to impress people like Innis Graham.

'Detective Calhoun,' he said. 'These days.' It sounded a little self-important but he had to make it known, in the circumstances.

17

The eyes widened briefly, then he looked towards where the body had been.

'I was with her, Michael. She must have been killed just after she left me, on the way back to her car.'

'You were with her?'

He jerked his head towards the sea again. 'Down on the boat.'

'Until when?'

'I don't know . . . must have been about ten o'clock, I guess.'

'So how did she get here?'

Innis repeated the question as if it didn't make any sense.

'From the boat,' Calhoun said. 'How did she get here from the boat?'

People used various ways to hide their guilt: grief, shock, belligerence . . . masks of innocence. If Innis wore a mask it was carefully chosen. There was grief and shock, certainly, and now a dawning comprehension.

'Oh, there's steps – up from the jetty. I watched her going up them.' He shook his head. 'I just stood and watched her.' The words seemed to catch in his throat.

'In the dark?'

He looked confused again and Calhoun pointed out it would have been dark at ten o'clock.

'Oh, I see. There's a sensor light – on the steps.'

Calhoun asked him how he knew it was Miss Ross who had died and he said Kate Wendicott had just called him on his mobile.

'She said it was a bear.' He looked at Calhoun for confirmation but Calhoun asked him how he'd come by the bruise.

He put his hand up quickly, as if to hide it. Or because he had forgotten it was there?

'She hit me.'

'She hit you?'

'She wouldn't let me walk her back to the car and when I tried to insist . . . she hit me.'

'I see.' They stood looking directly at each other for a moment. Calhoun thought there was an appeal in his eyes, a desire for some private confidence.

'Michael . . .' Innis began but then he just shook his head again as if it was all beyond him.

'I'm sorry,' Calhoun said, 'but we'll have to take a look over your boat.'

He asked Jensen if he'd mind going off to fetch some of the others to help in the search and followed Innis through the trees towards the headland. Now he could see the steps, hugging the side of the cliff, and the light Innis had mentioned – and the boat moored to the stone jetty below.

He paused and looked back to where they had found the body. It was obscured by the trees and if there was a path through them it was covered by the snow, but he figured it was no more than a couple of hundred yards from the top of the steps. He looked down again at the boat, trying to work it out.

'Weren't you moored out in the cove,' he asked Innis, 'a few minutes ago?'

'I've a couple of lobster pots I drop out in the bay,' he said.

'Who else uses this place?'

Innis shook his head. 'No one. Except sometimes you get the occasional boat put in over the summer for an overnight. It was built for the cannery owner. He had a cruiser moored here.'

It began to make a bit more sense. But how long had the cannery been closed now – a year, two?

'So what are you doing here, Innis? Besides fishing for lobsters?'

'I was working on the dig.'

Now this didn't make any kind of sense. At least, it didn't fit in with anything Calhoun had heard about Innis Graham over the last few years.

'I didn't realise you had an interest in archaeology,' he said.

'I didn't. Not then. My interest was entirely personal.'

'Miss Ross?'

'I met her back in the spring. I'd come home to see my mother and she brought me out here one day, to see how the dig was coming along. She *was* interested. I mean, in archaeology, local history. And this used to be our land.'

Of course it did. Most every cove and creek they'd sailed into when they were kids had been on Graham land and a good many of the islands, too. The Grahams had been the richest people Calhoun had known, until he went to Boston. They were timber barons, old Maine aristocracy. Owned whole forests along the Canada border.

'Used to be?'

'We sold most of it off when Dad died.'

'But you kept the house?' Calhoun said, almost in alarm.

Calhoun used to enter that house like it was a cathedral. Wiping his feet on the hall rug like he had six inches of mud on his boots, treading on eggshells.

Innis nodded. 'Mum's still there. By herself now.'

'But you stayed on the boat?'

'Not always. Just some of the time.'

Whenever he saw Miss Ross?

But he didn't ask that. Not yet.

The steps were quite narrow and Calhoun leant on the hand rail as they went down. The tide was well out now and the rocks on the strand draped with seaweed. It looked like a herd of shaggy beasts had died there, a herd of hairy mammoths driven over the cliff by hunters. He noticed the light Innis had mentioned, at the dog-leg. His stomach reminded him he hadn't eaten breakfast yet. He had a sudden vivid memory of a breakfast long ago, when he and Innis had been out in the dinghy one morning, checking the lobster pots. They'd gone ashore on one of the islands and cooked bacon and grits over an open fire. He could almost smell it, that breakfast.

He paused at the bottom of the steps and looked up. It was a steep climb, even with the dog-leg halfway up.

'Was it snowing when she left you?'

'Yes. It had just started.'

'And you say she wouldn't let you walk her back to her car?'

'No.' A small pause. 'To be honest, we'd had a bit of a fight. She was pissed off with me.'

'You care to tell me why?'

'Oh, nothing at all. I mean, just . . . she had a temper on her, you know, and, just something I said . . .' Again there was that mute appeal in his eyes.

Calhoun let it go, for the present.

'Shall we go aboard?' he said.

In the photographs Calhoun had seen in the magazines, Innis Graham had been pictured at the wheel of an ocean racer, a sleek, computer-designed machine stripped of anything superfluous to its primary function – its only function – which was winning races. But this was a boat from a different world, a classic beauty sculped in teak and brass. Her name was engraved in gold lettering on the stern. *Calliope. Calliope* of Providence.

They went below into the saloon. You could not grow up on the coast of Maine without having some knowledge of boats, but the ones Calhoun knew were working boats, fishing boats. They smelled of fish and diesel oil. They did not have saloons. Calhoun's only experience of sailing for pleasure had been those adolescent summers in Innis Graham's dinghy. And that had been a rugged, windswept pleasure, the often masochistic pleasure of going to sea in an open boat. This was pleasure of a different sort. Calhoun took in the leather upholstery, the wooden panelling, the polished dining table, the framed photographs on the walls . . . the trophies. A soft, diffused light from the companion. The smell of coffee. It reminded Calhoun of an Edwardian gentleman's club, hushed, reverential, a male sanctuary, but there was something seductively feminine about it, too. It was the womb, of course. A perfect reconstruction, furnished to suit an entirely masculine taste. Calhoun tried to imagine the woman whose body he had so recently inspected sprawled across the elegant sofa. He saw her empty eye socket, filled with frozen blood, and the gash that had been her mouth. Did Innis Graham see that?

Did Innis Graham *do* that?

'How many cabins are there?' he asked.

'Three. You'd like to see them?'

But then they heard footsteps on the upper deck and Jensen came down the companionway with two of the men from Dover barracks. Calhoun knew them by name – Gorridge and Mabbut – and considered, for a moment, introducing them to Innis. He felt like he had as a boy, when he had visited the Graham house and not known quite how to behave, falling back on the overscrupulous politeness he had been taught by his mother.

Instead he said, 'OK if they look around?' And Innis said, 'Sure, go right ahead,' but Calhoun saw the swift, reflex glance down to their boots.

Was it conceivable that a man who had just torn out his lover's throat and slashed away most of her face would worry about people trampling mud into his polished deck?

21

Calhoun's experience of homicide in Boston inclined him to the belief that it probably was.

He asked Innis if he'd show them the clothes he was wearing the night before.

Jensen wanted a word in private and Calhoun followed him back up on deck.

'We found a flashlight,' Jensen said. 'In one of the trenches, about twenty yards from the body. It was switched on but the bulb was broke.'

'Anything else?'

'Not so far. We're still looking.'

He went below again.

'When she left you,' he asked Innis, 'was she carrying a flashlight?'

Innis didn't think so.

'There was plenty light up the steps,' he said. 'She might have had one in her bag. She always had this shoulder bag full of stuff.'

They'd already been through it. There had been no flashlight.

'Excuse me, sir, are these yours?'

Gorridge had found a bunch of keys down the side of one of the leather chair cushions. He held them up so Innis could see. A small doll dangling from the key ring.

Calhoun looked at Innis and thought some of the colour drained from his face. Innis shook his head, slowly.

'Any idea whose they are?' Calhoun asked him.

'I guess they must be hers.'

Calhoun looked more closely. The doll was modelled on a young Indian maiden with braided hair wearing a dress made of animal skin. There were four keys and two of them had the VW logo.

So what did it mean? Only that she'd left without them. And been killed before she could come back for them, before she'd reached her car.

'Tell me about last night,' he said.

She'd arrived a little after eight, Innis said, and stayed a couple of hours. They'd eaten some supper, drunk a bottle of wine and then she'd left.

'After a quarrel.'

'I told you it was nothing.'

22

The first flash of impatience, the imperious irritation of the patrician, not accustomed to being questioned. Then he sighed and made a small placatory gesture, turning the palms of his hands towards Calhoun. I have nothing to hide.

'She turned up unexpectedly. I had things to do, things on my mind.'

'But you didn't get rid of her.'

'No. I'm far too polite. But I think she detected a certain lack of . . . enthusiasm on my part.'

What did that mean? That she wanted a fuck and he didn't want to fuck her? With anyone else, Calhoun might have asked precisely that. In Boston, he would have.

'Cal – will you come and look at this?'

Mabbut stood in the companionway and Calhoun followed him through to the cabin in the stern. It had the same wood panelling as the saloon and a large double bed. A fitted wardrobe door was slid half open to reveal a washbasin and mirror. Also a wicker laundry basket that Mabbut had emptied on to the deck. It was obvious what he wanted Calhoun to look at. He sensed Innis standing behind him.

'You cut yourself lately?' he asked him.

'No,' Innis said, surprised. 'Why . . . ?' Then he saw the towel.

'Any idea whose blood it is?'

Calhoun could see that he was thinking about it. He let him think about it for a moment or two more before he figured he wasn't going to say anything.

V

Calhoun was older than lnnis Graham by almost a year, but there had never been any question who was the leader. For one thing, Innis owned the boat. Calhoun could probably have owned a boat if he'd asked for one, maybe not so fine as Innis's but sound enough to sail around the bay. His folks weren't poor. Just not frivolous. Everything they made or bought had a purpose. They would have been puzzled if Calhoun had suddenly announced he wanted to sail to an island and lie there half the day in the sun. They would have wanted to know what for and he probably wouldn't have been able to tell them. His mother ran the smallholding and his father was a carpenter. The timber he worked with probably came from one of the forests the Grahams owned.

They'd met on the beach at Mill Cove where Calhoun sometimes went down early during the vacation to dig for clams. He usually went with his friend, Sam Killam, from school, but Sam was off on some trip with his folks so he was alone that morning. He saw the boat standing in from the headland with the sun behind it. Next time he looked up Innis was up to his knees in the shallows dragging it ashore. Except that Calhoun didn't know who he was then, he thought he was some vacation kid. He nodded to him amiably enough, pushing the hair out of his eyes, but he didn't stop digging. The kid looked at the little pile of clams he'd dug up and asked him if he wanted to trade. Calhoun didn't take him seriously, he thought he was trying to act big. 'Trade for what?' he said. But the kid had a pair of lobsters back in the boat. Calhoun gave him six clams for one. He had no idea who'd come best out of the deal, didn't even know if he wanted lobster for clams. This was somehow symbolic of his whole future relationship with Innis Graham.

In appearance they were not dissimilar. They were about the same height then, with the same sun-bleached thatch hanging down over their eyes. Maybe that was what first attracted them, the sudden discovery of a twin, not that it bore close scrutiny. Innis's face was longer, his features more delicately aquiline and his eyes an almost translucent blue, where Calhoun's were hazel, like his mother's. 'He's got sea eyes,' his mother said, 'you've got eyes like the forest.'

His mother often said odd things like that. She was regarded by her friends as fey. She made up her own cures for the animals on the farm, and sometimes for him. In another age they'd have called her a witch.

She was interested in his friendship with Innis Graham. She knew it was different from his other friendships. 'The rich are different,' she told Calhoun. He didn't know then she was quoting. She'd met his mother once or twice, she knew the house. Everyone knew the Graham house with the Greek columns all along the front. It had been built by Innis's great-grandfather when he was the biggest shipbuilder in Dover, and Innis's mother had filled it with antiques she collected from Europe. She went on collecting expeditions like J.P. Morgan. She even had antiques outside the house, statues and Greek vases and a gazebo. Even a folly she'd shipped back from England. Mrs Graham liked Calhoun because he was polite. Also, possibly, because he was good-looking like her son. Most of the year Innis was away at school or on vacation with his parents, and Calhoun was the only local boy he ever befriended. Eleven to thirteen, three perfect summers before it ended. Not dramatically, they didn't fight or have any other falling out, but the next summer Innis Graham wasn't there any more, not for Calhoun anyway. Calhoun saw him with a girl once out on the boat. Innis waved carelessly from the boat, and Calhoun waved carelessly back and then went on digging clams. But he cared.

'You're too easy-going for your own good,' his mother told him, once, 'like your father.'

She meant he'd get trampled on but like his father he was only easy-going when it suited him to be. When it didn't, he was inclined to be stubborn. When he was hurt he retreated behind a shield of assumed indifference.

He usually let Innis take the initiative. Innis was into navigation, even then. He'd haul out a map and find some island they'd never been to, and Calhoun was happy to go along. They went further and further afield. Sometimes they'd camp out on one of the islands and broil lobster over an open fire. Squatting there with the sun going down and the melted butter running down their chins. They saw whales. They had adventures. Calhoun consciously saw himself as living out an adventure, a story from one of the books he read. Tom Sawyer and Huck Finn. He supposed he must be Huck. Later, when he told people in Boston he had sailed with Innis Graham as a boy they'd asked him what he was like and he'd had to think about it.

'Bit restless at times,' he'd said, finally. As you'd expect from a round-the-world yachtsman. 'And very sure of himself.'

If he had a grain of self-doubt, Calhoun never saw it.

'He's a typical Leo,' said his mother, who believed in star signs. 'Fine when things are going his own way.'

And sure, sometimes when they didn't, he'd have terrible sulks on him. Sometimes going off without a word and Calhoun would think never to see him again, only he'd turn up in a day or two all sunshine as if nothing had happened.

Like most friendships between boys of that age, it was a kind of love affair but without any physical side to it. They never swam naked. They always wore swimsuits or kept their shorts on. It would never have occurred to them to take them off, they dried so fast in the sun and the wind. Perhaps there was an element of inhibition there but Calhoun didn't notice it at the time.

Yet he knew now there had been a physical awareness, a narcissus love. Maybe a female would have done just as well if either of them could have found one, but girls their own age went for boys two or three years older and younger girls were no good: they couldn't keep up and they were silly. They didn't have to rationalise any of this, or discuss it, it was just a fact.

And for Calhoun there was the added pleasure of being with someone who was rich. The sense of privilege, of drinking from the same golden cup. The increase in his own self-esteem that came from being a friend of the esteemed Innis Graham, the richest kid in the county. Why Calhoun should feel this, what need or insecurity made him value this, he never cared to explore, much less try to explain. The rich are different.

He took Innis to K-Troop barracks just outside Dover and left him in the interview room while he grabbed a coffee. He was surprised and slightly disconcerted that he hadn't asked for a lawyer. In Calhoun's experience of the rich, a lawyer was the first thing they reached for in a crisis.

When he went back to the interview room Innis asked him if they could talk in private. Calhoun thought it might be a confession, and it was, of sorts. But not the sort he'd fetched him in for.

'We were making love,' Innis said, 'and I got some blood on me. She'd just started her period. I wiped it off on the towel.'

Calhoun asked him why he hadn't told him that when they were on the boat.

'I wasn't thinking too clearly,' he said. 'My God, Michael, I'd only just heard she was dead. I wasn't exactly bursting to talk about the intimate details of our love life in front of a crowd of strangers.'

This was quite possibly true. It was also possible he'd only just thought of it.

'She started to bleed,' he said. 'She went out to the bathroom. I must have wiped myself on the towel and thrown it in the laundry basket. It didn't exactly stick in my mind, you know – what I did. When she came back . . .' He sighed and made that helpless gesture again with his hands . . . 'I just didn't feel . . . the inclination.'

'But she did.'

'I guess.'

'And that's why you quarrelled.'

'Well, let's just say it didn't help. I had things on my mind. Maddie could be very demanding at times. I guess I wasn't in the mood for it.'

'How long had you been lovers?'

He looked sharply up at Calhoun as if he was prepared to resent the question but it was rather to challenge it.

'It wasn't like that,' he said. 'It was more . . . complex than that.'

Calhoun waited for him to describe how complex it was.

'It was . . . how can I put this? It was not an exclusive arrangement.'

'You mean you had other lovers – or she did?'

'She was a very independent spirit. She went her own way.'

27

'Didn't you mind that?'

'Who was I to mind? Well, I might have. I suppose I did, at first, but . . .' he sighed as if he'd decided to make a clean breast of it. 'To be perfectly honest, I wanted Maddie to fall in love with me, and when I became aware that this was not going to happen I lost interest to some extent. I was still happy to accommodate her. Who wouldn't be? She's . . . she was quite extraordinarily . . .' He shook his head. 'We made love but we weren't what I would call lovers. Do you know what I'm trying to say?'

Calhoun cut through to what he figured he was trying to say.

'Do you know who else was happy to accommodate her?'

He saw by the look in Innis's eyes that he thought he was being mocked and didn't like it. 'Or maybe not so happy?' Calhoun added.

But Innis looked down his patrician nose at him and said he really had no idea, Calhoun would have to ask around.

VI

Shortly after five Calhoun had a call from the ME in Augusta. He'd just finished the autopsy. There was still no forensic evidence but the nature of the wounds inclined him to confirm Fentiman's initial conclusions.

'So it was a bear?'

'Or some other animal with curved claws between three and five inches long.' There was a small pause. 'Or a weapon, I suppose, of a similar design.'

Calhoun asked him if there was any evidence she was menstruating.

He heard the surprise in the ME's voice.

'She was, as a matter of fact. Do you consider that relevant?'

'It could be.'

'Well, you might also consider it relevant that she was wearing a contraceptive cap.'

When Calhoun put the phone down Jensen was waiting on another line.

'I've just been talking to one of the other students,' he said. 'She saw her going back to her car at about ten o'clock last night.'

'Who was this?'

Jensen sounded bemused. 'Madeleine Ross.'

'I mean who saw her?'

'Oh, sorry. Laura Jackson. She shared a trailer with the other student, Charlotte Becker, the one who found the body. She was looking out of the window and she saw her walking past the cannery towards where she'd left the car.'

'And she's sure it was Madeleine Ross?'

'Well, not 100 per cent. I mean, it was dark, snowing, but they keep a light on at night outside the trailers and she didn't have any doubt it was her at the time.'

'What made her look out of the window?'

29

'The snow. She was watching the snow.'

The first snow of winter. It was plausible, he supposed. And why should she lie?

'So she went back to her car, realised she'd left her keys on the boat and went back for them, is that what we're saying? And that's when she met whatever it was that killed her.'

'Could have been Graham. Coming after her.'

'But why would he leave it so late? So far as he knew she could have been in her car and away.'

'Not if he had her keys. He knew she wasn't going anywhere.'

'I see. So he turned into a werewolf, ripped her face and her throat out with his five-inch claws, wiped his paws on a towel, left it in the laundry basket and sailed off to check on his lobster pots. You think?'

'I don't know what to think,' Jensen said.

Calhoun felt sorry for him. You didn't do werewolves at the Police Academy in Augusta. Not in the first six weeks.

He drove Innis home. To the family home by the river, a few miles out of Dover. Not to the boat. Calhoun could understand him not wanting to go back to the boat, not by himself, not right away.

For the first few miles they didn't speak. Then Innis said: 'Are your parents still around?'

'My mother died,' Calhoun told him. 'Just over two years ago.' Innis said he was sorry.

'My father's still at the same old place,' Calhoun said, in the same non-committal way. The same old place. Their home.

After a few moments Innis said, 'I thought you'd have left. When you left school.'

Why had he thought that? Calhoun was the boy who was always there, the friend he took for granted.

'I did leave,' said Calhoun. 'But I came back.'

Then, because he thought it sounded abrupt, unfriendly, he said, 'And you?'

'I usually come home two or three times a year. My mother's alone now. Lives alone in that big house. I can't get her to move.'

No servants then. No Cook.

And Innis was an only child, like Calhoun. They had that in common.

'She lives in one room in the winter to save on heating. Sits next to the fire with her books around her.'

Calhoun couldn't remember her with books. What books, he wondered.

'I usually only stay a few days, but this time . . .'

They both knew why he had stayed this time.

The house looked the same from the outside. Big and white and grand, the great meadow dropping down to the river. In the summer they had walked down through the long grass and the flowers to the little jetty where Innis kept the boat. He could almost smell it, the warm grass of that meadow. Now it was covered with snow.

'You like to come in?' Innis asked, adding formally, 'Mother would like to see you.'

Calhoun didn't think so. He made an excuse about having to drive on to the dig to take more statements from the people there.

'What will you do now?' Innis asked him.

Calhoun said: 'About what?'

He knew he meant about the case. But he didn't know if it was a case any more. He certainly didn't know if it was *his* case.

'About the bear,' Innis said.

'Oh, the bear?' Calhoun said. He didn't do bears. What in God's name *did* you do about a bear that slashed women's faces? That stood them up against a tree and delivered a right hook to the jaw?

'I expect we'll have to kill it,' he said. 'If we can find it.'

When he drove off Calhoun looked out past the house towards the river, and saw the jetty where Innis had kept the little dinghy. He almost expected to see it there now, but it wasn't, of course.

31

VII

Jessica had dinner in hall where she met two women who had rooms on the same stair. Afterwards, more from mutual loneliness, she thought, than any more promising rapport, there was a move to go down the pub.

One of them had a car and they drove to the Eagle and Child in St Giles and found it full of students in Hallowe'en costume on their way to a party. They looked like a slightly grown-up version of the kids Jessica had seen earlier, escaped from their mummy and making the most of it. They wore their masks slung around their necks or twisted round to the backs of their heads, and Jessica found it somewhat disconcerting to be engaged in conversation by people with two faces, one animated but, generally, rather ordinary, the other lifeless and crumpled but resembling some fantastic grotesque from the Devil's Bestiary.

She caught sight of her own face in the mirror behind the bar and thought she looked like a tourist, lost in a foreign city, ignorant of the language and customs, with her expression contorted into a permanent frown of pained concentration.

It was almost a caricature of the way she'd been feeling since she came back from Italy in the summer.

England was like a foreign country to her, Oxford a kind of dream, nurtured from a glorious spring day when she was thirteen and had fallen in love with it all: the river and the water meadows and the medieval serenity of the college cloisters and an image of herself, older and more beautiful, drifting serenely through May bugs and apple blossom on a bicycle with a basket full of books.

But she should have come here at eighteen, when she left school, not now and near thirty.

'What do you think of the new Tom Waites album?' said a

man with a wolf's mask around his neck and the face of a flushed and drunken choirboy.

'I'm not sure,' said Jessica, politely, never having heard of Tom Waites or his album. 'What do you think?'

She felt like his mother.

'Well, if – you know – aliens came down to Earth, this is what I'd give them to – you know – and say this is representative of life on this planet.'

And Jessica nodded, still with that polite smile, her eyes flitting away across the crowded room and alighting, fatally, on the face of a man she half recognised – an older man, older even than she, who beamed and came over and said, 'Thought any more about wormholes?'

'I beg your pardon,' said Jessica and then she remembered and briefly panicked. He was a man she had met at a party in her first week here, a Fellow of All Souls who had trapped her up against a wall and lectured her for at least half an hour on the theories of Stephen Hawking. He had thought that, as an historian, she would be interested in Hawking's concept of wormholes which were, apparently, nothing to do with the passage of slimy invertebrates through the earth but hypothetical tunnels between black holes in space that formed a kind of short-cut through time. She had only vaguely grasped the concept – the conditions for concentration were not perfect – but understood that an object or being might enter the mouth of a wormhole in the present time and emerge in the same place in the distant past.

She had heard since that he was a man who preyed on young female undergraduates so perhaps she did not look as old as she felt – or else it was a bad evening for him.

'Well,' he said, 'have you come to any conclusions?' He wore a black monk's habit with a crucifix hanging round his waist and the mask on the back of his head. His own face was slightly vulpine, not unattractive, except for an almost permanent smirk. Mr Wormhole, she thought, Mr Pleased-with-Himself, All Souls.

'Not quite,' she said. 'I'm still thinking about it, but it's an interesting theory.'

'But of no practical application.'

'None that I can see at present,' she humoured him.

'Ah, but isn't that what they thought about cloning? Ten, even five years ago, all theory, science fiction, and look where we are now.'

'Identical sheep?'

'Ah, yes, but what will be next?'

'Identical cows?'

'Ha ha ha. But it's more or less accepted that we'll be cloning humans in our lifetime, probably for spare-part surgery – certainly in the less morally confused parts of the world. Time travel might take a little longer but who knows?'

'Well, if it's true,' she said, cheerfully, 'it's here now.'

He was momentarily confused, if not morally.

'Well, if it *has* happened – in the future – time travellers will already be travelling backwards, won't they. They'll be here now. I could be one myself.'

'Well, yes . . .' But his voice was uncertain.

She pressed her advantage.

'There could be people from various different times, in the past and the future, wandering all over Oxford.' This was, she reflected, a fairly accurate picture of Oxford as she perceived it.

'I don't think it's possible,' he said, 'for people in the past to be projected into the future. They didn't have the technology.'

'*Time present and time past,*' said Jessica, '*Are both perhaps present in time future, And time future contained in time past.*'

You could always rely on Eliot to muddy the waters.

'Who said that?'

She told him.

'The astrophysicist?'

'The poet,' said Jessica.

'Ah.' The frown cleared and was replaced by relief. Only a poet.

Jessica harboured a prejudice against scientists that was part of a broader resistance to people who tried to explain things to her – or anyone else, for that matter. Economists like her father or Marxists like her first boyfriend: people who constructed models of society, history, or the universe, and used them to explain away all ambiguity. She would not have minded this if they had not been so patronising of other less 'scientific' concepts like religion or spiritualism – or her own special subject, about which she admitted to a certain sensitivity. Why, she thought, was a belief in God or the Devil, in angels, demons and spirits, considered by such people to be a quaint relic of the primitive, superstitious past while the concept of wormholes through time and space was considered to be perfectly plausible?

Well, she knew the answer to that, of course. Because a physicist had thought of it and not a poet.

And yet here, surely, was an interesting contradiction – a crack in the construct, as they would doubtless say. It seemed to Jessica that after 500 years or more of pushing back the frontiers of knowledge, of clearing the mists of myth and superstition that hung over those areas formerly marked with the ominous but enchanting sign 'Here Be Dragons', some scientists were venturing into new realms of uncertainty, beyond the charted territories of time and space, into a region where many of their own laws of physics were turned upside down and inside out. Surely, if there were areas of the universe where time and space were themselves distorted, subject to no known laws, then all things were possible. If Black Holes could exist, then so could dragons, even unicorns. A witch might fly, a man turn into a werewolf. A hunchback could conceal an angel's wings. A scientist might become a poet.

'Well, in a sense, he is, of course, right.' He was more comfortable now. 'Imagine that you had an ultra-powerful telescope that enabled you to see events on a distant planet. You would be able to see things which, because of the speed of light, had actually happened in the past. And if you were looking into a giant mirror, you would be able to see things in your own present time, which had, in fact, happened in the distant past.'

As if, Jessica thought, this ultra-powerful telescope and this giant mirror were as conceivable and far more reliable than a crystal ball. But then, in the mirror behind the bar, she glimpsed the back of his head and saw that it was a grinning skull.

She felt the same shock she had experienced earlier in the library, but stronger now, almost like an ice cold wind on the back of her neck. She actually turned round to see if someone had opened a door behind her, but the door was closed.

They tried to persuade Jessica to come to the party.

'I'm not dressed for it,' she said.

A man in a Dracula mask offered to bite her neck so she could go as one of his brides. She thanked him politely but thought not. Mr Wormhole Pleased-with-Himself, All Souls, had found easier, younger prey who didn't quote Eliot at him.

Jessica had recently attended a lecture on the function of mask in seventeenth-century political protest, and discovered that it was not primarily to shield the identity of the wearer, but to diminish his humanity, to enable him to act the Beast – to wreck and riot, maim and kill. While Jessica thought there was little chance of the evening developing quite so dramatically, it was not improbable that it would prove embarrassing.

She walked off, alone, into the lingering fog.

It is a relief to be back in her lonely room.

She puts on the kettle and a CD. Callas live at Lisbon, *La Traviata*.

She watches her reflection in the window, as if she is out there, a ghost in the dark, drawn to the music.

She studies the photographs on the cork panel above her desk. More ghosts.

Her lover – her ex-lover – on a balcony in Rome, in the snow at Cervinia . . . Her sister, Maddie – one by herself and two with Freya, taken during the road protest when they lived up a tree – a pair of beautiful half-naked savages with warpaint and braided hair.

Her father and his new wife, the two little boys, her half-brothers.

She still thinks of Virginia as the 'new' wife, though they have been married for over five years now. Five years and two children. No wonder he had the heart attack.

Hating herself for the thought, saying a quick act of contrition in case God should punish her for it by giving him another.

The kettle boils and she floods the teabag and carries the cup over to the photographs for there is something to think about here, something to get straight. *Do I hate my step-mother? Truthfully now.*

Not hate.

Resent, then.

Yes.

Why? Because she has replaced my mother, or because she has replaced me?

Or – do I need this? – or is it because she is two years younger than me and she already has two children?

There is a knock on the door. Mr Wormhole of All Souls, popping in for a nightcap, masked and deadly?

But no, not Mr Wormhole. Just the bursar with two police officers, a man and a woman, standing there on the landing with their hats in their hands to break the news that her sister is dead, killed by a bear.

VIII

They asked her if she'd like a cup of tea.

'I've just made one,' she said.

'It's camomile,' she said when she saw the policewoman peering at it.

'Ordinary tea's better for shock,' the policewoman said. 'With lots of sugar.'

She sat down on the bed. They looked at her, their expressions concerned but also wary, uncertain, as at some unfamiliar animal whose disposition is unknown.

'A bear?' Jessica said.

'I know,' the bursar said. 'It's . . .' She shook her head at whatever it was. 'Oh, my dear,' she said, 'I'm so sorry.'

There was this line from Shakespeare that kept running through Jessica's head. *Exit, pursued by a Bear.* From *The Winter's Tale.* The silliest line in the silliest play he ever wrote.

'Bridport?' she said.

The bursar said, 'I know,' again. And the policeman nodded.

'That's what we thought,' he said, 'Bridport, Dorset. A bear. I mean, you know, did it escape from a zoo or something? But no, not our Bridport – Bridport, Maine. Near Canada. They get a lot of bears up there but they don't usually attack people.'

He sounded quite chatty about it. Sympathetic but chatty, as if he could tell her a lot more about bears if she wanted him to.

He was a sergeant but quite young, not much older than she was.

Then she remembered Freya.

They looked at her blankly. She was babbling, not making a lot of sense, the words were all there in her head but the part of her brain that put them in the right order wasn't functioning correctly. She'd had this trouble before, when she had a migraine coming on. She concentrated.

'She had a little girl,' she insisted. 'Freya. She's nine.'

'You were the only one they had down as next of kin,' the sergeant said. 'But we can ask.'

Next of kin. That brought another thought.

'Oh God, I have to tell my father,' she said. 'He's just had a heart attack.'

They said they'd send someone if she'd give them the address. The sergeant took his notebook out. But she shook her head.

'They live in Scotland,' she said.

'That's all right,' he said. 'We'll get on to the local police.'

But the last thing she wanted was someone like him turning up at the door.

What should she do? Phone him? Speak to Virginia. Then Virginia could tell him. Was that the right thing to do? What was the right thing to do?

'I'm sorry,' she said, 'I'm very confused. Will you try and find out for me where her little girl is? Or give me the number of the police over there?'

And then the full force of it hit her, like it hadn't hit her before, like it had been shunting her along in front of it and suddenly she'd hit the buffers. Her little sister was dead.

'I always looked after her,' she told them. 'I was the one who always looked after her. I always wanted to be there for her.'

'I know,' said the bursar, 'I know.'

But she didn't know, none of them did. The bursar sat with her arm around her, rocking her gently, and the policewoman on the other side, rubbing Jessica's thigh with the flat of her hand as if she was trying to rub some warmth into it.

She didn't know either of them. This must be terrible for them.

'She was only four when our mother died,' she said.

And Jessica two years older, having to make it better.

You have to look after your little sister, her father said. He said it to console her, to help fill the terrible void that had opened in her life, but it was an awesome responsibility for a child of six.

'Is this the little girl?'

The sergeant was looking at the photographs on the wall.

'It was a couple of years ago,' said Jessica.

'And is this your sister?'

'Yes.' She thought it needed further explanation, the warpaint, the single braid over one shoulder, the nose stud.

'She was a Donga,' she said.

'A Donga?' The sergeant was nodding again but without comprehension.

'The tribe,' Jessica said. 'The ones that try to save the trees.'

They'd lived in one for a while, trying to stop the highway cutting through the Downs. Jessica flew back from Rome to see them. They had bedding up there and clothes and Freya's toys, even a shelf full of books. Jessica climbed up the rope ladder and sat up there with them like one of the characters in the stories she and Maddie used to read as children, stories about more adventurous children who met in tree-huts to plan their secret assaults on the tricky grown-up world. But this was deadly serious. This was the New Age protest, to save the environment: Maddie versus the Motor Car.

Jessica was on Maddie's side but it made her uncomfortable. Jessica worked for the European Union, where everything was done through the proper channels, not by sitting up in trees. When it was dark she went back to her hotel in Winchester and soaked in a hot bath filled with the scent of lavender and geranium from a bottle of essential oils, and changed into a dress she'd bought in Milan, and sat alone at a table in the dining room where attentive waiters brought her the menu and a glass of champagne.

And she thought of her lover telling the story at a dinner party in Rome – of how his crazy girlfriend had gone to sit with her totally certifiable younger sister up a tree in England to fight the motorway.

So she went back to her room without having dinner and changed back into her survival gear and ordered a taxi to take her back to the tree. And in the morning, stiff with cold and discomfort, they had quarrelled. Over Freya's education.

'Don't you think she should be at school?' she had said, primly, watching her playing with the brats from the copper beech in the next block.

'Don't you think she's being educated here?' said Maddie. 'Don't you think she's getting a better education than any fucking school can ever give her? Learning what it's all about. Learning to fight the bastards.'

And Jessica had gone back, cross and lonely, to have breakfast at her hotel.

The sergeant had realised what a Donga was. His expression changed and he looked at the policewoman.

Jessica wanted them to go away now.

'I'll be all right now,' she said.

'Would you like me to phone your father?' the bursar asked.

'No,' she said. '*I'll* phone my father.'

But she asked the bursar if she'd ring the airport on another line and find out about flights to Maine.

II. CONVERSE WITH SPIRITS

I

The Abenaki, when hunting Bear, do not call it Bear. This is considered unlucky. Instead they call it Grandmother, or Cousin, or Chief's Daughter, or The One Who Owns The Chin. This ensures a degree of compliance with the rules of the game. It makes life a little easier for the hunter, death a little quicker for the hunted.

In the days when the Abenaki had the run of the place and made the rules, the hunting season was always in winter when the bear was asleep in its den under a thick blanket of snow. The hunter used a spear, or an axe, or a club – not a bow. Nor, when such an ignoble weapon became available, a gun. Arrows and bullets were not considered powerful enough to conquer the spirit of the bear and this was dangerous. The hunter had to feel the spirit go.

But first he had to find the den, and that was the biggest problem, because Grandmother was remarkably astute in covering her tracks. In the late fall before the first serious snow of winter she would scout a number of sites – in hollow trees, caves, uprooted stumps – until she found the one she deemed the safest, the most comfortable. Then, when the time came for her deep slumber, she would approach it backwards on her hind legs, sometimes leaping fifteen or twenty feet to the side to confuse the tracker. And even in the depths of winter, in the sleep of the near-dead, she could be awake in an instant and then the killing would be an altogether messier affair, the outcome far less predictable.

All this and more Calhoun had learned in the course of a few hours on Kitehawk Head with the rangers from the Blackwater National Park, half the Bridport police force and a dozen or so knowledgeable hunters who, Calhoun was assured, knew the difference between bearshit and bullshit, though he entertained private, unspoken doubts.

His particular informant on Bears, the Abenaki and related subjects was a man called Henry Savageau who had, for some reason, appointed himself Calhoun's general guide and counsellor. Savageau was about six foot six and looked to be at least half that across the shoulder. He had long black hair and a great solid lump of a face with a jaw as wide as his forehead, narrow eyes under a single thick straight line of eyebrow and a nose that was so flat and broken you could easily mistake it for an indentation. Calhoun had the disturbing thought that if you took his head off and stuck it back on upside down it would look exactly the same. His complexion was a reddish brown and Calhoun thought he was from the reservation, but he said he was one part Micmac and two parts French Canadian. He didn't say what the other part was but Calhoun figured it could easily be log. He said he was a trucker for one of the lumber companies, but that he spent all the time he could out in the forest, hunting.

The trees here were mostly pines and spruce, the upper branches still dusted with snow from the night of the killing. Calhoun felt it on his face as a fine mist whenever he looked up. It reminded him of downhill ski-ing in Colorado. He felt a momentary elation before he remembered why he was here, doing this, and he dragged his mind back to the present and his eyes back to the ground in the search for whatever traces a bear might have left in the thin layer of snow at the foot of the trees.

The trackers were assisted in their task by a number of assorted hounds, referred to as 'the pack', though in Calhoun's uninformed view this legitimised them with a sense of organisation, of collective responsibility, that was not always apparent to him and at times even threatened to depress their weary 'handlers'. For most of the short day, they rampaged through the timber, whining, slobbering, panting, barking, running around in circles and sometimes trying to run up trees. They reminded Calhoun of some police officers he had known.

On the other hand, they did find some bearshit.

It lay in the snow beside the uprooted stump of a tree about half a mile from where they had found the body. There were no tracks in the surrounding area so it was reasonable to suppose that the bear had deposited it here before it snowed – unless of course, it had leaped twenty feet, shat, and leaped another twenty in a bid to confuse the enemy. Calhoun, though he kept this particular thought to himself, did venture that one sample of bear poop did not prove the pooper had been here on the night of the killing. Could it not have been here for some time, he inquired.

They stood, the most important of them, in a small circle looking down at it. Others, less important, tried to look over their shoulders. From the wider circle beyond, the leaping dogs yelped complaint at being denied their greater expertise. The chief ranger, whose name was Grainger, hunkered down and peered more closely.

After a tense few seconds, he spoke.

'I'd say about two days, no more.' He was a small, bespectacled man who did not look as if he spent a lot of time in the Great Outdoors. Calhoun figured that appearances must be deceptive. What else would a park ranger do? How else could he speak with such laconic authority?

'Probably scouting for a den,' the ranger said, 'or maybe come down for the clams.'

Calhoun thought he said clams.

He looked for them in the trees.

'On the shore,' Grainger said. 'They dig for them on the shore.'

Through the trees they could sometimes glimpse the sea but it looked a long way down.

Grainger scooped up the evidence and put it in his specimen bag – for further analysis, he said.

'How will that help?' Calhoun asked.

Grainger and the other ranger looked at him blankly. The other ranger was about twice Grainger's size in every direction. He was called Moose. They were something of a double act. Ranger Grainger and his man Moose.

'Help us what?' Grainger said.

'I mean, can it help us find the killer?'

Moose said: 'No. But it'll tell us what she had for supper.'

Calhoun thought this was a joke but he couldn't be certain.

'She?' he repeated. 'You know it's female, then?' He thought this might be something they could tell from the bearshit.

47

'Just an expression,' Grainger said. 'We call all bears She.'

As in Grandmother, of course.

Grainger did not believe the killer was a bear. Not a black bear, anyway.

Or, as he put it, 'Not one of ours.'

There were over 200 bear on the reserve, he told Calhoun, and not one of them had ever attacked a human.

It was getting dark. They started to walk back to the cannery where they had left their vehicles. Calhoun stood there in the trampled snow looking around him, not knowing what he was looking for. Not knowing if he'd know it if he saw it. For a boy who'd been brought up in the country he was woefully ignorant on the subject of bears, or, at least, he had been before he met Henry Savageau. They used to come into his mother's garden sometimes after the strawberries. He remembered seeing her run out from the kitchen once with a large spoon shooing one of them away. It had run from her on all fours and a guilty, shamed look over its shoulders, a great lolloping fat-assed clown of a creature, more brown than black.

Clowns. Clowns and bears. Wasn't there a connection there, somewhere? Some myth or other? Or was he thinking of the circus?

The One With The Chin. Grandmother. *Oh grandmother, what big teeth you've got . . .*

He saw that Henry Savageau was waiting for him and joined him for the trek back to where they had left the vehicles. They must have taken a slightly different route back, though, because after a few minutes they emerged into an area that was clear of trees except for a few silver birch standing in their stark, naked way out of the snow. Calhoun stopped and looked about because there was something about the place that struck him as strange, almost unnatural. He thought that it might have been cleared by the archaeologists. Maybe there were the foundations of some other old buildings buried here. But then Savageau said: 'Souriquois.'

'What?' Calhoun looked at him like he was crazy, or playing some child's game set in the past, pretending they were Indian fighters or something. There were just the two of them in the clearing and Savageau's hound, and to Calhoun's astonishment he saw that its hackles were raised and it was showing its teeth and growling.

'The hound knows,' said Savageau. 'They reckon it's an old Indian burial ground. Someone keeps it cleared. Fucked if I know who.'

He turned and walked around the edge of the clearing, rather than straight across, his dog slinking after him, and after a moment or two Calhoun followed, feeling slightly irritated with all three of them, but most of all with himself.

Calhoun took the rangers back to the Dover barracks and showed them the photographs.

'You're not going to tell me a bear did that,' Grainger said. A fierce little man, holding his anger in, not knowing where to go with it.

'So tell me what else did,' Calhoun said.

Grainger shook his head. Then he said: 'I don't know, polar bear, grizzly maybe, but . . .' He shook his head again.

Moose said: 'There was a grizzly in Banff killed three people before they shot it.'

'Yeah, but not before they'd slaughtered every black bear in a hundred-mile radius.' Grainger let some of the anger out. 'And that's what's going to happen here if we start panicking people.'

'It went for the faces,' Moose said. 'That's what made me think about it. Every case it went for the faces. One guy, it didn't kill him. They kept him alive on a drip. Then when he saw what it done to his face he pulled the tubes out.'

Calhoun thought this was probably the wrong way to go about reassuring people.

'Theory is they don't like people staring at them,' said Moose.

Calhoun said he was no expert but he understood that neither polar bears nor grizzlies were native to Down East Maine and that had one of them wandered a couple of thousand miles off course he assumed it would have been noticed before now.

'All I'm saying is I do not believe a black bear is capable of inflicting those kind of injuries.' Grainger was stubborn in his repetition.

'Are we talking physically capable, or mentally?' Calhoun asked.

Moose took it as a serious question.

'Some of them can get pretty grouchy at times,' he said, 'specially this time of the year, close to hibernation. They're like people when they're tired.'

Grainger still wouldn't buy it. The only time he'd known a black bear turn nasty was when she was defending her cubs. Otherwise they gave you a wide berth.

'What if you ran into one in the dark?' Calhoun suggested. 'I mean, literally walked into it.'

'You wouldn't,' Grainger said. 'She'd hear you coming. She'd be out of there before you catched a sight of her. These animals are not naturally aggressive.'

Calhoun looked at the information he'd picked up off the computer.

'Thirty-five deaths attributed to black bear in the last fifty years,' he read. 'Haven't got a figure for non-fatal attacks but I guess it's plenty.'

But Grainger wasn't impressed.

'More people die from bee stings,' he said. 'Or get struck by lightning.'

'Still – it happens,' Calhoun insisted. 'You post warnings. You tell people to give them a lot of space, don't leave food in the tents if they're camping, that kind of thing. Also,' he consulted another print-out from the computer . . . 'it says here the Parks Department put out special warnings to women who are menstruating. Not to go into the forest where there's bear. Says bear are attracted to the smell or something.'

'Was she menstruating?'

'She was. That make a difference?' He could tell by their reaction that it did.

Grainger reached for one of the photographs and studied it again.

'You got the measurements for these wounds?' he asked, 'like depth of penetration, distance between them, that kind of thing.'

Calhoun said it would be in the autopsy report when it came through.

'Fax it over to us,' Grainger said. 'But I can tell you right now, injuries like that, you got to be looking at something the size of a cave bear.'

He saw something in Calhoun's expression. 'And before you ask, they've been extinct for about 10,000 years.'

Polar bears, grizzlies, now cave bears, Calhoun thought. Anything but *their* bears.

II

Calhoun lived, temporarily as he insisted to everyone including himself, in the house his father had built in the woods on the outskirts of Dover when Calhoun was two. Calhoun, of course, remembered nothing of the building of it, but he grew up thinking his father had built it like a boat, or ark, first laying down the keel in an east-west direction and then building up from there. It had the feel if not the look of a boat, long and low and narrow, and firmly anchored on the wooden slopes above the river to the north of town. There was one main room running the length of the house with a large window at each end so you could see the sunrise through one and the sunset through the other. When there was a sun. Through more windows in the roof, as a further aid to navigation, you could see the stars.

Off this main room there were two small bedrooms, like cabins, just about big enough for a bed and a wardrobe, and in Calhoun's case a desk where he could do his homework. Outside, looking north, there was a deck. Sitting out there and looking down through the trees in winter you could just see the river, very narrow here and rapid. The far slope of course was Canada.

On squally days the house sprang leaks and had to be bailed out and have its timbers caulked. It made a tremendous noise in a storm, creaking and groaning and sometimes releasing loud and inexplicable cracks, as if invisible sails had filled with a sudden excess of wind. Calhoun had always found these sounds more comforting than not. When he had first lived in Boston, above a busy street, he was unable to sleep.

In the first few years, Calhoun's father had attributed these noises to 'weathering'. As in, the timbers weathering in. When this explanation began to lack conviction, his mother declared more forcefully that it was a fault of the plumbing or the central heating, both innovative works of his father's. For Calhoun's father, though a carpenter by trade, did not confine his ingenuity to works of wood. He hated buying anything he believed he could make just as well. This frequently drove Calhoun's mother to the limits of distraction, for his father's manufactures, while boasting a certain originality and durability, frequently failed the acid test of use – as compared to the mass-produced versions readily available in the nearest store.

Calhoun was kinder to his father than his mother was, though he, too, suffered from his father's excesses of craftsmanship. Most of Calhoun's toys were handmade. They included a beautiful fairy-tale castle, based on the Imperial Castle of Nuremberg, which his father had seen in a book, and which had a keep and a barbican, eight turrets, an inner and an outer bailey and a gatehouse with a drawbridge and a portcullis that you operated with chains and a small wheel. There was a garage for his toy cars, with an inspection pit that moved up and down and trapped your fingers if you weren't cautious, a working windmill that could really grind corn – and the fingers the garage missed – and a medieval siege engine that fired small rocks and was the terror of his mother's hens. But easily the most wonderful were the two warships: the Japanese battleship *Hirohito* with its towering superstructure and its great guns and the little American submarine, the *Franklin D. Roosevelt* with its wooden torpedoes that really fired. The *Hirohito* had a small yellow 'target' in the side of the hull which, if you hit it with one of the torpedoes, released a catch that exploded the superstructure high into the air, so that it took all day to find the pieces and build it up again. This was the problem with Calhoun's toys. Like the house itself, they demanded the same loving care of the user as they had of the builder. They required heavy maintenance and were frequently immobilised, awaiting repair. Or else their very artistry defeated their intrinsic purpose, which was play. Sometimes, though he would never say so, Calhoun wished for a simple plastic toy that did what you expected of it for as long as the novelty lasted and then broke and was thrown away.

He remembered now, returning home along the dark, straight, empty road between the trees, how his father had once built a bear trap. Perhaps this was after one of those raids on the strawberries. Doubtless his mother had complained and his father had finally got around to doing something about it but had, as usual, neglected to discuss the exact method of doing. Ideas came to him, he would explain, 'all in a rush when he had time in his hands'. Time *in* his hands, not on. Calhoun's father often used the wrong word in a way that was curiously *right*. Time often did appear to lie, complacent, in his father's hands like a tricky piece of machinery requiring delicate adjustment.

The bear trap was, like so many of his father's devices, a complex arrangement of poles and stakes and heavy logs and sly little Celtic catches, but the basic idea was devastatingly simple. The Bear, in pursuit of the Bait, put its head in the Noose and so triggered the Tossing Bar. And the Tossing Bar jerked the Bear's head tight inside the noose and up against the Choke Bar. And the combination of the Tossing Bar and the Noose and the Choke Bar and the Bear's own terrified struggles slowly strangled it to death.

Calhoun's father had described this process, not without a certain understated pride in his own craftsmanship, while constructing the device and Calhoun, with the cold-blooded curiosity of the child, had rather looked forward to seeing it put to the test. But this was not to be. His mother, arriving home from the store where she worked four days a week, had been outraged by the murderous 'object' and had demanded its instant decommissioning. She would prefer to belabour the 'poor critters' with a wooden spoon, she said, than permit them to suffer such a fate and at the hands of a man who called himself a Christian. Grumbling but ever compliant, Calhoun's father had dismounted it and doubtless rebuilt it, when time was once more 'in his hands', as the *Hirohito*, pride of the Imperial Japanese Navy.

But now his mother was dead, the strawberry patch gone, her treasured rose garden rank with weeds. The bears could come and go with impunity, safe from attack by spoon or other kitchen weaponry. The goats and the pig and the ducks that reminded his mother of her own mother's farm in Wisconsin had all died. Only three of her hens remained. His father wouldn't get rid of them but he wouldn't replace them either. Sooner rather than later the fox or old age would take them all away.

When he got home Calhoun was greeted by a smell of fried onions and overheated oil. His father was in the kitchen area, glaring at a cookbook through his spectacles. A solid, stocky man with his thick, carpenter's fingers, he was entirely the wrong design for a cook.

He was cooking a Spaghetti carbonara, he replied to Calhoun's faintly anxious enquiry. He pronounced it Sphagetti.

Calhoun saw the cream and the fatty bacon and winced. Cooking was a new venture for his father. Normally he ate out or made a sandwich or opened a tin of something but recently he had taken to cooking evening meals for them both, aided by a cookbook that one of his women friends had given him. Probably his intentions were good but Calhoun wondered if they overlaid a subconscious resolve to drive him out and find his own place to live. His father didn't think it was good for him, 'living with his old dad', didn't think he should have come back home at all.

He seemed to feel Calhoun had let himself down, coming home to Maine. Or, more likely, let down his mother, who'd had such ambitions for him. The local paper carried a regular weekly police report and he would read some of the entries out to Calhoun in a dry, mocking voice reflecting his opinion of detective work in Russell County.

'The Bridport Police Department received a complaint on September 24 at 7:15 pm that two flower pots on Pleasant Street had been smashed. The incident is under investigation.'

'On September 31 at 6 pm, the police received a report that a roving gang of juveniles was drinking and making noise in the wooded area by Constitution Street. Upon the arrival of four police officers ('Four! Hell, how many d'you think they'd send for a shooting?'), the juveniles scattered in different directions. Left behind were empty beer cans. ('Hey, d'you think they'd been drinking BEER?')

'On October 4 at 9:30 pm the police received a report that there was screaming behind the elementary school. Upon inspection, the officer found two cats engaged in a sexual act.'

'What d'you want to come back here for?' he'd said, when Calhoun first told him he was thinking about it. 'You must be mad.'

What could he say? Punishment? Atonement? A desire for the cold, purifying earth of my roots? He wondered how his father would react if he came out with it one day, the whole story.

Calhoun knew how he would react. His father was a Puritan at heart. He could be tolerant but he had a rigid, unbending sense of integrity, of what was right and what was wrong.

'There's a bottle of wine if you want some,' his father said. He indicated it where it stood, unopened, on the table. Calhoun picked it up and inspected the label.

'Any good?'

'Fine,' Calhoun lied. But he was touched by the thought. His father never drank wine. Calhoun would have got some in, some decent stuff from mail order, but somehow that would have suggested permanence and Calhoun was not quite ready for permanence. He loved his father but the thought of them continuing to live together, two lonely old bachelors in their ship in the woods, could not be considered with total equanimity, not yet.

'Want some?'

His father shook his head.

'I'll have a beer.'

'Want me to do anything?'

'No, I'm fine.'

Was his father lonely? Calhoun thought about it while he sat with his wine at the far end of the room, as far as he could from the smell of frying onions and bacon fat. He had plenty of friends though he never brought them to the house. He met them at the place he called 'the club' in town which was more of a den, a bear's den, where he drank beer and played pool and the English game of darts he'd taken to recently. Calhoun thought he might have a particular woman friend, just over the border in Canada, a Mrs Williams he'd mentioned once or twice that he 'did some odd jobs for'. Calhoun hoped there wasn't a Mr Williams. One philanderer in the family was more than enough.

Calhoun could never have asked him a direct question about it. He and his father did not communicate like that. Sometimes they

56

did not communicate at all, for days on end. When they did it was a bit like a game of chess. A considered move, a long pause for thought, a considered response – the occasional careless exchange when their minds were on other things. He could sometimes get his father talking about the people he worked for. He worked for a lot of small businesses in town but more often, now, it was in people's homes. He was good with people. They liked to talk to him. He seemed to listen. And he was perceptive about them. He said things that surprised Calhoun sometimes.

He knew Hannah Crew quite well, had done plenty of work for her in the Old Barrack House when she converted it to an inn. But he'd not met Madeleine Ross, only the daughter.

'Strange kid,' he said.

'In what way?' Calhoun asked him.

'Quiet for a kid. Bit wrapped up in herself.'

Long pause. Then, when you thought he'd stopped thinking about it. 'Like an elf. A little elf. You feel her watching you. Big eyes, brown eyes, dark. Bit . . . not creepy, but you know what I mean, you don't know what she's thinking.'

'Poor kid,' said Calhoun.

He should speak to Hannah Crew, see what she knew about the woman. He still wasn't happy about the bear. But he had to tread carefully. The State police hadn't officially been called into the case yet.

His father knew a bit about the archaeology team from the university. He'd done some work for them at the old cannery when they'd first moved in, making it a little more habitable, which amounted to boarding up some of the broken windows and putting up a few shelves. He knew a lot more about the site than Calhoun did.

'French came here in 1604,' he said. 'First settlement on mainland America.'

After a while, Calhoun said: 'How come no one ever knew it was there, so close to the cannery?'

'You ever smell that place?'

'People worked there.'

The cannery had been a thriving concern when Calhoun was a kid. Maybe a couple of hundred workers at the peak of the season.

'They just went in, did their shift, went home. Didn't stroll around the headland. It was pretty well overgrown till they came here in the spring. Cleared a lot of timber. Besides, even if you'd seen something it was just some old ruin. It was only when they found the bodies. They reckoned it was the cemetery. Lot of them died. Scurvy, she reckoned, or starved.'

'Who's she?'

'The one in charge, Dr Wendy something.'

'Wendicott. What d'you make of her?'

'OK. Bit kind of distant. Nose stuck in her work, I guess, stuck in the past. Very clever woman, though. We don't know a thing about the past, do we, *our* past? Who came here before us, all that. Place like that and we know nothing about it. They were carpenters, the first ones.'

'Who were?'

'First lot of settlers. Carpenters. From France.'

Calhoun wasn't sure he was right about that but someone must have told him.

'Go easy on the cream,' he said.

'What?'

'Goes a long way,' said Calhoun. His father acted like he'd never heard of cholesterol.

'Says here a carton of cream,' his father said, peering at the book.

'That's probably for four,' said Calhoun. 'It's usually for four. Or six.'

After supper Calhoun went outside to feed the chickens what he couldn't eat. He reckoned his father neglected them, wanted them to die. They were more trouble than they were worth, he said. His mother reckoned they were therapy for her. She liked the little clucking noises they made, said they were soothing. Calhoun listened to them now in the dark as they bickered over the carbonara. She had names for them all. Greek and Roman names. Heroic names. There was a rooster called Agamemnon. They called it Aggie. It died. He didn't know what these three were called, the survivors.

'Medea?' he tried in the darkness. 'Andromeda? Hecate?'

Calhoun always reckoned he was lucky his mother hadn't called *him* after one of her classical heroes. Hector, perhaps, or Ajax. Maybe his father had put his foot down for once.

There was a frost on the snow. It sparkled in the moonlight. A fat, full moon and a sky full of stars. The tops of the trees trembled in what was left of the wind. He looked out over his mother's garden, pale and clear in the moonlight and the snow, a few roses still blooming even this late in the year. It looked smaller than he remembered it as a child. The forest was moving back. Sometimes he even thought he saw it move, out of the corner of his eye, a furtive, almost imperceptible creeping up. As if it was playing grandmother's footsteps with them. When he'd come back here in the summer he'd spent a weekend weeding, pulling up the shoots of new trees, pruning the roses. But it needed more than a weekend. The forest always grew back.

He went back inside the house and told his father he was going out for a while, there was someone he had to see.

III

It took Calhoun twenty minutes to drive to the cannery. He thought maybe he'd find one of Jensen's people there, keeping an eye on the place, and he was figuring out what he was going to say to explain his continuing interest in the case. He had even less of an excuse to be here now than on the bear hunt. But there was no one there. Just the VW, still in its shroud of snow.

He left his own car next to it and walked down the side of the cannery. A sensor light came on and he felt momentarily exposed as if there was someone, or something, out there in the darkness, watching. More lights ahead, from the little cluster of trailers and RVs, and as he approached he heard music, a violin, sharp and sad in the frozen air. He gave them a wide berth and the music faded and there was just the sound of his footsteps, crunching in the snow.

He switched on his flashlight and the wavering beam found the darker patch of snow where they had found the body – and the flowers that had been scattered over the blood, as if they could somehow neutralise the stain. He stopped to pay his own silent respects, and as he stood there he sensed, rather than saw, a sudden movement at the edge of his vision, a fleeting shadow against the forest. When he swung his light there was nothing there but he began to run across the site in that direction, leaping the trenches and slipping on the icy mounds of earth, hurting his hand. The beam of the flashlight bounced from tree to tree and threw grotesque shadows, and he had the absurd thought that the trees froze when the light hit them and moved as soon as it swung away. He switched it off and stood in the darkness, listening. Silence. And then, what was it? It sounded like a laugh. But very light and distant, almost like a child laughing, or crying.

'Who's there?' he shouted hopelessly into the trees, and the trees threw his voice back and there was nothing. He searched a little longer with the flashlight but could see no footprints in the snow beside his own.

He knocked loudly on the door of the camper so they would know he wasn't a bear snuffling at the door. A pause, then a woman's voice raised above the sound of the music: 'Who is that?'

He told them. A longer pause before the door was opened. It was the man, pale and whiskered and anxious, a white rat sniffing the air. Calhoun, too, sniffed – and smelled illegal substances thinly disguised with incense and quick burst of eau de toilette. He had to ask if he could come in and the man stepped reluctantly back from the doorway with an apologetic glance over his shoulder into the dimly lit interior.

Dr Wendicott and her two students were sitting around a table, glasses and a bottle of wine up front, the spliffs not. The younger women looked guilty, Dr Wendicott merely irate.

'What is it?' A schoolteacher disturbed by a troublesome child. Calhoun felt he should apologise. He just wanted to check they were all right, he said. He was still standing in the doorway.

'I'm sorry,' she said. A deliberate adjustment of manner. 'We're a little on edge, as you can imagine. Won't you sit down? Will you have a glass of wine?'

One of the younger women made a space for him on the bench seat and the headmistress told the white rat to open another bottle. Pete, she called him. He looked a little unsteady on his feet, drunk or stoned or both, but he managed to open another bottle.

'You're obviously not too bothered about staying on here,' Calhoun said, not entirely to make conversation.

'Oh, I wouldn't say that. Why do you think we're all in the same truck?'

'You're all sleeping here?'

'Cosy, isn't it? And between us we have an axe, a hunting knife, a mace spray and a large bunch of garlic.'

He had seen the axe.

'Garlic?' he said.

'Don't you think?'

'We're not too much troubled by vampires round here,' he said.

'That's what they said about the bears.' He thought her manner curiously flippant in the circumstances, but perhaps it was protective.

'Did you find anything today?' This was the woman sitting next to him – Laura? – who seemed the most nervous of them all.

He told them they'd found 'bear traces'.

'Do you think it will be back?'

'Clearly not.' Dr Wendicott spoke before he could make reassuring noises. 'Or I assume they'd have left several of those large men here with their dogs and their guns.'

'I could arrange to,' said Calhoun, 'if it would make you feel better.'

No one said if it would or it wouldn't.

'We don't think it will be back,' he said, 'but it's probably not a good idea to go wandering around the headland at night.'

'Don't worry. We won't.'

Another silence. He was starting to feel sorry he'd come, though probably not as sorry as they were. He felt all the awkward intrusiveness of the stranger who intrudes upon the company of intimates. More than that, he had intruded upon their grief and burst the thin bubble of consolation they had begun to construct from booze and dope and their own shared emotions. If he knew what he was doing there, if he had any business being there, he would have lived with that, but he didn't, none he could think of anyway.

He asked them how long they were thinking of staying on here.

'Funny, we were just discussing that,' said Dr Wendicott. 'The general consensus is that we move out tomorrow.'

He had a feeling that the general consensus was not her own.

'Will that interfere with your plans?'

'We were hoping to get a little more done here before the weather closed us down but . . .' A small shrug that might have been resigned, could as well have been petulant . . . 'No one's very keen on staying on, given the . . .' She didn't trouble to finish the sentence.

'So what will happen to this place?'

'Oh, we'll leave it pretty much as it is and come back in the spring and hope it's pretty much as we left it. That's what we always intended. It's just that we were hoping to get a little more done, that's all.'

She reached for the wine again, leaning across the table towards him and a bunch of her hair coming loose from where it was pinned at the back and falling forward across her cheek. It worked on Calhoun like a sudden sexual exposure, this unexpected flash of femininity, and there was something else, perhaps in the slight sulkiness of her mouth, as if the drink and the drugs were tugging loose other pins, that made him think of things that were entirely inappropriate to the occasion.

'You've hurt your hand,' said Laura.

He turned it up to the light. He'd taken the skin off the side of his palm beneath the thumb. The Mount of Venus. How did he know that? Then he remembered – and the way she'd touched it with her hand as she explained it to him, and then her mouth. The Mount of Venus and the Mount of the Moon and the life line between. The graze was the shape of a kiss, raw in the yellow light.

'I slipped on the snow,' he said.

Dr Wendicott twisted round and half knelt on the seat to reach for something on the shelf above her head. She wore tight blue jeans and he was too busy observing the way they fitted around her bottom to realise it was a first-aid box until she opened it up on the table and produced a tube of antiseptic. But she didn't offer to rub it in for him. As Calhoun did, mixing the ointment with the blood, he felt the eyes of the two younger women on him, staring at the graze in a kind of fascinated horror, as if it was somehow significant.

'So what have you found here?' he said, more to take the attention off his hand than because he really wanted to know. 'Anything interesting?'

'Depends what you're interested in,' said Dr Wendicott.

'You found some bodies?'

'Are they interesting? I suppose they are to some people. Yes, we found some bodies. In a cemetery, right on the headland.'

'Not here?'

'Not on the site of the fort, no. People don't tend to bury their dead right next to where they're living. They leave a discreet distance.'

'Is this relevant?' It was Jarvis. The first thing he'd said since he'd opened the door.

Calhoun looked at him. He was probably Calhoun's age, maybe a little younger, pale-faced with that wispy brown moustache and round-rimmed glasses that gave him an intense studious air, even if he did look a little dazed at the moment.

'Relevant to what?' said Calhoun.

'Well – to your inquiry?'

'I didn't mean it as such but . . . I guess if there were a lot of bodies around it might attract certain wildlife, that's all.'

Rats, for instance. Why did he instinctively dislike this man?

'It was last year we found them.'

'But you expect to find some more?'

'Do we?'

'It was a question.'

'Possibly. We haven't so far.'

'How long had they been there?'

'In the cemetery? Between three and four hundred years. Apparently undisturbed by wildlife.'

'OK,' he said, backing off. 'I was just curious. Another theory is that with all the digging you've been doing round here the bear might have come looking for a place to hibernate and Miss Ross just picked a bad time to bang into him. Her.'

'Her?'

He shook his head. Now was not the time to expound on Henry Savageau's history of Grandmother, the Chief's Daughter. 'Him, her, whatever,' he said. 'Is there a drop more wine?'

He'd had only one glass of his father's and this was better. Besides, it might make them relax if he drank a bit more. Might make him relax, anyway.

'And if you want to finish off the dope,' he said, 'it's OK with me.'

A difficult moment. Then Kate Wendicott smiled.

'Charlotte,' she said.

The woman called Charlotte shot a glance at Laura, rolled her eyes and then stood up and fished around behind one of the speakers for the CD player.

'It's sort of medicinal,' said Dr Wendicott, 'in the circumstances.'

Calhoun took a couple of puffs to be sociable, though it was not his particular medicine. But his participation in this small crime lightened the atmosphere considerably. If it did not make him one of them, it opened the door a crack into their exclusive world and they began to tell him about the dig. Or rather, Dr Wendicott did: Kate, as she invited him to call her, her fingers tugging loose the knot of hair at her neck with a frown of impatience as if it was really too much trouble and letting it tumble to her shoulders as she spoke.

IV

They weren't all carpenters. There were gentlemen adventurers and Swiss soldiers of fortune and a handful of *vagabondes* they'd rounded up from the streets of La Rochelle to make up the numbers and to do the skivvying. But the carpenters were the most plentiful and the most important; it was they who did the skilled work, it was they who built the fort. They'd been sent by Henri Quatre, King of France, to build a base for the ones that would follow and they brought most of their building materials with them. The land they came to was one vast forest, bigger than the whole of France, bigger than all the forests in Europe, but they had no experience of building houses of logs. So the boat they sailed in from La Rochelle was loaded to the decks with planks and joists, prefabricated doors and windows, even chimneys.

They landed in the last week of June, 1604.

By late August they had built a small village, like a village in France. It had a meeting hall, which they also used as a mess, a storehouse, a communal oven, a blacksmith's and a kitchen. There were several houses for the gentlemen adventurers, their walls ornately carved with the *fleur de lis* of the French kings, and there was even a watermill for grinding the corn they would grow to make the small white rolls they would eat, the *petit pain*.

There was also a chapel and a cemetery, of which they were to have much need in the months to come.

All these buildings were linked with a palisade of felled trees as protection against the people they called *Les Sauvages*, the people of the forest. But *Les Sauvages*, who had watched them come ashore, kept their distance and stayed watching from their forest until they saw which way the wind blew.

The settlement was a little below the 45th parallel, which was the same latitude as the south of France, and for most of the summer these men of Gascony and of Bordeaux felt that they had discovered a new Provence, a land of sunshine and song where they would grow grapes and olives and citrus. Between the houses they dug gardens which they planted with the seeds they had brought from France and which would give them a crop of vegetables, perhaps before Christmas if the winter was mild. For the present, however, they had a plentiful supply of French and Spanish wine and cider from Brittany which would last them until the spring, and though they had no women they entertained themselves with regular carnivals when they wore fancy dress and sang and danced and told stories, like the troubadours of old. There were disagreements between them, inevitably, for they were French. But on the whole they were content. Their commander, the first Lieutenant-Governor of Acadia, wrote to his sovereign in Paris and told him it was the most beautiful province of his kingdom, a garden of Eden.

And then on 30th October, it snowed.

They thought it might be a freak of the season but it snowed the day after that and the day following . . . By mid-November they were snowed in. Through the whole winter the snow lay four or five feet deep against the walls of the stockade, and the cold north wind brought blizzards that at times would bury the houses altogether and force its way through the gaps the carpenters had left in the thin wooden walls. It was so cold even the cider froze in its casks. They had to break it with an axe and distribute it in chunks to be thawed in pans over an open fire. They were too afraid to venture into the forest and besides had no means of walking on the snow, so they lived on their supplies, which consisted mostly of salted meat. The only thing they had to eat that was fresh was bread, and by January they had run out of flour.

The snow lasted until April. Long before that they were afflicted with a deadly disease they called *mal de la terre* which putrefied the living flesh and turned the blood black in the veins. It rotted their gums so their teeth fell out and clogged their mouths with decaying flesh so that they could not eat. Early in the New Year, they began to die. By April, when the snow finally started to melt, almost half of them were dead and the rest so ill they could scarcely move from their beds. At night, towards the end, many of them thought they heard a large animal moving around the settlement between the houses. They heard it snuffling at their doors. But it might have been the wind. They were then in a twilight world, between life and death. When the relief ships came from France they took off the survivors and the place was left abandoned for many years. The French, when they spoke of this first settlement, called it Fort Hiver – Fort Winter.

Fort Winter was something of an Eldorado among historians and archaeologists, sought after, argued over, written about in many a learned article, but never discovered. The English had come here about fifty years after the French, but they, too, had survived just one winter, and the fort had been abandoned in circumstances that added to its sinister legend. Both settlements had left documentary records: scraps of journal, more detailed if less compelling reports from the commanders and priests, even plans of the fort and sketches of individual buildings, but in all cases the descriptions of the actual geographical location were confusing. In those days there was no precise way of fixing longitude and the names of the places given by both expeditions bore little or no relation to the names they now had. There were over a hundred creeks and inlets on Narragasco Bay and the scrappy details in the archives could have applied to any number of them.

The discovery of the cemetery on Kitehawk Head aroused immediate interest in the university archaeology department because this was one of the places that had always been considered among the more likely sites. In the graves they found buttons and coins, belt and shoe-buckles that gave them a fix on the dates and the nationalities of the corpses. Kate Wendicott was a specialist in the archaeology of the early colonial period. She took a small field team up to Russell County and they set up camp on the headland. The whole area was densely forested and they had no permission to fell trees. All they could do was pull away some of the undergrowth and probe with metal detectors and ground radar. It took them two weeks before they found the ruins of the fort. It was about 200 yards inland from the cemetery, on the cliffs immediately above the jetty built by the owners of the fish cannery. The cliff path ran right through the middle of it, but all that remained were the granite foundation stones, buried under several inches of topsoil and overgrown with thick vegetation.

It took them almost a year to raise the necessary funds from the National Endowment for the Humanities, and it was the following spring before Kate took her field crew back to the site.

They had maps and plans of the fort drawn up by the French commander for the Intendant of New France, and by Captain James Russell who had led the English expedition there in the 1650s – but there were discrepancies between the two. The French plan showed a regular fort neatly laid out in the conventional European star shape – earthworks topped by a palisade of white oak and spruce and with platforms for cannon at each corner – but this may have been wishful thinking, or an attempt to impress superiors back in France. Russell's description was of a more primitive structure. 'The French lay close under a work of earth,' he wrote, and his own plan showed only a few of the buildings so meticulously laid out by his French predecessor. He claimed to have built up the walls substantially and to have stripped eight cannon from his ships and four 'murtherers', or mortars, to defend them. He also built a magazine for the powder, a barracks and an infirmary, and where the French had planted gardens he laid out a central courtyard, or parade ground, with cobbles from the beach.

The first settlers arrived from Boston in May, 1655. When Russell came back with supplies the following spring, the entire community had perished, depleted by scurvy and malnutrition, the survivors either massacred or carried off into captivity by the Indians.

Kate's preliminary survey had used ground-penetrating radar to reveal the foundations of the buildings, but the readings bore little relation to the historical plans. She decided to clear half the site and dig trenches intersecting eight of the buildings they'd discovered. The rest would have to wait for more funding in a year's time. They marked the site out in sections a yard square and started digging.

As well as the four full-time staff from the university, they took on six local people as labourers or, more flatteringly, field assistants. Three of them were fishermen whose boats were laid up most of the year because of the embargo on the cod fisheries, two were from the Souriquois reservation on the edge of Bridport – and the sixth was Madeleine Ross. Each of them was given a target of two square yards a week.

They found a rich haul of artefacts in the clay sand and gravel between the granite stones of the foundations, but at first nothing particularly interesting or surprising. There were ceramics from south-west France and Staffordshire in England, gun flints and the metal parts of firearms, musket balls and coins, clay tobacco pipes, buttons and buckles by the score. Kate, who was making a special study of the diet and health of the early settlers, spent most of her time in the three kitchen middens they had discovered, happily poking about among the vertebrate remains of the domestic animals that had formed their staple fare and afterwards identifying and cataloguing them in the laboratory she had set up in the cannery. It was the kind of work archaeologists and anthropologists revel in, this obsessive picking through the leavings of the long dead, if of scant interest to anyone outside their own professions.

They began to paint a detailed picture of how these people had lived as they clung to the edge of a wilderness, space travellers on the dark side of the planet, but they still had no clear idea of how most of them had died. Only one of the corpses found in the cemetery showed signs of having met a violent end and they could only assume from the scant documentary evidence that the rest had died of malnutrition, probably hastened by scurvy. It was a familiar disease among mariners and not unusual in isolated communities cut off in the winter. But so far they had found no signs of the massacre recorded by contemporary authorities in Boston.

Traditionally the natives stayed inland during the winter, following the herds of caribou, deer and moose, and came to the coast only during the summer months to fish for pollock and herring and indulge themselves in great blow-outs on clams and oysters. Shell middens had been found on the strand below the settlement above the high-tide mark, and there was an ancient burial ground on the headland which was sacred to the Abenaki. But the only signs of a native presence on the site itself were a few pieces of coarse pottery and a pair of primitive bodkins made from the shin bones of moose or deer. Jarvis, who was the anthropologist among them, claimed that the initial reports in the archives suggested the local tribes were friendly to the settlers and there had been a fair bit of trading between them.

There were conflicting accounts of why they had turned hostile. The most widely accepted was that they had been stirred up by the French, but Jarvis preferred the Bear Story.

Calhoun detected a sudden return to the tension apparent on his arrival, at least among the women. But Jarvis, who was probably numb to all feeling by now, ploughed on regardless.

Apparently, one evening in the fall, a group of settlers had spotted a bear trapped on the beach by the rising tide. As it attempted to climb the cliffs towards them they hurled rocks and stones at it, until someone fetched a firing piece and shot it, so it fell down into the sea. From then on none of the natives would come near the fort. A story went round that the Souriquois believed the bear to be a powerful shaman who practised the art of shape-shifting. In killing him, particularly in such an improper way, the settlers had offended the bear spirit *Memekwesiw*, and would bring extreme ill fortune upon themselves and all who had dealings with them.

'And the bears have been hitting back ever since,' said Jarvis. 'One way or another.'

The sheer crassness of the remark deprived Calhoun of speech for a moment. But not Kate. 'Thank you, Pete, for sharing that thought with us,' she said, with a dangerous softness.

He flushed, either with anger or embarrassment or both.

'I was thinking of the stories,' he said, 'about the winter.'

'What stories?' Calhoun found his voice.

'I think that's enough fairy tales for one night,' said Kate with a firmness that had been absent from her voice since she had let her hair down.

Jarvis shrugged and continued to roll another joint.

'About the winter?' Calhoun pretended not to notice the change of atmosphere. 'What winter?'

But Jarvis was silent.

'He means the winter they all died,' Kate answered for him. 'There are all kinds of ghost stories attached to this place, like any place where people died in – well, when there's some mystery attached to it. But, I don't think it's very helpful to repeat them in the circumstances.' With another cold look at Jarvis.

Calhoun persisted. 'How do you mean?'

'Well, I would have thought it was obvious, even to a detective.' This was a return to the old Dr Wendicott, her tongue newly honed. 'Given what happened to Maddie, if the press get hold of anything vaguely . . . weird, they'll be all over us. We need to keep a very low profile at the moment or when we come back in the spring we'll find the entire place has been dug up by ghouls.'

This was probably true, but Calhoun would not be so easily diverted, even at the risk of losing a new friend. *The bears have been hitting back ever since*. What did he mean? He was considering how best to put this question when his phone rang.

'Saved by the bell,' Jarvis murmured, just loud enough for him to hear – and Calhoun caught the look Kate gave him before he answered the call.

It was Jensen. He was at the Old Barrack House where Madeleine Ross had been staying. Her little girl was missing.

V

The early morning flight from Heathrow landed at Boston at three in the afternoon, and Jessica had to wait an hour for the connecting flight to Bangor. It was dark when she arrived and whipping up a storm. The man in the rental said it would take her two or three hours to drive up to Bridport and there were snow warnings. He told her to stick to Route 1 and not take any short-cuts.

As Jessica drove from the airport the leaves came flapping out of the night, beating against the windscreen, but the snow held off. After an hour or so she reached the sea, and the road began to twist and turn along the jigsaw coast, hugging the edge of dark inlets or plunging recklessly out on causeways across the black water. She was confused, disorientated, her brain like an ants' nest after the Nipon attack. As if the individual brain cells were still logged into the certainties of yesterday, scurrying about the archives of Oxford, while the central control struggled to grapple with the enormity of what had happened or refused, absolutely, to accept it – this impossible reality.

There were frequent intersections where she missed the road signs and had to stop to check the map. It told her the dark void out to her right was Frenchman Bay and the lights in the far distance Bar Harbor, the last town in large print before the Canada border. Sometimes she saw another car, not often, always going the other way. There was snow along the sides of the road and the occasional flurry in the headlights but it didn't last.

She drove in a grief blacker than the night. Whenever she passed a house she saw a ghostly figure left over from the junketing of the night before: a cardboard skeleton, or a scare-crow of pumpkin and straw, or just a plain old sheet tied to a tree, dancing in the wind. And tonight was All Saints, the holy

Catholic response to all this pagan mummery. She remembered the school chapel with its smell of beeswax and incense and the nuns rustling their rosaries, and the long lines of girls on their knees in the hard wooden pews saying their ritual prayers for the dead.

And later, when the Mass was over, she would take her little sister up to the side altar where they kept the candles and they would light one each for their dead mother, placing them side by side in the red plastic lanterns beneath the statue of the Virgin. Long after she had stopped believing in the certainty of salvation, Jessica continued to light candles to the memory of her mother, if not her soul. She lit them in churches all over Italy, one for herself and one for her sister.

Now it seemed to her that there had been some terrible significance in those two candles, burning side by side.

She drove along deserted stretches of coast with occasional signs for places called Starboard and Whiting and Bucks Harbor, lonely sea places, names out of the cold night. Once she nodded off at the wheel and lurched off the road, hitting soft earth instead of a tree. It was 8:40 local time but nearly two in the morning by her own mental clock, and she had not slept at all the night before, and only fitfully on the plane. She opened the car door and let the shock of cold air slap her awake. The wind had dropped but it had scoured the sky clear of cloud and the stars were out. There'd be no more snow tonight but the frost formed a crystal glaze over the snow that had fallen already. She thought of Maddie lying alone on that frozen bed of snow through the long night and it seemed impossible that she had not known, had been unable to help, even to come and lie there with her.

She had always wanted to be there for her little sister.

Whenever Jessica was in trouble and in need of a friend she would console herself with the thought of how an older, more competent version of herself would turn up out of the blue, like a fairy godmother, to comfort Maddie in similar straits. She would invent little scenarios in her mind in which Maddie was dumped by a boyfriend or was stranded, without money, in some remote part of the world, and Jessica would come dashing to the rescue, dispersing all the demons with a wave of her magic wand. She didn't want Maddie ever to suffer. She didn't want her to be unhappy. Even when Maddie showed an alarming predilection for making life difficult for herself and everyone else at every opportunity, Jessica still thought she could save her from the consequences of her own actions.

But Maddie didn't want to be saved.

'You've got to let people go their own sweet way,' she said, 'learn from their own mistakes. You're not the bloody Virgin Mary.'

So Maddie went her own sweet way, which was not an easy way and involved a great many mistakes, and never once did she ask Jessica to help her out.

Except there was just once – and the nature of it only emphasised her independence – when Maddie had gone with some friends to a restaurant round the corner from their father's apartment in Chelsea and spent far more money than they were able to pay and then had to ring him to come and bail them out. She had been so humiliated and angered by the public bollocking he had given her she had phoned Jessica the same night and asked her if she could send her a postal order so she could pay him back immediately. She was sixteen at the time.

At eighteen she was pregnant with Freya. It was an accident. The condom burst, she told Jessica, at the far end of a telephone again. The bloke was called Kieran, 'some Australian' she'd met in a pub. She thought he might be in California now. 'He was lovely,' she said, wistfully, but had no plans to see him again.

'You're impossible,' Jessica told her.

Jessica thought she would have an abortion. Later, she found this was what her father had assumed and so Maddie, being Maddie, had decided to have the baby. Either that or some residual Catholicism had reasserted itself.

Jessica was there for her then. She went with her to Natural Childbirth Classes. She learned all the things she had to do to help her through. When it got close to the time, she had a bag packed with all the things Maddie would need in hospital, even a book for herself. (Eliot, again, the *Collected Poems*, with a citation inside to Jessica Ross, the Prize for Service to the School. 'You try reading that to me, I'll fucking kill you,' said Maddie.) She held her hand through the long and difficult labour, wiped the sweat off her, urged her on, was sworn at and swore back so imaginatively Maddie was laughing between screams. When Freya finally came out, they first handed her to Jessica, and for two or three seconds she held her before passing her on to her mother, and Jessica walked away dazed with the emotion and the effort of it all.

'You'd think you'd had the fucking child, not me,' Maddie said before she went to sleep. And Jessica went back to university in Edinburgh.

Having a baby did nothing to cramp Maddie's style. She brought her to see Jessica in Edinburgh wrapped up like a papoose on her shoulders and took her everywhere, even to parties. Everyone said she seemed to know how to look after herself. Only Jessica was unconvinced.

'How will you live?' she asked her when Maddie was going home. Their father refused to give her any money. He said she was irresponsible and had to learn the hard way. Maddie said he'd never forgive her for making him a grandfather before he was fifty. Jessica sent back what money she could, but Maddie never asked for any and seemed to get by on remarkably little. For a while she lived in a one-bedroom apartment on a rundown council estate in Hackney. She was on benefit and had her rent paid by social security but she picked up money-in-hand working part-time in a local pub. She and another single mother shared the baby-sitting. When Jessica visited her she couldn't believe she could live like this, her beautiful sister.

'What else can I do?' Maddie said, shrugging. She'd left school without a single qualification. She was dyslexic and the difficulty of overcoming this had built up enormous frustrations. She was never satisfied with anything that was less than perfect. If she couldn't do something perfectly, she wouldn't do it at all. She'd been a talented artist at school but if she couldn't get something right she would give up in a misery of self-loathing. Sketches and paintings, things that other people, especially Jessica, thought were brilliant she would find some fault with and destroy before they could save them from her. She had tremendous energy, but all too often it seemed to turn inward on itself and become destructive. She would burn up with great rages against the world.

But suddenly all the fires seemed to be burned out. It was almost as if, bruised by the hurts she had inflicted on herself, she had stopped caring. She would no longer paint or make things. She would just take care of Freya and let life take care of itself.

'There's nothing I can do,' she said. 'I'm practising passive resistance.'

'With your looks you could be a model,' Jessica told her. Maddie thought that was hilarious.

'That's what they all say,' she said.

But next time Jessica rang her she said she'd taken her advice and was posing for life classes. She was much in demand. Hackney was full of aspiring young artists. She lived with at least two of them in turn, but they seemed to have less money even than Maddie. Jessica longed for her to meet someone rich who would look after her and bring up Freya somewhere nice. Maddie was testing all Jessica's feminist convictions and finding them wanting.

Finally Maddie persuaded their father to relent. He put down the deposit for an apartment and Freya got a place in a nursery school. Next thing Jessica knew Maddie was living on a bus with some New Age travellers. Their father had said something that had infuriated her and she refused to be 'beholden' to him.

That was when Maddie became a Donga. At last she had found something to believe in, something that harnessed her creative energies. To save creation itself. The last time Jessica saw her, she was helping to organise another protest against yet another motorway through the vanishing English countryside. She'd just been on television. She had developed an appreciation of public relations. The protesters used her as their spokesperson. Her looks were a formidable asset and the TV cameras loved her. She argued with impressive eloquence and Jessica suddenly felt very proud of her, but a little startled, too, as if this was a different Maddie from the one she had always thought was her little sister.

She even had a boyfriend Jessica liked, one of the leaders of the protest, who had studied law at Oxford. Jessica watched him with Freya and hoped. Freya, despite the lack of a formal education, was growing up a bright, thoughtful child. A watcher, like Jessica herself, with the same Latinate features, the same dark eyes, but her straight black hair cut in an uncompromising pudding basin round her head. Jessica had come over for her Oxford interview and was looking forward to seeing more of them if she moved back to England. She even thought they might share a house together in Oxford, when Maddie wasn't living in a bus or up a tree.

That was in February. In May she'd had a card from her in Maine with a moose on the front and a few careless, carefree words on the back about picking berries and digging up roots. There was no explanation of why she'd left England. She would write more later, she said, but she never did.

For the last part of the journey the road skirted another great bay, and Jessica could see the lights of a town in the distance like a ship far out at sea. For an hour the town played hide-and-seek with her in the darkness, sometimes seeming nearer, sometimes further away and at times vanishing altogether. In one of those latter times she found herself travelling inland through dense forest, with a sign warning of moose on the road and another indicating she was just a few miles from the Canada border. She thought she must have missed her turning and was thinking of doubling back when an intersection suddenly appeared ahead of her with the other sign she'd been looking for. It took her out to the coast again and beyond, across a long, bleak causeway to an island out in the bay, and finally into the town of neat white shingle-clad houses where her sister had come to die.

The Old Barrack House was on the cliff road climbing out of the harbour and there was a police car in the drive outside.

The door was hauled open almost as soon as she touched the bell and a stout, grey-haired woman filled the porch with a confusion of glaring, owl-eyed anticipation.

'Miss Crew?' Jessica said, puzzled by her expression.

'Yes?' She stared at Jessica with that same desperate expectancy and then Jessica told her who she was and her expression changed to one of unambiguous despair and she pressed a knuckle into her teeth and let out a little moan.

Her panic was infectious.

'Where's Freya?' Jessica said in sudden alarm.

The woman stepped back away from the door. Jessica stepped into a large dining room, empty except for the two police officers.

'Where's Freya?' she repeated.

But they didn't know where Freya was. That was why they were there.

VI

Another man turned up, a detective this time. Jessica sat at one of the empty tables, trying to take in what they were saying. The initial reaction to her had been a solicitous but embarrassed, almost shamefaced, concern but since then she had been ignored. They had placed her to one side like a parcel that has arrived unexpectedly from some distant country marked fragile, open with care. They did not care to open her. She was a bomb that might go off at any moment – or, with luck, if ignored long enough, go away. At least they had not offered her tea.

The detective wanted to see the bedroom at the back where Hannah Crew said she had put Freya to bed, and they all trooped in after him, with Jessica bringing up the rear.

The bed had obviously been slept in, and there were several dolls and furry animals on the chair beside it. Freya's travelling menagerie, Maddie called it. Maddie, who always travelled light, who kept nothing she could not stand to lose. The window was slightly ajar. It had obviously been opened from the inside, one of the officers said, there was no sign of a forced entry. The detective shone his flashlight into the area at the back. There was a number of cabins out there, log cabins, scarcely discernible among the trees. One of them until recently Maddie's.

And Freya's – until the night of the killing, when Hannah had moved her into the main house.

'If I'd had any idea she was going to do something like this I'd have put her in one of the upstairs rooms,' Hannah said. She was a large lump of a woman, exuding an air of anxiety so palpable it was as if she were constantly wringing her hands and wailing. Jessica picked up one of the cuddly toys. It was a badger she had bought for Freya at the airport in Rome on her way back to Scotland to spend Christmas with the family. The awful last Christmas with Virginia and their new family in Cumbria. The badger was a last-minute extra and Jessica thought it might be a mistake, that Freya was now too old for cuddly toys and would think she was trying to baby her. But she had loved it. One of the few good memories of that Christmas was seeing her hugging it to her chest and stroking the fur. She called it Scrodger.

Jessica holds it to her face, hoping for a lingering smell of Freya but there is none. She feels a small but perceptible rise in the level of grief, as if her soul is a cup that is almost full, and someone has just tilted the jug and added an extra few drops.

'Have you checked the cabin?' the detective said.

'First thing we did,' one of the officers told him. 'It was still locked and Miss Crew has both the keys.'

'What about school friends?'

'Yeah, well, I asked that, too. No go. Miss Crew here says she doesn't have any.'

'She doesn't have any friends?'

Her own voice, but surely she isn't here, or shouldn't be speaking. But they are all looking at her now. Hannah's eyes swimming with worry behind the overlarge spectacles, worry and guilt.

'Not according to the teachers,' apologetically, as if it is all her fault. 'But she's only been there since the start of term . . .'

'Excuse me, but what exactly is your role in all of this?' The detective was looking at Jessica and there was something in the look and the accompanying tone of voice that suggested a level of impatience, or restraint, as if he'd have been happier with 'And who the fuck are you?'

One of the other men told him. 'This is Miss Ross – the Sister.'

So now she has a title. She is the Sister.

'I'm sorry, I had no idea.' He made it sound like a criticism, and perhaps it was, but of whom? 'You've just come over from England?'

She nodded. She was still clutching the badger.

He came over and took her arm and led her back into the other room and sat her back on the chair, which was clearly where she belonged. But at least he sat next to her. He told her his name was Calhoun and he was with the State police. She was not too sure what else he said to her, but it was about Maddie, and there was an element of sympathy in his voice, or simple human feeling, that threatened to bring on the tears again. Gently, he reminded her that the priority now was to find the child.

Yes, she nodded, she understood.

'My guess is she's gone to see somebody,' Calhoun said. 'Somebody close to her mother, perhaps.'

'She knew I was on my way,' Jessica said. 'Perhaps she didn't want to see me.'

But his eyes had drifted out of focus as if his mind was off somewhere else. 'So if there's anyone your sister told you about that . . .'

She was already shaking her head.

'I know nothing about her life here,' she told him. 'The last time I saw her was . . . I don't know, six months ago, I suppose.'

The last time I saw her. That brief encounter in early spring and *she did not know* – none of them knew that it was the last spring Maddie would ever see.

'She didn't phone – or write?'

'I had a postcard a couple of months ago, telling me where she was, that's all. Until then I didn't even know she was over here.'

It sounded like they weren't very close. Perhaps they weren't. How many times had she seen Maddie over the last few years? Twice a year at best? A couple of holidays in Italy. Perhaps she had thought they were a lot closer than they really were.

'I lived in Rome until a month or so ago,' she added, as if it needed an explanation, a lame excuse.

'Rome,' he said, nodding to himself as if it should have been obvious. Then he was talking to Hannah Crew again and Jessica, feeling ever more lost, looked around the room. The tables and chairs were of a certain style she identified with New England – was it Shaker? – and there was a huge open fireplace of brick, hung with cooking implements from a different age.

They were talking about Maddie's friends now.

Maddie, it appeared, unlike Freya, had plenty of friends.

'She got along so well with people. She worked on table, you know, three, four nights a week. Everyone knew her by her first name.'

But when it came to special friends, people she might have seen on her nights off, she was not so sure. Her mind had gone blank, she said.

'Innis Graham?' the detective prompted her.

'Innis? Yes, of course, Innis, but . . .'

'Did he know the child?'

'Oh yes. He took them sailing a few times over the summer, but then he seemed to drop out of favour.'

Jessica looked at her, puzzled. *Drop out of favour.* Like a queen surrounded by her courtiers. Is that how Maddie had appeared to these people?

She managed to get a word in. Who was this Innis Graham?

Calhoun answered distractedly while he punched numbers on the phone. 'Your sister was with him when she . . . she'd just left him when she had her . . . her encounter.'

Her encounter. And suddenly the horror of it is there, that has been lurking in the undergrowth of her mind, and she can almost smell it, the pungent animal smell of it. She pushes it back, not able to deal with this, tries to concentrate on what Calhoun is saying on the phone, but it is a short conversation and clearly fruitless.

'He says Maddie knew a lot of people on the reservation.'

He had put the phone down and was speaking to Hannah Crew. Jessica was aware of a sharp increase in the level of anxiety.

'Well, I know she spent a bit of time with them but . . . they never came into the inn.' Emphatically.

'Any names at all?'

She shook her head. 'A couple of them worked with her on the site. Probably Dr Wendicott would know. I think Maddie might have mentioned somebody called Joe but I can't recall his second name. She was very interested in the Indians, the culture and so on . . .' She was looking at Jessica now and Jessica finally knew what they were talking about. 'She said her mother was . . . native American. And that her family came from these parts.'

And now they were all looking at her.

'Is that true?' Calhoun said, as if an accusation had been made.

'My mother died when Maddie was four.' It sounded, even to Jessica, as if she had suddenly been thrown on the defensive. But why? Why should she feel defensive about her mother – or was it Maddie and the crazy ideas she had?

'I don't know where her family came from,' she said. 'We never met them.'

When she thinks of her mother she thinks of heat and dust and the smell of diesel. Of travelling somewhere in a jeep or a truck or a bus, of excitement and discomfort in more or less equal measure. Of her mother's face looking back at her across the seat, to make sure she is all right. A brown, smiling face and long dark hair, a young face. On Khan's Flying Coaches up the Grand Trunk Road to Peshawar – Jessica still has the ticket in the cardboard folder of her life, the yellowing papers and the pressed bits of flower and the smudges of accidentally squashed insect and the photographs. Or a birthday party in a garden in Lahore – *her* birthday, when she was three or four – and her mother carrying out the cake. Bending over her as she blows out the candles. One of Jessica's earliest memories is the kites of many colours soaring in the blue sky over Lahore and the brown-limbed children who flew them from the rooftops, stepping from roof to roof still holding them, like little puppets attached to their strings. She would watch those children open-mouthed, wondering what would happen if they missed their footing. Would they soar with the kites, or plunge to their death in the street four or five storeys below? She never satisfactorily resolved this mystery. Once her mother took her on to the roof and held her so she could watch the kites writhing and twisting in the invisible heat waves of the air, but her eyes were drawn down, down into the blue-shadowed canyon between the ancient houses.

She remembers the feel of her mother's arms around her waist as she knelt to hold her and the soft touch of her hair against her cheek and a fresh, warm smell that was like . . . what? Flowers, spices?

But is it real or imagined? Wishful.

So much is derived from the memories her father gave them, like gifts: the stories he told of her in the first years after her death when he still did speak of her, and when he still wanted her daughters to be with him wherever he was, before he packed them off to school in England. Later, Jessica would wonder whether these sudden recalls of touch and warmth, of smells and

84

caresses, were not of her mother at all but of their amah, Selma Kuresh, the two women confused in her mind.

The only definite memory of her mother is on that bus up the Grand Trunk Road. Khan's Flying Coaches to Peshawar. That look in her eyes back down the length of the coach to where Jessica sat with another little girl she had just met, sharing a bag of sugar cane. It impressed itself on her mind, that look, and in later years she remembered it as one of quizzical amusement but loving, too, and with pride, as if she approved of what she saw, and Jessica held on to that, to the one memory that had to be real.

Her father and mother had met in India and on such a coach. On the hippie trail to Katmandu. It was the 1960s. Her mother was the hippie. Louise. Lou, people called her. She wore long print skirts and carried a guitar on her shoulders and sang the songs of Joan Baez and Buffy St Marie. And was a full-blooded Algonquin Indian. This was the expression her father used when he first told the girls. This was confusing to Jessica. For many years she thought her mother was a real Indian, from India. Only later did she realise she was a Red Indian, as they called them then, the politically correct Native American coming later, perhaps not at all for her father.

He was enchanted by her, by the romance of her. He was not a hippie himself, only pretending. He worked for a development agency and was six years older than she was.

He took her back to Scotland and they were married in Edinburgh, where he grew up. Hippies did, apparently, get married. Or perhaps she, too, was only pretending. Later, when her father grew more cynical and her mother had been dead many years, he told Jessica she was not really an Indian. Her own mother had been half French, he said, her father a white American from the southern states, a drunkard and a wife-beater who had left them when Louise was only seven. So far as Jessica was aware they were both long dead or disappeared and she knew of no other relatives.

Something had happened. Jessica could tell from the way the officer was speaking on the phone.

'What is it?' she said. 'Have they found her?'

'She's all right,' he said. 'She's safe.'

'Thank God,' she heard Hannah say and Jessica, too, made her silent acknowledgement to the Almighty or Fate or whatever it was that had failed so abysmally to take care of Maddie. 'Oh, thank God for that.'

'Where is she?' said Jessica. But the officer spoke to Calhoun: 'Some people who knew the mother. They phoned the reservation police a few minutes ago. She just turned up at their door.'

'You'd better come with us,' Calhoun told her.

Jessica had no idea what an Indian reservation would look like. From what she saw of it by the sparse street lighting it seemed not unlike a housing estate in some parts of Britain, the kind of place they built for the less affluent retired people on the south coast, little single-floor cabins – in England they'd have called them bungalows. The house they stopped at was set a little apart from the others and seemed more substantial. A sign outside advertised 'Native American Handicrafts, Jewellery, Basketware etc'. When she got out of the car, Jessica could smell the sea.

The door was opened by a small, elderly man with rheumy, anxious eyes who looked at them like they were the trouble he'd been expecting for most of his life.

Freya was curled up on the sofa watching television with a mug clutched in her hands. She was fully dressed but with a blanket round her shoulders, an Indian blanket, brightly patterned. Jessica stooped down beside her, wanting to hug her, but something restrained her from doing more than touch her hand with the tips of her fingers. Freya did not look at her. She looked past her at the television set.

'Freya?' Jessica said. 'It's Jess, it's your Auntie Jess.'

Freya had never called her 'Auntie' but Jessica felt the force of the barrier the child had wrapped around herself and used the term of endearment like an invocation to break it down. It didn't. Freya's eyes drifted back to the television as if there was something there she couldn't bear to miss. It was a police series, as mysterious and meaningless to Jessica as the real world had suddenly become.

'She's still a bit frightened, but she's better than she was.'

Jessica looked at the old woman sitting beside Freya on the sofa. Small, grey-haired, birdlike. Perhaps not so old: her eyes were bright, almost youthful, with just a fine web of lines at the corners and her hair was shoulder-length and slightly dishevelled. She gazed at Jessica with the gentle curiosity of the wise or the barking mad.

'You are the sister.'

She spoke with quiet assurance as if she did not need Jessica to confirm it.

'You look like your mother,' she said.

'I beg your pardon?' In her distress Jessica fell back on the stock British response to the impolite, the intrusive, the insane . . .

What could this woman possibly know of her mother?

'We never met,' she said, 'but I've seen a photograph. You are very alike.'

Jessica couldn't deal with this, not now. She turned back to Freya, who was still determinedly tuned in to the other crazy conversation on the TV, and told her she'd come to take her home.

The child's eyes went to the woman in sudden alarm, panic in her voice.

'Tante Yvette?'

The woman shushed her gently, stroking her hair.

She saw the way Jessica looked at her.

'Your mother and I were cousins,' she said. She stood up and walked over to an old wooden cabinet that stood against the far wall.

Jessica looked confusedly at Calhoun.

'I think we should get Freya to bed,' he said, 'before we do anything else.' The voice of authority to which the man – the husband? – responded.

'That's right. Poor child. She should be . . . asleep.' His voice tailed off lamely, as if he had long since given up hope of anyone listening to him.

The woman ignored them both, rummaging in the drawer of the cabinet.

Calhoun wrinkled his nose.

'Is that sea-grass?' he said.

The smell, musky but not unpleasant, pervaded the room. Calhoun picked something up from the table. It looked to Jessica like a straw doll, or it might have been an animal.

'We sell them. To raise money for the community centre.' The man pulled nervously at the sleeve of his cardigan. It was frayed, presumably from doing this a lot. He had slightly flattened features, as if he'd been trodden on but bore this humiliation with quiet dignity.

'Here it is.'

'Tante Yvette' had found what she was looking for. She presented it to Jessica like a trophy – a faded black-and-white photograph that showed a man and a woman and four children in full native costume of head-dress and beads and fringed deerskin, outside a log cabin. They looked toward the camera with a stiff self-consciousness, like exhibits in a museum, Jessica thought.

'That's your gran'mere.' Pointing to one of the two little girls, a child of about eight or nine. 'And that's my mother beside her. They grew up on the reservation. It looked a little different then. But your gran'mere left when she was eighteen, to join the American army. It was 1942.'

Calhoun stooped down to nearer Freya's level.

'I think we should get you back to Miss Crew's,' he said, 'with your aunt, yes?'

Freya made a sound like a sob and ran to the woman she had also called aunt.

'I think you must go back tonight, little one,' she said, 'but we'll see you soon. And I'll never be far away from you.'

She looked over Freya's head to Jessica as if this were a challenge, or a threat.

'She can come here again, yes?'

'Of course.' Jessica would have said anything to get away, to get Freya away. She wasn't sure why she felt so uneasy, except that there was a weirdness here she could neither understand nor cope with, not right now. She felt claustrophobic, almost suffocated.

'I'll come with you to the car,' the woman said.

She whispered something to Freya that none of them heard and then put her arm round her shoulder and steered her out of the room. She held her all the way to the car, the others following without speaking. Calhoun opened the door and the woman gently urged Freya into the back seat and then put a restraining hand on Jessica's arm.

'Come back tomorrow,' she said, 'and bring the little one.'
It sounded almost like a command.

As they drove off Freya twisted round in the seat, and Jessica looked back with her at the diminishing little figure outside the house. None of them waved but the woman watched them out of sight. She hadn't once mentioned Maddie, Jessica thought, and there hadn't been a single word of regret or condolence.

'We'll come back tomorrow,' she said reassuringly to Freya. She wanted to put her arms round the child and cuddle some feeling, some love, back into her. Always in the past they had been very physical, very huggy, but now she was afraid to touch her. She felt something soft and furry on the seat beside her. It was the badger. She must have brought it with her from the Old Barrack House without thinking. She picked it up and placed it gently in Freya's lap. The shriek made the police officer who was driving jerk his head round, swerving across the centre of the road and throwing Jessica hard against the side of the car.

Freya swept the toy off her lap, lifting up her feet and curling into a little trembling ball in the corner of the seat. Jessica reached out for her then, but Freya recoiled even further, and the look in her eyes caused Jessica to drop her arms in confusion, not so much from the terror and the panic she saw there as from something more alarming and altogether more inexplicable, something that seemed very close to hatred.

VII

Jessica wakes to sunshine and melting snow. Outside, through the streaming window, yesterday's world is dissolving, creating an illusion of spring. She looks across the room to where Freya is lying, curled up in the foetal position with one hand resting on the pillow close to her mouth, the index finger slightly raised so that she seems to be shushing someone in her sleep.

She looks such a baby, but she will be ten on her next birthday.

Jessica watches her, recalling other images, snapshots from the family album in her head.

There is the gypsy girl, the ragamuffin who lives in a bus, climbs trees, sticks up for herself, the bruiser. A countryman's peaked cap set on her head at a jaunty angle, a cheeky, catch-me-if-you-can grin, a smudge of dirt or warpaint on her cheek. The sense of instant readiness for flight.

She runs the way Jessica did as a child – and still does when the occasion demands – no soppy girl's scamper, elbows in at the waist, fingers flapping at invisible insects, but a sprinter's run, hands curved into a cutting edge, aimed like a dart at an imaginary finishing line. Jessica is proud of this child, of the self-reliance she projects, the bravado. But there is another picture: the little girl who likes to be mothered, treated like a baby, indulged, wrapped in a large dry towel after a hot bath and given a cuddle. Jessica remembers the feel of her damp warmth through the towel, the wet tangled hair against her cheek. The cosy intimacy of such moments.

Now she will have to rely on the tougher side of her nature.

What is to be done with her? She can no longer roam with travellers.

Probably Virginia will have her and probably that will be best for her. To be with a family in a safe, solid home and go to school and be in the same place from one year to the next.

But just thinking it makes Jessica feel like a traitor.

Looking at her as she sleeps, Jessica feels instantly protective. *Maternally* protective. She will take her back to Oxford and wrap her in a large, warm towel.

She imagines them sharing a small apartment, caring for each other, consoling each other for the loss of the sister, the mother. Sharing their lives together . . .

And through the layers of love and grief, there is a rising sense of panic.

She came downstairs to the smell of coffee and something sweetly nauseating and freshly baked – and Calhoun, sitting alone in the dining room reading a newspaper.

Something in this domestic scene jarred, like a picture puzzle which contained a number of deliberate errors, the lurking suggestion of ambush.

He told her Hannah had gone into town and left him to fix breakfast for her. He offered her a cake, which she declined.

'They're blueberry cakes,' he said. 'She makes them herself. She's famous for them.' He looked at them, frowning, as if they posed a problem that needed to be resolved.

She observed him as if for the first time and saw that he was much younger than she remembered from her disordered impressions of the night before, younger and less confident. He reminded her of someone she knew, or perhaps a well-known actor, but she couldn't put a name to the face. His expression was solemn but there was something strained about it, as if it had been assumed for the occasion, like a black tie for a funeral. When he looked directly at her she saw that his eyes were a pale, washed-out blue, and she had the impression you could look at them for a long time without having the slightest idea what he was thinking, or even if he was thinking anything at all.

It was a surprise to her that she could make these observations, just as it was a surprise that she could drink the coffee he put in front of her, that there were clearly parts of her that still functioned normally.

'Are you staying here or something?' she said.

'I stayed the night. I live the other side of Dover . . .' He checked himself, realising she had no idea where or what Dover was. '. . . Up on the Canada border – and there were one or two things I wanted to check out with you – when you weren't so . . .'

'About Maddie?'

'If that's OK?'

He wanted to know if Maddie had spoken or written to her about anyone she had met while she was here.

She told him no, that Maddie had only sent her one postcard and that had contained very little information at all.

'And you didn't know you had any family here, on the reservation?'

'No,' she said. 'My mother died when I was six. I knew she was half Indian but not where she came from.'

'You think your sister came here because she found out?'

'I suppose so, it would be typical Maddie. But I don't know how she knew. She didn't talk to me about it – just suddenly took off, but that was typical Maddie, too.'

'Impulsive.'

'You could say that.' Then, after a moment: 'Those two people we met last night on the reservation . . . Do you know anything about them?'

'The man's called Urbain Selmo. The woman's his sister, Yvette. I'll check them out today with the reservation police.'

'You called them Souriquois.'

'That's the name the French gave them. They speak Algonquin and they're a branch of the Abenaki, the People of the Dawn, so take your pick. They're related to the Micmac in Canada and the Maliseet and the Penobscot.'

Names that meant nothing to her.

'And what do they do?'

'What do they *do*?'

He looked at her a little sharply and she felt like one of those ignorant English women of a certain class and prejudice who know nothing of the world outside their own family and their own village but consider it entirely inferior.

'I meant what kind of work do they do?' she said.

'Some of them work in the lumber trade, or they do seasonal work, picking fruit, blueberries, that kind of thing, but there's not a lot of work around. You planning to go back there?'

'I don't know. I said I would. It depends on Freya.'

He nodded thoughtfully and asked how she was.

'Still asleep.'

'It was a long way to walk, for a child,' he said. 'I'm surprised no one saw her on the road.'

'Perhaps they did.'

'This isn't the city. A child that age, that size, they'd have stopped, or called the police. Besides, there's only the one highway along the coast. If she'd just arrived there, like they said, I'd have seen her myself on my way here.'

'Perhaps she kept out of sight.' He nodded, but she could see he still wasn't happy about something. She said she thought Freya would be better when she could get her away from this place.

She thought he looked uncomfortable, even a little shifty.

'It might be a while before we can release the body,' he said. Her sister, who was now 'the body'.

'Why is that?'

He told her the medical examiner wanted a second opinion. 'We're trying to find somebody – a doctor in Canada who's dealt with a lot of these cases – I mean, injuries caused by a . . . a bear. Only he's on vacation.' He spread his hands in a gesture of what? Apology, incompetence?

'When you say "a while"?'

'A few days.'

She nodded, thinking it would take her a few days to organise things, anyway. It wasn't something she'd ever done before, organise a funeral. But she wondered why they wanted a second opinion. If it was something to do with the nature of the injuries she wasn't sure she wanted to know, not just now.

'Will I have to identify her?' she asked him.

He said if it would cause her too much distress they could ask Hannah Crew, or the woman who was in charge of the dig.

'I'd rather remember her as she was,' Jessica said.

Neither of them said anything for a moment. Then he said, 'What will you do? I mean, for the . . . will you take her back to England?'

Where will she bury her lovely sister?

Where does she belong?

Is there a forest somewhere they will not dig up for a road?

She could bury her with her mother if she knew where her

mother was buried. In India somewhere, or Pakistan. Why has she never asked?

She told Calhoun that Maddie had no real home, except the road.

'She'd probably like to have her ashes scattered in the wind,' she said. 'I don't think she'd be particular which wind.'

And that was when she first thought of burying her here, where she'd died, where she'd come to find her roots.

VIII

She waited until midday to ring her father so it would be early morning in Scotland. Virginia answered. 'Your father's still in bed,' she said. When Jessica told her what she was thinking she sounded relieved.

'I think that's a marvellous idea,' she said.

A marvellous idea?

Then, as if aware that this was not quite the response for the occasion: 'I mean, I think that's very sensible.'

And finally, striving desperately for the right note: 'I think that's exactly what she would have wanted.'

'Will you want to come?' Jessica said. 'I mean, will Dad?'

He and Maddie had been at loggerheads since she was an adolescent. Whenever they met they fought. She had blamed him for everything bad about the world, especially highways that cut through beautiful downland. That was the problem with Maddie's protests. Jessica couldn't help thinking that they were all part of her lifelong battle with her father and all he stood for.

When Jessica had first spoken to him, to break the terrible news, he had sounded sad and subdued but not devastated, not life-threatened. A dark thought insinuated that he had written Maddie off a long time ago, like one of his investments that had failed to live up to its initial promise. But that was unjust. She knew that somewhere deep inside he must be bleeding, grieving for his lost daughter, but a carapace protected him from the damage she could still cause him. He seemed to accept – to expect – that Jessica would pick up the pieces, bring back the body. Bury the dead and arrange the requiem Mass. He had insisted on paying for her flight by credit card, and she had let him, because she thought it would make him feel better.

A moment's silence. Then Virginia spoke for a long time, and

Jessica could tell she was picking her words with care. This was unusual. Virginia was not normally careful about what she said or how she said it. She was so entirely self-absorbed she rarely noticed the devastating effect her remarks had on others, but occasionally, when confronted with an obstacle she could neither bully nor charm into submission, she attempted to manipulate.

She told Jessica her father had taken Maddie's death very badly. He woke up in cold sweats, she said, and suffered from what she called an ectopic heartbeat which was worrying his doctor. It was an awful thing to say, she said, but her prime concern had to be for the living. A trip to America for the funeral might kill him. All this was quite reasonable, but the way Virginia put it induced in Jessica a perverse desire to do the exact opposite of what Virginia wanted.

'I think I should talk to him about it,' Jessica said, 'all the same.'

'Of course you should talk to him,' said Virginia, 'Of *course* you should talk to him.' She frequently repeated a sentence, sometimes as much as three or four times, as if this would convince people of her sincerity or her enthusiasm. 'But I'll mention it to him first if you like.'

Then she asked about Freya. Jessica told her she was in a state of shock. She said nothing about the incident of the previous night, nothing about the reservation. She was thinking, I can't let Freya go to this woman. Maddie would never forgive me.

Then it hit her. *Virginia wouldn't take her.* Or she'd pack her off to some awful boarding school the moment she arrived on her doorstep. Probably the same one her father had sent his own girls to. She would consider this Sensible, or even A Marvellous Idea.

'And what about you?' Virginia said. 'What about *you?*'

When Jessica returns to the bedroom, Freya is still sleeping. She looks alarmingly lifeless, and Jessica lowers her head until her ear is almost resting on the pillow, until she feels the whisper of breath through the faintly parted lips.

She used to do this when Freya was a baby. She was convinced she'd stop breathing in her sleep. She would creep into her room in the middle of the night just to reassure herself. She was so tiny and vulnerable. 'I just don't see what keeps her *working*,' she'd say to Maddie.

And Maddie said: 'You'd be useless as a mother, you worry too much.'

Jessica remembers this now as she backs slowly away and sits on the edge of her own bed. Maddie was right for once. She has too vivid an imagination and there are so many things that can go wrong. What is it like to be nine? How does a nine-year-old *think*?

There must be books that will tell you. She thinks back to what she herself was like at that age. She recalls the words in her school reports: *Jessica is a very bright and capable child. Jessica is very mature for her age. Jessica is a very responsible girl and a good example to her classmates.* When Jessica read them they seemed to be describing someone else entirely, someone whose skin she lived in but who wasn't *her*. Inside, she had felt completely lost and bewildered, but she couldn't ever give in to that. She had to look after her little sister.

Until she was a little older than Freya is now, Jessica lived in India and Pakistan, mostly in cities, in Delhi, Lahore, Peshawar . . . Her memories are of narrow streets filled with bullock carts and bicycles and buses and camels and motor scooters; shops that spilled out into the sidewalks, huge round wooden trays piled high with ground herbs and spices like dyed sand, the pleasing clash of saffron and cinnamon and turmeric; the intricate lace-work of the overhanging wooden balconies and the shutters and the dark mysterious rooms within; gun shops and silk shops and copperware shops and brass-band shops and sweat shops and sweet shops, all with their own screaming discord of colour and sound and music . . . and the darting kites in the gold and blue skies above.

From all of this, she was abruptly transported to the cold, bleak border country between England and Scotland, a land of rain and heather and grey-stone walls draped with a sodden mat of moss and lichen. A land where the hills were called 'fells' and the streams 'becks'.

A land of sheep. Ugly rain-sodden sheep with shaggy grey coats that looked like bits of wall had broken off and been scattered across the hillside; and black crows that nested in the twisted beech trees of the churchyards and flew down to eat the eyes from new-born lambs; and the gaunt-faced market towns where lambs were brought for sale to slaughterers and the little 'fashion' shops selling cotton print frocks and felt hats from another age, and underwear that looked like it had been designed with a view to chastisement; and DIY shops that were called 'chandler's' or 'ironmonger's' and sold galvanised iron buckets to catch the drips from leaking roofs; and low-roofed pubs with even lower doorways that led to dark, forbidden interiors smelling of sheep and cigarettes and stale beer and the terrible old men who came out of them smelling worse.

And the wind-driven rain that swept in off the fells and lashed the empty villages, and the sky that for most of the year was like the opaque plastic containers the nuns gave them for their packed lunches when they went out on Nature Study. Tupperware containers they were called in other parts of the world, but in the border country tup was the word farmers used to describe what rams did to ewes and so was subject to censure. Sometimes, remembering the skies over Lahore, Jessica thought it was as if someone had turned a giant Tupperware container upside down over the whole county.

The only thing she liked about it were the rivers that issued from every crack and fissure in the grey-green hills and seemed always to be cheerful, whatever the season. It came to her one day that this was because they were on their way to somewhere else.

But Jessica endured. She became a stoic, and took a certain pride in passing the constant tests of physical and mental insensibility, in not being 'nesh', which meant week and weedy, like an effete southerner. She read books and lost herself in other worlds, and was good at lessons and sports which were called 'Games' (they even had a teacher called a 'Games Mistress') but were deadly serious affairs. You could not play hockey on a bone-hard pitch with a wind from off the fells without acquiring what the nuns called character. Jessica took a certain masochistic satisfaction in this kind of outdoor cold. Worse, far worse, was the cold indoors.

Jessica imagined this cold as her personal demon, her succubus, her penance for forbidden thoughts, her flagellator – the ghost of a defrocked priest who watched her with malignant eyes from the frozen walls and wrapped himself around her at nights or when her spirits were low, breathing his graveyard breath on her neck, insinuating his bony fingers up her skirts, inside her sweaters, feeling through flannelette nighties and knickers penetrating to the bone.

One of the books she had read was *Wuthering Heights*, and she thought often of poor dead Catherine Earnshaw, her cold white face pressed to the windowpane, her lips forming frozen rings upon the glass. Sometimes she mixed Catherine up with her sister Maddie, who had the same wild beauty, the same wild thoughts.

Maddie was not made for acceptance, only rebellion. Sometimes Jessica thought she would die, as Cathy had – of heartache or her own unrestrained frustration. When she ran off and the police sent search parties out for her across the fells, Jessica imagined they would find her in one of the becks, but instead they found her outside a pub in Carlisle with a couple of local Jack-the-lads, smoking and annoying the passers-by, and the nuns sent for her father, who took her away and enrolled her at a more liberal school with a reputation for dealing with difficult children by letting them do pretty much as they liked.

But Jessica stayed on, not entirely displeased at the enforced separation. Perhaps even then there had been some primitive sense of survival in her that knew she had to be distanced from Maddie and the wildness in her – that did not *want* to be responsible for her errant sister.

So she made the best of things and things turned out to be not so bad. The memories of India receded. She grew to appreciate the fell country, though she would never love it. She learned to look for the blossom on the hawthorn tree. Later, in Italy, in sunshine and warmth, she even missed the sense of mortal combat with the elements that been a feature of life in the border country. She watched the Romans, huddled and miserable in their winter rain, and, remembering the rain of Cumbria, thought them, 'nesh'.

But wherever she was, the Tupperware container went with her.

Jessica has become accustomed to her enclosed world. She has replaced the opaque skies and the convent walls with institutions, going from school to university to bureaucracy and now back again to university, as if she feels exposed and vulnerable without this protective skin, this blind that hides her from the light. Jessica is comfortable with her life. She does not want to change it. And if she ever does, she wants it to be from her own choice, not because it is forced upon her. She does not want to be obliged by circumstances: by poverty, by accident . . .

By Maddie's child?

She begins to think of the practicalities. She'll have to move out of hall. She'll have to find an apartment big enough for both of them. She'll have to send Freya to one of the local schools. She'll have to borrow more money . . .

The prospect is entirely without enchantment.

She is startled out of these considerations by a sudden yell and Freya is sitting up in bed with her eyes open wide, staring across the room as if she has seen a ghost.

'It's all right.' Jessica moves quickly to embrace her but she flinches away with another sharp cry.

'It's all right, pet. It's me. Jessica. Remember?'

'Where am I? Where's Mummy?'

Jessica's voice is gentle but there is no gentle way to put it.

'Mummy had an accident, darling, do you remember?'

And Jessica sees that she does.

IX

They drove along the cliffs towards the reservation on Nagwind Cove. The sun had conspired with the melting snow to produce a low but dense mist which hung over the sea, so that only the headlands and the highest points of the islands stood clear of it, like the tops of mountains above cloud. It made it impossible to differentiate between the mainland and the islands out in the bay, so that it seemed to Jessica that she was in the middle of a vast and mysterious archipelago linked by hidden causeways.

She almost drove past the reservation, it was so tucked off the highway on its little inlet. Even with the sun breaking through the patchy mist it had an air of bleak abandon. Signs of occupancy were apparent only from the lines of washing and the accumulation of domestic objects in the small patches of grass between each house and the road: broken bits of furniture, old cookers and refrigerators, children's toys and beaten-up old cars. She saw no people, just a solitary dog, tied to a washing line by a rope so it could run up and down, though it showed no inclination to do so.

Freya guided her to the house where they had found her the night before. It was at the end of a street, right on the edge of the sea, with a fishing net draped out over the grass. A soon as Jessica stopped the car, she was out and running towards the figure that had appeared in the open door.

'Your gran'mere was crazy to get out of this place.' Yvette sat at the kitchen table among the faded old photographs, the brittle-leaf letters of the dead. 'The war was a blessing for her. She was a nurse with the army. She went to England and then to France, then Germany, ended up in Berlin, just a step behind the front line all the way. We had letters from her . . .' She laid the tips of her fingers gently on them as if they might crumble to dust. 'She didn't write much but she kept in touch.

'She met her husband in Berlin – your *gran'pere*. Yes . . .' seeing the expression on Jessica's face, who had never before considered the existence of this *gran'pere*. 'He was with the American army. Laurie, his name was. She brought him back for the marriage. A handsome man, my mother said. He was a sergeant. He didn't like it here. It was much worse then. Hard to imagine how it could be, I know, but it was. My mother said you could see him wondering what he'd married into. And your *gran'mere*, she was ashamed of us, it was obvious. He took her with him down south, wherever it was he came from, and my mother didn't hear from her for many years. He beat her. So what's new? The men always beat the women unless . . . Well . . . But he left her, eventually. Or maybe the beating was so bad she left him, I don't know. She went back to nursing, made enough to see your mother through college. They came back here once or twice, during the summer, to rake blueberries for some extra money and to see the family. But I'd left by then. My own mother married a Micmac from Nova Scotia and we lived on one of the reservations there. I only came back a year ago.'

She was a funny woman, Yvette. A strange mixture of the mysterious and the mundane with her family snapshots and her cryptic little remarks. She wore a pair of little granny glasses perched on the end of her nose and her grey hair was tied back in a ponytail, but she wasn't so old, not nearly so old as Jessica had thought at first sight of her. From the stories she told about the family she must be in her mid to late fifties, a little older than Jessica's mother would have been had she lived. She was dressed conventionally enough in shapeless pants and sweater with a leather waistcoat over the top. The only ethnic touch was a collection of charms she wore on her wrist that made a soft clinking sound whenever she raised her arm, like a hanging ornament of shells or cymbals that moves in the wind. Through the kitchen window behind Yvette, Jessica could see Freya standing at the water's edge. She seemed to be staring out to sea, and as Jessica watched, she tilted her head in a listening attitude. Jessica herself could see nothing, except the tops of the pine trees on a nearby island protruding eerily above the mist and catching the last rays of the sun. Perhaps it was a bird she could see.

'Sooner or later we all have the urge to return to our roots,' Yvette said, 'if we know where to find them.'

'Like Maddie?'

'Perhaps.' She had still not spoken of Maddie, yet she must have known her. Freya would not have come here, surely, unless Maddie had brought her. 'You, too, I think.'

'Me?' Jessica shook her head. 'Not me.'

The woman shrugged as if she couldn't be bothered to argue.

'You have no curiosity?'

'Curiosity, yes, but . . .' Through the window behind her a boat emerged from out of the mist, heading towards the shore, a little fishing boat with its decks piled high with lobster pots and a single figure standing upright in the stern. Freya raised her arm in an almost solemn greeting and the man returned the gesture, a young man, tall and striking, with long black hair down to his shoulders. He brought the boat in to a little wooden jetty at the bottom of the garden and made it fast. Tante Yvette turned to see what had caught Jessica's attention.

'This is Joe,' she said, 'My brother's son.'

'He's a fisherman?'

'No. He is not a fisherman.' Her tone was without emphasis but Jessica felt some kind of a point had been made. 'But sometimes he fishes.'

Freya had taken hold of his hand and was leading him up to the house, talking all the while, but suddenly he stopped, looking straight at Jessica through the window. Then he turned on his heel, letting go of Freya's hand, and walked back to the boat.

They watched without speaking as he untied the rope and headed back into the mist.

Jessica turned to face Yvette, frowning a question.

'Maybe he forgot one of his pots,' she said, but she looked angry.

Freya was standing on the shore, a lonely figure staring after him.

'I think I'd better call her in,' Jessica said.

When she went outside she could hear the faint sound of the boat engine, fading into the mist.

'Why did he go away again?' she asked. But Freya just shrugged and walked back towards the house.

Tante Yvette was still in the kitchen, folding away her little scraps of family history, like old linen you only get out for best.

'I'd better be going,' Jessica said. 'There are things I have to do.'

X

'You shouldn't be doing this, not by yourself, not in the dark . . .'

Hannah's plaintive voice from the door of the inn and the sound of music from the bar, the world of the living.

'I'll be fine – just keep an eye on Freya for me.'

Jessica walks on towards the locked and shuttered cabins in the darkness of the trees, towards the world of the dead.

'I'll keep the door open . . .'

But already her voice is a distant cry from that other world, and now there is just the sound of the wind threading through the pine needles and the growl of the pebbles on the beach below.

Jessica turns the key in the lock and opens the door. A fetid, vegetable smell out of the darkness and a sense of having been here before.

She feels for the light switch, *on the right facing the door*, and there it is, just as Maddie left it, as she has left so many rooms – in a mess. The dirty dishes piled up in the sink and on the draining board, the remains of a meal on the little table, a pair of boots in the middle of the floor as if she has just kicked them off . . . Jessica treads softly through the ghostly room as if not to disturb its hidden sleepers. The bedrooms are side by side at the far end, not much bigger than cupboards, one with a double bed that almost fills the entire space, the other with two bunk beds and a chest of drawers. The bed is unmade and strewn with Maddie's clothes. A bra and pants, a pair of Levi's, a T-shirt, an odd sock . . . Jessica trips over another shoe in the doorway and picks it up, a leather sandal with a low heel and a strap that needs stitching. She holds it in her hand, fingering the broken strap. Such a personal thing, a shoe, more personal even than under-wear. A sudden image of them as little girls in a shoe shop. Where would that have been? Was their mother with them?

It was probably their amah, Selma Kuresh. She used to buy them the same outfits, like twins, until their father stopped her. They're individuals, let them be different, he said.

How can two sisters be so unalike? Jessica overheard one of the nuns say after yet another scrape that Maddie had got herself into at school, and had felt a disloyal sense of gratification that no one could possibly think she was like Maddie, her hopeless sister. But later, at university, when she got into a few scrapes of her own, she sometimes wondered if they were so very different after all, and that perhaps she had repressed those aspects of her character that might be considered 'troublesome' because when they were younger one of them had to be responsible, and Maddie had made it perfectly clear it wasn't going to be her.

What a burden to be responsible, how much easier to be Maddie, how much easier to be dead.

She is startled by the knocking on the window but it is just the branches of a tree, moved by the wind. She drops the shoe on the bed and gets on with the job she came to do.

There is a small partitioned section off the main room with a washbasin and a shower. A towel left lying on the floor, still damp. Jessica sniffs the soap. Sandalwood. And now, with the front door open, there is the smell of pine trees and the sea. At least it was a good place for Maddie to be, this last home of hers. There is a consolation in this and also a terrible sadness.

Methodically, she starts on the dishes. How many times has she done this before on some visit to Maddie's latest slum, and Maddie would come back and never even notice?

There is a bookshelf with some childish paintings stuck to the wall above and a number of photographs. Freya at Glastonbury, Freya again on the chalk Downs in the south of England, dressed like a young Indian maid with her beads and her bands and the yellow caterpillars gouging a wide white scar on the hill behind her, the battle lost and the plunder just beginning. One of Jessica on a balcony somewhere in the sun looking . . . slightly cross, Jessica thinks. Why did Maddie choose that one? A group picture with Maddie in it. One of the group is holding a skull, posing with it like Hamlet. A sun-tanned Hamlet with a golden beard. Are these the people from the dig? She looks more closely, her eye taken by a young man with high cheekbones and long black hair down to his shoulders. Surely that is Yvette's nephew, but smiling now, at ease.

The paintings are presumably by Freya, simple pictures of flowers or butterflies or children playing. But there is one that has the complexity of allegory. It shows a little girl sitting on the top of a rock or a cliff looking down at a strange-looking boat in the sea below. The boat has masts that resemble trees in winter and on the branches or spars are a number of creatures that could either be hairy, bearded men in fur coats or bears in boots.

A sudden shiver that has nothing to do with the cold.

Jessica peels the pictures from the wall, one by one, mechanically rubbing off the blue tack with her thumb and looking for a large envelope or folder to put them in. Instead she finds some papers stuffed among the shelves: notes in Maddie's untidy scrawl and photocopies from a book.

Jessica heard the tapping noise again but louder, now, more insistent. Looking up she saw a man standing in the open doorway.

Adrenalin is supposed to prepare you for fight or flight, but the shock wave that hit Jessica was entirely debilitating.

'I'm sorry, I didn't mean to startle you.'

He had the palms of his hands towards her. See, I have no weapons. In the photograph he was holding a skull, for this was surely Hamlet.

'Hannah Crew said you were out here. I was a friend of Maddie's. My name's Innis, Innis Graham . . .'

The bar looked like the whaling fleet was in port and this was the only place they'd found that was open. Innis steered Jessica through a ruck of large, bearded men in dungarees and greasy sweaters who looked at her like she might be the floor show. She sat at a table by the window while he fetched drinks from the bar. Outside she could see the lights of the harbour and beyond them the untroubled darkness of the sea. When Innis returned he told her the scallop season had just begun and that it brought in fishermen from all along the coast.

His voice was low and husky as if he was short of breath and she had difficulty in hearing him above the noise of the bar.

She had asked him for a mineral water but he'd also bought a bottle of wine and two glasses, in case she changed her mind. Jessica's mind was divided on the subject, as it was on Innis himself. The cold, reasoning part told her she should stick to the mineral water, that alcohol would unloose her inhibitions and she'd end up crying in front of all these people. The more emotive part told her to go for the alcohol, that there was nothing wrong with crying, worse things than embarrassment. And there was need of some form of anaesthetic, after all, when you were about to hear of your sister's last moments on earth from the man who let her walk to her death.

But first he told her how they had met.

The first time he saw her she was crouched in a hole in the ground brushing the dirt away from a human thighbone. When he made some remark, she looked up and frowned and asked him to move his shadow out of her light. She was wearing a pair of shorts made from hacked-off Levi's and a grubby T-shirt and her limbs were brown and her hair was tied in a red ribbon at her neck. He walked straight back to the tent where they were logging the daily haul of artefacts and asked if they needed any unpaid labour for the summer.

Maddie already had more than her fair share of admirers. Her looks would have turned heads in New York City. In Russell County she was a major phenomenon. At first, Innis couldn't figure out what she was doing there. She seemed to have no particular interest in archaeology and she could hardly have been working for the money – it paid less than she could have earned in a bar. When she told him about her links with the Souriquois he thought she was romanticising. Wisely he didn't tell her this. She was obsessed with what she called her native American heritage and there was a time when he thought he was only going to get somewhere with her by dressing up in buckskin and feathers and doing a war dance.

She spent most of her spare time on the reservation with the people she claimed were her kin. She had discovered them, she told Innis, from a picture or postcard she had found in an old book of her mother's, though he was never entirely convinced she had come to the right place. He could not fit her into the picture he himself had of Nagwind Cove and the people who lived there.

He found her, at times, infuriatingly naïve. She was a woman of passionate opinions and simplistic solutions. She was prone to unpredictable mood swings. She could transform a dull evening in a bar into party night. Other times she could throw such a dampener on the atmosphere you wanted to crawl under the nearest rock. She possessed a freedom of thought and action that was as admirable as it was alarming. She couldn't be controlled or manipulated. You never knew where you were with her. But Innis thought she was wonderful.

'I loved her,' he said, without emphasis, his tone almost resigned, and Jessica believed him. Lots of men had loved Maddie.

There was a wildness in her that was irresistible to them. They wanted it but they also wanted to tame it, or rather, to bottle it up and keep it for their exclusive use, and when they found they couldn't, they retired hurt. To some extent, this was what had happened with Innis. He'd think they'd become close and the next day she'd treat him like a distant acquaintance. Or he'd talk about spending an evening together and she'd blithely announce she was seeing some other man and appear surprised, even angered, when he complained that she was using him.

He was too proud to love where he was not loved. He retreated behind a shield of indifference – or amused tolerance.

Jessica knew that nothing was more calculated to get under Maddie's skin. She was not easily reconciled to indifference, especially not in someone who had once been passionate about her. She had to stir the embers into flame.

'So suddenly she was . . .' He shook his head and didn't speak for a moment. She thought he was going to cry and that this would start her off, too, and then she wouldn't be able to stop. He couldn't look at her but when he spoke again his voice was stronger and more emphatic, as if it was important Jessica should understand this, even if he didn't quite understand it himself.

'She needed some place to belong and she thought she'd found it on the reservation, but something happened . . . I don't know what it was but . . . she got disillusioned about it all. And kind of . . . needy. And I – I hadn't seen that in her before . . .' He looked at her then and Jessica, who had seen it many times, nodded. 'She just became sensitive to the slightest hint of rejection and . . . I couldn't cope with it.'

He sounded surprised at himself, that there was something he couldn't cope with.

'I'd put up this barrier as if I was afraid to . . .'

He looked directly at her then.

'There was something in her that . . . I guess it scared me. Yes. I had to keep . . . a distance.'

'I know,' she said.

He continued to stare at her as if he was making his mind up about something and she saw the appeal and the despair in his eyes and braced herself for the confession.

'You know I was with her when . . . ?'

She nodded, not trusting herself to speak. She knew only what Calhoun had told her, and she wanted to hear it from Innis, but was afraid to. Even now she was afraid to let Maddie get too close to her, afraid to see her body, even in her mind, afraid to think about how she had died.

'I know what you must . . . How I could have let her walk off like that in the . . . snow.' He held his fist clenched beside his bottom lip and now he began to tap it against his chin, like he was knocking on a door. She could see the red mark it made. The expression in his eyes was distant, turned inward. 'She was angry with me . . . she left . . . in anger. I'm sorry.' He held himself then, very still, looking down at the table, holding in the tears.

They sat at their table in the rowdy bar and the noise made a barrier for their private grief.

'I didn't mean to make any excuses for myself. I should have followed her but you just don't . . . I just didn't think. I'm sorry,' he said again, but this time not for the catch in his voice, not for the tears. He wanted absolution and she couldn't give it to him, she was not a priest; she was like the nuns who could only pour guilt on guilt.

But there were times when she, too, had let Maddie walk off into the night after a quarrel, could not have stopped her even if she had wanted to.

She could at least understand.

'I know,' she said, 'I know.' Weeping now, as she knew she would, as she held his hand across the table.

XI

She wakes in the middle of the night and listens for the sound of Freya's breathing in the next bed. She hears only the nocturnal creakings and fidgetings of the inn, like the painful stretching of rheumatoid joints. She can see from the luminous dial of her watch that it is just after two in the morning and she knows she will lie awake until dawn.

Time is no longer playing by the rules.

This time between death and disposal is like a badly edited film running on a constant loop in Jessica's head. It keeps jumping frames, sometimes a whole sequence. Scenes seem to repeat themselves or to be inserted in the wrong place, or juxtaposed from a different film altogether. And there are far too many flashbacks. Jessica gropes her way through this time, trying to separate nightmare from reality and not always succeeding because so often they are inseparable. She finds herself clinging to moments of apparent solidity, trying to hold on to them, to prolong them, as she does to people who seem normal and solid, like Hannah Crew and Innis Graham. People she can lean on and who do not seem to bend as time does.

Her mental clock is impossible to regulate, like the images that suddenly jump out at her when she is insufficiently on her guard. And there are greater problems. Maddie's body is still with the medical examiner in Augusta. They are still waiting for this bear doctor in Canada to give his opinion. So there is no limit to this time. It is something she must endure, finding brief moments of sanctuary to nurse her pain and the even briefer moments when she can forget.

The inn is itself like a sanctuary. Large and comforting, it too has endured and survived. It is classic Cape Cod, Hannah Crew tells her, unable to hide her pride of possession, and has weathered two-and-a-half centuries of storms, a revolution and a military occupation. Its first owner was a merchant adventurer who ran guns from France during the Independence War and then, when the port was occupied by the British in the war of 1812–14, the house was used as a barracks for the Redcoats. It is one of the oldest houses in Bridport, but despite its antiquity it has a peculiar air of impermanence, like so many of the houses in the neighbourhood, as if they could at any time draw up their wide-skirted verandas and stomp off in a huff and set themselves down somewhere else.

'After the Revolution,' says Hannah, 'the loyalists moved their houses on rafts and towed them across the bay to Canada. You can still see them there if you go to New Brunswick, all along the coast, flying their British flags.'

And Jessica looks out over Narragasco Bay with its maze of wooded islands and imagines the fleet of houses in full sail with the Union Jack at their chimneys.

There is no more snow. Every day she is greeted, almost as if in mockery of her grief, by a sky of carefree, almost cloudless blue. An Indian summer. A phrase she was always associated with the India of her childhood and took to mean a *long* summer – a lazy extension of August into autumn, a mature if dying warmth, a *safe* season. But now she learns from Hannah that it was a term used by the New England settlers to describe a spell of fine weather in the fall when the Indians came out of the forest for a spot of slaughter before the winter, a season of bird cries at dusk that were not birds at all but the prelude to the arrows and war cries and the tomahawks and the terror, a season of sunny days and dangerous nights.

Jessica lies awake in the darkness of the old inn or sleeps fitfully, wary of her dreams. The forest has entered her sleep and in it there are indistinct shapes that might be people or animals. Some part of her wants to stop and confront them but something stronger urges her on in blind panic, not wanting to see their faces, the nightmare faces of the bear and the wolverine, the psychopathic goblin and, worst, the gorgon face of her mutilated sister. But the voice pursues her in the darkness: *Look at me, look what they did.* And she is just a backward glance away, a glance into the pit, the primitive terror.

Never can she slip too deeply into such a sleep. And besides, there is another more urgent need to lie just beyond the surface of wakefulness, a part of her brain on permanent alert for the first slow moan or the sudden nightmare shriek as frightful as any war cry. And Freya will be sitting upright in her bed, eyes rolling in terror, bathed in sweat. Or worse, scuttling around the walls like some wild animal locked in a cage and scrabbling at the shuttered window with her broken nails.

The Devil's mirror has shattered and a piece has worked its way into Freya's heart and transported her into the world of the ice queen. Jessica can see her but she cannot reach her. *Where are you?* she wants to say.

She sees her in this way, like a child in a fairy tale.

There are glimpses of the Freya that was – the wilful but affectionate child of her sister. For reasons that Jessica cannot quite fathom, but for which she is infinitely grateful, Jessica insists on going to school every day. Perhaps she welcomes the distraction from her terrible world of the imagination. Hannah, who is on the School Board and seems to spend quite a bit of her time there, says she has no close friends but that since the accident the other children are kind to her and treat her with a certain awed respect. Jessica helps her get ready in the morning, makes her a packed lunch, drives her in. She hugs her before she runs off and in the afternoon she waits for her with the mothers and minders. It is all so normal . . . until the darkness comes and with it the fear. She can see it in Freya's eyes, as if a thin film of ice is forming over the conjunctiva, and the child she knew is sliding away behind it.

The child she knew.

There is a problem here that Jessica must confront if she is to accept responsibility for her in the future.

Does such a child exist, or is it a child of her imagining – a pretend child they invented, she and Freya between them, for their amusement, sustained for the brief periods they spent together?

It is not the child Maddie knew, she made that clear enough.

'She can be a right madam,' Maddie said, 'though you'd never think so to look at her now.' Watching her sleeping after Jessica had read her some bedtime story.

'She hides from me,' she elaborated when pressed. 'She retreats inside herself, where no one can reach her – not me, for certain sure.'

Jessica said nothing but privately blamed Maddie for it, thinking: *the life they lead, it's probably the only way she can make any space for herself.*

Jessica was inclined to endow Freya with her own character-istics as a child – the self-reliance, the need for solitude combined with warmth and comfort, the much-valued, much-denied luxu-ries of a child at a boarding school for girls.

Physically, Freya resembled Jessica at the same age, with her dark complexion and high cheekbones and big brown eyes, while Maddie had more of their father's looks, was bigger-boned altogether, her features bolder, less elfin.

Elfin. Another word she must examine more closely.

Jessica often used the word to describe Freya to her friends in Rome, meaning 'scamp-like, cute', not thinking then of its more chthonic connotations, of furtiveness, secrecy, even slyness, of the dark creepiness of the forest. But Freya was half Celt, half native American; it had to be in the genes.

Then with surprise she thought, *No, this is not Freya* – whose father, so far as she knew, was a New Zealander – *this is me, this is Maddie.*

It was not something she cared to examine too closely.

'You fear the pagan in yourself,' her ex-lover told her, 'the Dionysian.' And Jessica dismissed it, quite rightly, as part of his sexual goading, but she knew there was a part of her that did fear the darkness, the wildness, in her – just as she feared and part-despised it in Maddie, and now in Freya?

It was something that had to be kept firmly under control, otherwise there was no knowing where it might lead.

'How is she in school?' she asked Freya's teacher, Miss Carter, a woman of about Jessica's age but seeming older, with what Hannah Crew called 'sound opinions'.

'She seems OK,' Miss Carter began, cautiously, even ner-vously. 'I mean, there are no outward signs of . . . distress.' Then, after a pause, and perhaps observing that Jessica was unwilling to leave it there, 'In fact, she's almost disturbingly normal in the . . . circumstances.'

114

'Has she made any . . . reference to . . . what happened?' Jessica asked her.

'No. Not at all. In fact . . .'

'What?'

'Well, I'm sorry, but . . . she's always had this thing about bears.'

Jessica inclined her head, waiting for her to elaborate, and then, when she did not: 'What thing about bears?'

'Well, she . . . just has a thing about them. She draws them.'

'She draws them?'

Jessica thought about the picture she had found in the cabin at the back of the Old Barrack House.

'All the time. I mean, she *did*. Whenever you asked her to paint a picture, you could be pretty sure bears were going to feature in it somewhere. And she was always kind of, wanting to know about them. Like it was some kind of . . . obsession with her.'

'But not any more.'

'Not any more. No. Not . . . openly.'

'What did she want to know about them?'

'Well, everything, like how they behave, what they eat . . . I'm sorry, this must be very distressing for you.'

'That's all right. I'd rather know what's going on in her head. Have you any idea what made her so . . . obsessed?'

'I guess . . . I used to think it was because she was British, she hadn't seen a bear before. Not like . . . I mean, here we . . . But once, when I asked her, she said her aunt told her stories about them.'

'Her aunt?'

'She didn't mean you?'

'No,' said Jessica, 'she didn't mean me.'

Later, driving Freya back from school, she asked her: 'What is it you like so much about . . . Tante Yvette?'

A shrug. 'I don't know. She's nice to me. She talks to me.'

'What about?'

Another shrug. 'All kinds of things.' Then, after a moment. 'She doesn't talk like . . . grown-ups.'

'You mean, she doesn't talk *down* to you?'

Do I talk down to her? Jessica wondered. *Do I talk baby talk?* She wanted to ask her, *Did your mummy like her?* But she couldn't. She couldn't talk to her about Maddie at all. Perhaps that was why she was so relieved that she wanted to go back to school.

XII

While Freya is at school, Jessica walks along the beach, if the tide is out, or sits in the shelter of a wind-crabbed old pine on the low sloping cliff below the inn. She watches the push and pull of the waves against the rocks, expending their energy in this fruitless but strangely consoling assault, watching for the greater seventh wave that rushes down the granite cutting like an express train and surges upwards in a giant spout that almost reaches her feet before it falls back in a frenzy of foam, leaving her face wet with spray, her lungs filled with the breath of the sea.

Her recent life has been spent in cities, her eyes adjusted to the proximity of buildings, trained in the study of detail – the patina of a statue in the niche of a church wall, the epitaph on a tomb, the expression on the face of a stone angel, a crucified god, just as her ear is tuned to the throbbing of a thousand stalled cars, the irate hooting of horns, police whistles, sirens, the computer hum of hermetically sealed offices.

Her senses reel in this enormity of sea and sky. This is why she likes the rocks. In such boundless space there is comfort in a rock.

Some mornings she will sit in the diner at the Old Barrack House reading a book or looking through a window at the busy little scallop boats, that the locals call draggers, ploughing their invisible furrows across the bottom of the sea.

Her appetite, normally quite ravenous, has returned, treacherously, defying her sense of mourning, but she confines herself to the simpler dishes on the menu, like a fasting monk declining meat but ensuring that the fish is palatable.

Mostly she sits alone but sometimes the barman, Little Raymond, comes over to talk to her. Raymond is about five foot nine and weighs around 160 pounds. Here, in Down East Maine, this makes him 'Little' Raymond. Or perhaps there is a Big Raymond she has not yet encountered who is nearer the

117

average height, and this is a means of distinguishing them in conversation.

Little Raymond was until recently a property dealer in New Hampshire but left because of The Pressure, he tells her. She thinks there is probably more to it than that, or why would he work in a bar? His manner is stage camp but there is possibly something going on between him and Hannah, even if it is not exactly sexual. His manner towards her – and the inn – sometimes verges on the proprietorial. Perhaps he has a stake in the business. Perhaps Hannah simply indulges him in his fantasies of ownership, to bolster his damaged ego. Hannah seems to have a soft spot for misfits.

Half the buildings in Main Street are occupied by people who have left the cities because of The Pressure, she says, and opened art galleries or craft shops in Bridport. The other half are closed and boarded up. The entire town has an air of undramatic but irreversible decline. The newcomers have brought colour and character and a degree of optimism, but they never seem to do any business. It is the wrong season for trade, they say. They spend a lot of time in the Old Barrack House with the out-of-work fishermen who don't have draggers. It is a town without a future, Raymond tells her cheerfully, pouring more coffee.

He claims his ancestors settled here from France 300 years ago but were driven out by the British, part of the mass exile to Louisiana. Now, he says, the exiles are drifting back, looking for their lost Acadia. He is trying to form a Cajun band. There are three of them so far and he introduces them to her one day in the bar, stressing the French names: Jerry Rougere, Buddy Chagnon and a giant of a man called Henry Savageau.

Sometimes she is joined here by Innis Graham, or Calhoun. She is on equally friendly terms with them both but for some reason she never calls Calhoun by his first name. Innis will always come in as if he is looking for her and walk straight up to her table. Calhoun is more oblique in his approach. He ambles through the door with a slightly perplexed frown as if he has forgotten something, or even why he is here, and his eyes appear to stray accidentally in her direction and he smiles and nods and then hangs around for a while talking to Little Raymond or some other acquaintance and then, when he has sufficiently established his pretext, he comes over and loiters, leaning against the back of a chair, until she asks him to sit down. She knows now who he reminds her of: not an actor but the writer, Jack London, a picture she saw accompanying the review of a recent biography. He had the same square, chunky features, the same slightly unkempt look. Perhaps, too, it is an association of ideas: the forest, the climate, a sense of remoteness – alcoholism, suicide?

It is a strange courtship, this business between Jessica and her Detective, as she thinks of him, in this vacuum of time between a death and a funeral. Awkward, of course, hopelessly constrained, but a courtship all the same, and with all the formal and self-conscious courtesies that such an old-fashioned word implies.

Jessica can permit herself no such romantic notion of her friendship with Innis, her dead sister's lover. And yet there is a definite sexual *frisson* between them and they both know it and it is all the more intense for being so impossible of fulfilment.

Both men treat her with a gentleness she appreciates but finds faintly embarrassing, as if they have mistaken her for someone else and she cannot bring herself to tell them who she really is.

There is still a sense of not being here. She feels almost as if she is a passenger in a time-and-space machine that has taken a wrong turning. She wants to get back on course and return to her own world, where she was safe and comfortable and where people she loved were not killed by bears or altogether more dangerous, more frightening apparitions. In the meantime she concentrates on getting through each moment, each day, until she can fly back to the world she came from, only she has the terrible feeling that when she does it won't be there any more.

When she talks about this world to Innis, or Hannah, or Calhoun it already seems somewhere very distant and fantastical, almost as if she has imagined it.

'I lived in Rome for a few years,' she says, 'but now I'm at Oxford.' And the words feel like breath on the glass of her windows, misting briefly and then fading. She would rather hear about them than talk about herself.

'How do you get to be a Round The World Yachtsman?' she

asks Innis, not without a degree of mischief. 'Do you tell your careers teacher at school? Do you go on a course?'

She cannot take it seriously, it is like something out of a *Boy's Own* adventure story, a yarn of blue water, a game for grown-up boys.

There is, she thinks, quite a lot of the grown-up boy in Innis, but then someone once told her that most men are aged about eleven.

'First you have to have a yacht,' he tells her, 'then you take it on races.'

He names them for her: the Transatlantic, the Newport to Bermuda, the Sydney to Hobart, the Fastnet, the America's Cup . . .

So it must be serious, if they have names – and cups.

But he has sold the ocean racer – to pay off the family debts, he says – and now he has *Calliope*.

Her first thought is that this is a dog or a cat but no, it's a boat. A Maine schooner, he says.

'*Calliope*?' she repeats. The name is familiar, but from where?

'The muse of heroic poetry,' he says, mocking, as if at his own pretension.

She is impressed. 'You named her that?'

'No. That was the name when I bought her. But I did look it up.'

'And can't you race *Calliope*?'

But *Calliope* is too much of a lady to be raced, he says, and 'besides,' he adds, a little grimly, 'I have to make a living, like everyone else.'

Clearly a cause for genuine regret, this, the need to be like everyone else, a loss of innocence – a loss of childhood? She senses some grief in Innis beyond what he obviously feels for Maddie, some deep, unreachable hurt.

It seems to be there in Calhoun, too. Perhaps it is a condition of being born on the coast of Maine, something to do with the sea, perhaps. In the film, *Il Postino*, when the poet asks the postman for an adjective to describe fishing nets the postman says 'sad'. The sad nets.

She is surprised to discover that the two men were boyhood friends, but could not say *why* it is a surprise, for in some ways they are not so dissimilar. When she mentions this, Calhoun says that some of the breeding must have rubbed off on him. Perhaps some of the sadness, too. Perhaps they dragged it up together in the same sad net.

As a boy, he says, he was as much in love with the sea as Innis. Or perhaps it was the idea of travel. He read books on explorers and searched maps for the names of their discoveries. He recreated their journeys in his own solitary ramblings through the forest, or sailing with Innis among the islands of the bay. They would pretend they were Elizabethan sailors searching for the North West Passage, or discovering fantasy islands in the North Atlantic: islands of strange peoples and mythical beasts.

They would sit on a lonely beach trying to light a fire of driftwood and seaweed with a box of matches, soft and damp from the sea air, and Innis would tell him about the places he had visited in Europe with his parents, places that were almost as magical to Calhoun as the lost cities and vanished civilisations of his story books. His own parents had never left America. They rarely left the state. Vacations were spent on his grandparents' farm in Wisconsin. When he left school, not having money or a yacht, he joined the navy: a disastrous career move for, to everyone's irritation, not least his own, he was hopelessly sea-sick. He could sail an open boat in swell or squall without the slightest discomfort, but something in the motion of a larger vessel, or the smell, or the confined space below decks, or a combination of all three, made him instantly nauseous, even in the calmest of seas. He thought he would get used to it but he never did. It was a chronic condition. Apparently Nelson had the same problem. This was no comfort to Calhoun.

They decided it was all in the mind, and sent him to a navy psychiatrist who suggested that he might have a deep-rooted fear of foreign places; that he was a home boy from the backwoods of Maine who did not really want to go anywhere. Calhoun thought this was bullshit, but the very expression of it depressed him, that someone should even think this of him. On his next leave, as an experiment, he took a cheap package tour to London. The only nausea he suffered was after drinking three pints of English beer in a pub in Chelsea. Next time he went to sea he was so ill they had to treat him for dehydration.

Finally they transferred him to Naval Intelligence. It seemed to them a logical move. But he thought there was no point in being in the navy if he couldn't go to sea, so when he'd served his time he signed up with the Boston police department.

He does not strike Jessica as having the temperament for a policeman, though in truth, she is not at all sure what temperament a policeman should have.

It seems to puzzle him, too.

'I couldn't think what else to do,' he says. And then, more puzzlingly. 'I think it must be the carpenter in me. Trying to make things fit. Only I'm not much good with wood.'

She is intrigued, too, to know why he came back here, to the place where he grew up, where he doesn't seem to fit at all. She senses some mystery and wonders if he had some kind of a breakdown and fled from The Pressure, like Little Raymond and the rest of the refugees from the cities.

He seems fascinated by the idea of her living in Rome. Almost, she thinks, as if it was *ancient* Rome. And it might as well be, for all it means to her now.

'What did you do there?' he asks.

She tells him she worked for a department of the European Community that distributed grants for the preservation of historic buildings. He nods, thoughtfully, as if this is a subject of interest to him, though it can have no relevance to his world.

'And where did you live – in Rome?'

'Do you know Rome?' She asks him.

No. He has never been there. She suspects he has a romantic notion of what it must be like to live there and of herself for being someone who once did.

'And why did you go and live in Rome, was it the job?'

No, she says, it was a man. Her lover got a job there so she went, too. It seems pathetic now.

And suddenly it is there, as if she has caught the smell of it. The smell of the city baked in the heat of an August afternoon, of a pavement café in the evening, of fresh basil and garlic and tomatoes, of geraniums on a roof garden – of her lover's body when he lies naked beside her. Smells of sex and the sun.

'So it didn't work out?'

'Not really. It did for a while. He was much older than me and at first I was more easily led. Then I started to act more . . . independently.'

'And he didn't like it.'

He was confused by it. I suppose. He was a bit of a control freak, really. There was no formal break but we both knew when I went to Oxford it was over. It was my own decision, you see. He had no part in it.'

It is the first time she has talked about this, the first time she has seen it so clearly.

She shrugs as if it can be so easily dismissed and, trying to keep her voice just as light, asks: 'So why did you leave Boston?'

He doesn't answer at first and she is sorry she asked. But then he says: 'I had an affair with a married woman and it ended badly.'

'Oh. I see.' But she does not see, for *ended badly* has a multitude of meanings just as a flat, matter-of-fact tone can hide a multitude of hurt.

'There was an accident. Their daughter died, their little girl.'

'Oh no.' She presses her knuckle into her bottom teeth as she did when the police came to her room at college and told her about Maddie. As if it can somehow stop the greater pain of knowing.

'It was widely reported at the time. In Boston, anyway. They were . . . quite well known. He was a lawyer. This isn't something you want to know, is it? Not when . . .'

'Sometimes it helps,' she says, 'to hear other people's . . . to take your mind off your own.'

But more because she thinks it will help him.

'She blamed herself. I suppose you would.' It is easy to see who Calhoun blames. 'He was driving – her husband – but . . . they were quarrelling at the time.'

'What happened to her – the woman you . . . ?'

'She went away. To the west coast where she . . . to her family.'

'And you came back here to yours.'

'Yes.' Bleakly, then after a long moment, 'I stopped liking myself and I thought . . . I don't know.'

'To go back to the source, where the water's pure.'

He looks at her in surprise. She is surprised herself. It is not the usual kind of thing she comes out with.

'Something like that.'

With the melancholy smile of *Il Postino* inspecting the catch in his sad nets.

XIII

Calhoun wakes early and in a mood that might almost be taken for optimism if it were more familiar. He feels lighter, as if he has shed some weight in his sleep, or some knot inside him has become unloosed.

He dresses quickly in his track suit with an extra sweater under the top and moves quietly through the empty house on stockinged feet to where he has left his trainers, out on the deck. They are stiff with cold but there is no frost on the ground.

He runs along a well-trodden route that descends gradually to the river and follows it for three miles or so towards the rapids. He moves through tall pines and spruce that impose a strict regime of gloom and silence, like some ancient monastic order. A fog hangs in the topmost branches and the air is chill. All he can hear is his own harsh breathing and the slap and scuffle of his trainers on the padded earth beneath the trees. Then there is the distant roar of the rapids and the rising sun breaks against the tops of the pines and splinters through the forest, and suddenly all is light and sound. He quickens his pace, in a fierce joy now, leaping the tangled roots, descending ever more swiftly to the fury of the river.

He pauses above the rapids, taking his breath in great gulps, drinking in the cold liquid air. Below him the river fragments against the rocks and the white gobbets of spray rise towards him and briefly catch the light of the sun before they fall. He sits with his back to a pine, his hands hanging loose between his legs, relaxed, enjoying the view and his own mood, the first time he has taken pleasure in either since his homecoming in the spring.

But how much of this is down to Jessica?

He considers this carefully, wary of the pitfalls. You do not fall in love with someone who is suffering the pain of a recent loss, or rather, they do not fall in love with you, and if they do, it has to be a suspect love, born of extreme need and vulnerability. Besides, she will be leaving soon.

But it is as if this new affliction, this new desire of the blood, has killed off the old virus, or at least numbed the pain. For the first time in months he feels glad to be alive.

The roar of the rapids drowns every other sound so he does not hear the bear's approach. Certainly it cannot have been aware of the man sitting in the shadows of the tree, and the spray must have confused the scent. Calhoun climbs to his feet to continue his run and it is there, just a few yards away, on all fours with its nose to the ground. It is alerted by the movement and rises up on its hind legs, and for a moment they stare at each other, both equally startled. Then it turns and drops on all fours again and runs off into the forest.

Shaken, Calhoun leans against the tree and wonders what he would have done if it had gone for him. Yet he did not feel it was at all dangerous. Maybe because it looked so shabby – a burly old tramp, shabby and shambling, its coat more a dingy brown than black and the burrs and the pine needles sticking to its fur.

He is left with the impression, which must be entirely in his imagination, that the expression in its eyes, just before it turned away, was one of mild reproach.

XIV

The Wildlife and Forestry Department have sent in a team of experts – and a helicopter with heat-seeking radar that can, Calhoun is assured, detect a chipmunk in thick undergrowth. It circles the National Park, day after day, just above tree height, sending vital messages to the hunters on the ground.

But whatever the chipmunk tally, very few bears have been detected within the confines of the Reserve.

'They're all across the border in Canada,' says Ranger Grainger, 'watching with interest.'

Not quite all, judging from the number of carcasses Calhoun has seen hanging up outside the houses backing on to the forest. Every hunter in the county wants to be the man that killed the killer bear.

'They could kill every black bear between here and Oregon,' Grainger insists, 'and they wouldn't get the animal that killed that girl.'

'So what did?' Calhoun asks him, but he just shakes his head, not willing to commit himself.

They are asking the same question at headquarters in Augusta – only a little more forcefully.

'Either it's a fucking bear or it isn't,' Lieutenant Beckman points out with the incisive logic that has made him what he is today. And if it isn't, he'll be on the first plane into Bridport with a team from homicide and all the media he's got room for. The only thing that has stopped him so far is the fear of making a fool of himself. That's what Calhoun is paid to do.

'No, Detective,' says Ranger Grainger, 'bears are not more dangerous when there's a full moon and so far as I am aware, they do not celebrate Hallowe'en.'

'That's not what I asked,' says Calhoun with more patience than he feels.

'But that's what you meant, isn't it?' Grainger persists, rolling his eyes at his main man Moose. 'He thinks it came dancing up to her for a trick or treat. Okay, sorry. Sorry. But you'll be wanting to shoot it with a silver bullet next.'

'Why d'you say that?'

'Because you've been listening to Henry Savageau, that's why.'

This is true.

'You said yourself it's out of character for a black bear to attack a human being,' Calhoun reminds him. 'Henry Savageau thinks it was something more than rage, that's all, that . . .'

'I know what Henry Savageau thinks,' says Grainger. 'He thinks it's the ghost of an Abenaki shaman shape-shifter stoned to death 300 years ago, for Jesus sake, and he's got you half believing it, hasn't he?'

'Get the fuck out of here,' says Calhoun, but it is an expression he has learned in Boston and it lacks conviction, even to himself.

There were bear societies among the Abenaki in the old days, composed of men who dreamed of bears and who had taken the animal as their guardian spirit. They were known as Bear Dreamers and before a battle they would plaster their bodies with mud and draw red scratch marks on their cheeks. They painted black circles around their eyes and shaved the middle of their heads, tying the hair on each side in bunches to resemble the bear's ears. Their favourite weapon was a knife with a handle made from a bear's jawbone, and when they charged the enemy they growled like a bear.

Bear Dreamers believed the power of the bear would protect them from harm. They had the duty of rescuing men who had been wounded or taken prisoner, regardless of the risk to themselves.

In their minds they *were* bears, and they were respected and feared as such by other members of the tribe.

There were also women Bear Dreamers, and although they did not fight battles, they were more feared than the men. Their rituals were more secret, their membership more exclusive, passed down from mother to daughter. They practised magic associated with the mystic powers of the bear goddess. There were powers of healing but also of harming. In their secret dances and ceremonies they were believed to have the power of shape-shifting, of changing into bears whenever they willed it.

Real bears were present at all the meetings and ceremonies of the Bear Dreamers, although they were not always visible. The Sauk and Fox of Lake Huron had a bear clan called Mu'kwa whose members claimed descent from a bear that had come from under the ground. They gave their children Bear names such as Long Claws, Twinkling Eyes, Fat, Imprint Of Buttocks On Sand, Sit Tight In Hollow Tree and Bear Shit.

Calhoun listens to the stories of Henry Savageau with a quizzical smile on his face but there is a part of him that is not amused, a part of him that knows that although Henry speaks of the past, there are still people crazy enough to act out their fantasies, especially if it involves women and violence.

After killing a bear, the hunter would speak to it, saying, 'Friend, I have killed you. Now we have pressed together our killing hands so that your wild hands may come to me, that I may be feared as you are feared and kill as you kill, for now I have inherited your power.'

XV

There was a small sitting room at the back of the Old Barrack House, a private room for Hannah which she shared only with the most privileged of guests. On quiet nights when she was not needed in the kitchen – she was rarely in front of house, she left that to Raymond – she sat there reading or catching up on her council work.

Hannah Crew was a power in a small community like Bridport. She was on the City Council and the Police Board and the School Board. But more than that, she had the power of knowledge. Calhoun knew she could tell him a lot more about Madeleine Ross if she chose to – about her lovers, about the people on the reservation. But she had locked it away – out of respect for the dead, or something else?

Calhoun was with her in the back room one night, gently probing and not getting anywhere, when there was a knock on the door and Jessica came in wearing a bathrobe and rubbing her wet hair with a towel.

Calhoun felt the usual kick in the stomach, perhaps a little stronger than usual. Her eyes widened in surprise at seeing him there in this sanctuary, but she smiled and they both said hello.

'I was wondering if you had any nail clippers,' she said to Hannah. 'But it'll keep if you're in the middle of something.'

Hannah went to fetch them from her room and he and Jessica sat on opposite sides of the big old fireplace, with an awkward silence between them. Calhoun felt a constraint that was absent in the crowded dining room. He felt like some tongue-tied farmer from a different age who had ridden into town to pay embarrassed courtship to the daughter of the house. He saw her smiling and wondered if the same thought had occurred to her.

'What?' he said.

'Nothing,' she said, but then: 'I was just remembering when I

130

used to sit in front of the fire with Freya and read her stories before she went to bed.' She frowned as if something in the memory bothered her. 'I wonder where that was. Where would we have had a fire?' She looked at him as if he could tell her, but he only shook his head, smiling, watching her. 'Perhaps I imagined it.'

'What sort of stories?'

'Oh, the usual. Little Red Riding Hood, Peter and the Wolf, Hansel and Gretel. They were our favourites.' She frowned, as if another thought had just struck her, not so pleasant. 'They all had the same kind of message. Don't trust adults, not even your own mother – she might betray you, she might die . . .' the pause was slight . . . 'Stick to the footpath and if you're in trouble, use your own resources.'

He saw the quiver in her upper lip, the tension in the muscles of her throat. There were dark prints under her eyes as if someone had pressed a dirty thumb into her skin. He wished he could stroke away the strain, kiss away the thumb-prints. She was small and fine-boned but not thin. Not thin at all. He thought she was probably naked under the bathrobe. Does sex transcend all other emotion? Or is it just him?

You're all animals under the skin. And not very far under either.

That must have been his mother. Why? What had he done? Some childhood atrocity buried in his subconscious, in the file marked guilt, a lingering sense of unworthiness.

He tried to think of something to say.

'Do you still read to her?'

'Last time I saw her I did. I haven't now. I don't know if she'd like them any more.' She stared into the big, old-fashioned fireplace where the fire should have been. 'Strange, isn't it. We bring children up to believe in magic, in fairy tales, in the idea that all things are possible. Animals can talk, trees can run through the forest, cows can jump over the moon. A frog can change into a prince. Then we take it all away from them. We say it isn't true. A frog is just a frog. Look, you can dissect it, spread it out on the table, see its heart, its lungs, its bowels. Eat its leg if you like, cooked in garlic and butter. We take away the magic and say, you're too old for it now. People can't change into animals . . .'

131

He wondered what was bothering her – something more than this, surely – but before he could ask, Hannah had returned with the nail scissors.

Then they heard the noise. It seemed to Calhoun like a cat or a dog was scraping at a door. Then there was the sound of breaking glass. Jessica was up the stairs two steps at a time with Hannah panting behind her. Calhoun hesitated a moment and then followed them.

He stood at the door of the bedroom taking it in: the smashed windowpane, the blood on the wall. The child crouched on the floor in the corner of the room.

Jessica was speaking to her soothingly, trying to take her hand. It was tightly clenched and Calhoun could see the blood welling up between her fingers. But it was her face, and the sound she was making, that disturbed him the most. Her upper lip was drawn back from her teeth and the sound came from deep in her throat. Like a picture of a lynx he'd once seen, caught in a trap. He didn't go any further into the room in case he scared her. He saw that the window had a security lock and the shutters were closed.

Hannah pushed past him without meeting his eyes and came back with a first-aid kit. Together the two women managed to calm her enough to prize her fist open. Calhoun could see the cut at the base of her palm.

'Does it need stitches?' Jessica said.

Hannah said she didn't think so, it wasn't too deep. She wiped it with disinfectant and put a plaster on it. All the time they soothed her like a baby, and then Hannah spooned some dark syrup from a bottle and coaxed it into her mouth. Freya was silent now. She looked bewildered and very small. Calhoun left them to it and waited downstairs.

Hannah came down first.

'How long has she been like this?' Calhoun asked her.

'It comes and goes. Not usually as bad as this, though.' She opened a cupboard and took out a bottle of brandy. 'Yes?' Calhoun shook his head and said he had to drive back. She covered the bottom of a balloon glass and a fair bit of the sides and collapsed into the nearest chair.

Calhoun was looking at the graze on his hand from when he'd fallen over chasing shadows in the snow.

'Has she been out again at night?'

He might have been asking about an animal rather than a little girl.

Hannah was shaking her head.

'Not that I'm aware.' Then, anticipating his response: 'The window's got a lock on it and Jessica's moved her bed across the door.'

'So she obviously thinks there's a risk?'

It was a moment before she replied.

'Apparently she walks in her sleep.' Sniffing at her brandy, keeping her eyes closed.

Calhoun asked: 'Does she know how her mother died?'

She nodded. 'I told her. I had to tell her something.' She drank and made a noise between a cough and a sigh.

'Did Maddie have many men friends?'

She opened her eyes and looked at him as if to say, What has that got to do with anything?

'Men she went out with,' he said. 'Besides Innis Graham.'

'One or two,' she said cautiously. 'I guess she was a bit of . . . what we used to call a flirt. I don't know what you'd call it now. It didn't mean anything. Except, maybe, there were some who thought it did.'

'Like who in particular?'

She considered him for a moment, troubled. Then she said: 'That boy Joe Selmo. I call him a boy. Too much of a boy for her, too. Henry Savageau, others I can't immediately recall. Why d'you ask?'

'Henry?' Calhoun repeated. 'She was seeing Henry?'

'I didn't say *seeing*.'

But then Jessica came down, putting an end to it for the time being. He did not want to talk about this in front of Jessica. Freya was sleeping, she said. Hannah poured her a brandy. She didn't bother sniffing at it. Head back and a decent gulp, enough to bring tears to her eyes.

He said: 'I know it's none of my business, but I'd say you could use a little counselling.' He didn't mean for the drink.

Jessica looked at him. 'Well, one of us does,' she said.

XVI

She eased her foot on the gas, almost coming to a halt, looking down the long tunnel of trees that led to the headland where Maddie had died. Some part of her wanted to go there, to stand beside the place where it had happened, to lay flowers on the desecrated earth in some primitive gesture of atonement – an appeasement of the spirit – but the dominant, more frightened, part resisted, protected her from the pain and the terror, just as it did in her dreams when she sensed the shadow behind her. So she pressed her foot down hard on the pedal and drove on towards the reservation.

When Calhoun said counselling he probably did not mean Yvette Selmo and, in truth, Jessica was not sure what had made her come here. What could the woman tell her that she didn't already know? That Freya was bound to be traumatised by the death of her mother, bound to have nightmares, that all she could do was hold her hand and help her through it.

But perhaps it wasn't Freya she wanted to talk about. Perhaps it was Maddie, perhaps it was herself. The closer she came to Nagwind Cove, the more doubts she had about the wisdom of the visit. As if, in some unfathomable way, she was subjecting herself to a harmful influence. As if Yvette's knowledge of her own background, her own roots, made her vulnerable to something she'd shut out of her life, rejected as too disturbing, too dangerous.

Just before the turn-off for the reservation there was a church by the side of the road. She knew it was Catholic from the statue of the Virgin outside the front porch, and she found herself slowing down again. Only this time she stopped completely and read the sign. Saint Ann's Roman Catholic Church, with the times of the Masses and the name of the priest – Fr Francis O'Neill. The statue was not the Virgin then, but her mother Ann.

Though how they knew the name of Christ's grandmother was one of the Catholic mysteries Jessica had never satisfactorily resolved.

On impulse she left the car and walked up the stone steps to the door. It was locked. She turned away, feeling unreasonably let down, and was about to get back into the car when she heard a shout and turned to see the black-cassocked figure in the porch of a house by the side of the church.

'Hold on a minute now, and I'll be right with you.'

He was gone before Jessica could protest that it didn't matter, only to reappear a moment or so later with a bunch of keys, a thin, balding man with the ruddy nose and broken veins of the desolatès she saw on the streets of Oxford. He even had the obligatory graze on his forehead.

'We've had a spot of trouble with the vandals,' he said, 'so we keep the door locked now. But I don't like to put off a genuine worshipper, we have few enough of them, God knows.'

'I just wanted to light a candle,' Jessica said.

'You'll find them in the usual place by the side altar,' he said, as he opened the door and gestured for her to enter. 'I'll leave you to your devotions. If you wouldn't mind turning the key in the lock and dropping it off in the presbytery before you leave. You'll need to give the door a good pull now when you close it.'

She was glad, at any rate, to be left alone.

It was not a handsome church. The walls were painted a dingy cream and the stained-glass windows depicted stern-faced angels and submissive women. It was a masculine church in a style she characterised as Victorian suburban Gothic. She wished for something more feminine. She wished for the mellowed sanctity of a country church in Italy, its worn stones softened by centuries of peasant worship and unburdened sin.

She walked down the left-hand aisle towards the side altar, her footsteps loud in the hollow silence, and stopped before the statue of Our Lady.

She lit the two candles, one for Maddie, one for her mother, beginning the ritual that would last now as long as she did. She made the sign of the cross but said no prayer for the dead, as a true Catholic would. A true Catholic would have held on to the consoling image of the pair of them in Heaven together, or, at worst, serving their time in Purgatory. A fair bit of time for both of them, probably, and for Maddie without a doubt. She remembered the way they'd uttered the words of the Creed every Sunday at Mass, so confidently, so unthinkingly: *We believe in one God, the Father, the Almighty maker of heaven and earth . . . We believe in one Lord, Jesus Christ . . . We believe in the Holy Spirit, the Lord, the giver of life . . .* Stumbling over them now in her mind, meaningless, offering no comfort, no consolation. But she remembered the sense of absolution she'd had as a child when she came out of church after Mass, clutching her missal and looking forward to breakfast with the satisfaction of the righteous and the renewed. As if the communion wafer and the wine really was the body and blood of Christ and that He was inside her, filling her with a sense of purity and purpose, His holy Grace. *Lord Jesus Christ the only Son of God eternally begotten of the Father . . .* God the Father was always a remote, even frightening figure, a figure of judgement and retribution, believable as a figurehead but never as a real person, someone you could talk to. Not like Christ. It was always Christ she talked to in her prayers, her own personal god, the Lamb of God in his white robe with his halo and his shepherd's crook and a real lamb tucked under his arm. *Lamb of God you take away the sins of the world have mercy on us, Lamb of God you take away the sins of the world grant us peace . . .* She wished she could recapture that peace, even if it came of ignorance, the simple uncritical faith of children and peasants. *We look for the resurrection of the dead and the life of the world to come. Amen.* If there was any grain of belief in her now it was in that third member of the Trinity, the Holy Spirit, a much less comforting figure, of ambiguous gender and even mortality, at least in her own mind if not in the creed of the Apostolic Church. She pictured this Spirit as a flame, eternal possibly, but bearing no guarantee of personal immortality, no caring arm around the placid lamb. Just a flame burning in a dark world, as inscrutable as a Buddha and much more cold.

She was watching her candles flickering in the empty church when a familiar feeling came upon her that something was not quite right. She turned swiftly, half expecting to see a figure in one of the pews beside her, but there was no one. Still, she knew there was something wrong, something out of place.

She looked around.

This is Jessica's skill, her special gift. She will enter an old building and know by the shape of a room, or some sensitivity to atmosphere, that it has been altered, that here there was a window, there a door. Similarly with an old painting. She can sometimes sense that there is another painting hidden beneath, or a face that the artist has painted over. She does not know how this is, or how to make use of it. It is her party trick.

'I'm sure there was a door there once,' she will say, and there will be an exchange of glances. Jessica, in touch with the other world. Once she found a priesthole behind the wall of an Elizabethan manor that the owner had not even suspected was there.

'The ghosts must speak to you,' he said.

But it is not so clear as a voice, just a vague feeling of having been somewhere before, an affinity with the past.

She looked up at the roof of the church and around the walls. There was nothing here that could be hidden. It was too plain, too modern. It contained no mystery within its walls, no secret, dark niches. And yet . . . she looked back at the statue. And saw there was something wrong with the eyes. There was a cast in one of them – and the other looked slightly bloodshot. Then she realised that the face had been recently painted over, and none too expertly. She looked more closely. Someone had touched up the eyes and gone slightly over one of the pupils and for some reason added a touch of red to one corner. The robe, too, looked as if it had been recently repainted. She could smell it now, the fresh paint under the stronger scent of incense and beeswax. She looked around the walls again. Surely one was a different colour from the others, a slightly paler shale of magnolia. She walked up the aisle, inspecting it more closely, and under one of the stations of the cross she saw a mark, like a shadow, that the paint had failed to entirely cover. It looked vaguely like a human hand, except that it was bigger than a hand. It was more like the pad of a large animal.

XVII

'That's the kind of thing I have to put up with,' said the priest.
'That's why I have to keep a lock on the door.'

Father Francis O'Neill was a thin gangling beanpole of a man
leaning towards sixty, with bright, moist eyes and a pronounced
Adam's apple that wobbled when he spoke. His accent reminded
her of the priests of her childhood, the priests of the confessional.

'It looked like an animal . . .' she began.

'An animal is right, whoever did a thing like that.'

'I meant – I saw the shape of a paw that you hadn't quite
managed to cover up.'

'Have I not? Well my eyes are failing, so, like the rest of me.
Yes, all over the floor and one of the walls. But the statue was
worse. I suppose the idea was she'd been clawed.'

'Clawed?'

'All down her face and the front of her robe. Red paint. I'd a
divil of a job painting it over and if I could lay my hands on the
bast . . .' He asked her to forgive him the odd lapse into the
vernacular. 'I'm not used to female company, apart from my
housekeeper, and she so deaf you could swear with the lungs of a
seraphim and she'd think you were whispering absolution. Will
you come in, now, and I'll make us a drop of tay as they say in
Ireland, for I judge from your accent it's a beverage you'll be
accustomed to yourself at this time of the afternoon.'

Stage Irish, clearly loving the verbosity of his own tongue, but
under the heavy varnish of booze and blarney, in the appeal of his
eyes, she sensed a desperate loneliness.

'Thank you,' she said. 'Tea would be very nice.'

He fussed her into a room that was halfway between study and
lounge and all the way to being a total shambles, the housekeeper
clearly being deficient in more than just hearing, though the fault
was more likely the priest's. Newspapers and magazines littered

the floor or were stacked here and there in some semblance of an order known only to himself. The bookshelves on the walls were filled to capacity, and the books that weren't squeezed in vertically were perched horizontally on top of the ones that were. The furniture was old and ugly and the only religious icon in the room was a simple wooden cross above the old fireplace. There was a smell of damp, old clothes.

Jessica read book titles while the priest made tea. They were mostly the theologies and histories to be anticipated of a man in holy orders, but she was intrigued to find a few from her own reading list of witchcraft and demonology.

He returned, steering a loaded tray through the door, and successfully negotiated the paper obstacle course on the floor. She saw that he'd taken the trouble to put a few biscuits on a plate. It was a pleasure, he said, to meet someone who voluntarily sought admission to the house of God on a weekday. He had trouble enough getting anyone to Mass on Sundays and on Holy Days of Obligation you might as well save yourself the trouble of getting out of bed.

She said she understood most of the Souriquois were Catholics.

'Baptism and funeral Catholics,' he said, 'and the occasional marriage, but it rarely goes any deeper than that. The Jesuits, in their infinite wisdom, converted the heathen by first converting their gods, but you can dress up all the boggles and banshees and flibbertigibbets in the world and call them Saint This and Saint That and they'll still be as pagan as Paddy from the bog.'

His hands shook, she saw, as he poured the tea.

'Is that the reason for the animal paws, do you think?'

'I'm sorry, you've lost me on that one.'

'St Ann is one of the conversions, isn't she? Ursanna, the Bear Goddess.'

He looked at her more carefully and there was an edge to his voice.

'Is she so? And is this a bit of a hobby with you now?'

She told him she was a student of primitive religions and she sensed him relax again, though he viewed her with a keener interest.

'Well you've come to the right place,' he said, 'if it's primitive you're after.'

He was, he said, a bit of an expert in the subject himself . . .

And so they talk of gods and demons – like some old sorcerer and his apprentice having a tea break, Jessica thinks – amid the decay of old news and ancient knowledge, and he tells her of Tabaldak, the Abenaki creator of all living things, and Glooscap the Trickster, of Tsimchian the Mousewoman who works to keep the world orderly and free of troublemakers, and Michi-Pichoux, the water lynxes of the Cree who cause unexplained deaths and steal children.

And she tells him of the gods of the Celtic forest and the Nordic snows who were too terrible or too amorous to be sanitised and sanctified, and of the Church Council at Toledo in Spain in the fifth century which defined the most terrible and amorous of them all as a large black monster with horns on his head, cloven hoofs and the ears of an ass, savage claws, fiery eyes, terrible teeth and a sulphurous smell, who was ever after known as The Beast.

She spares him the detail of the Immense Phallus out of deference for his cloth and if he knows already, he is too polite or embarrassed to mention it.

They exchange these stories as the emissaries of alien cultures meeting for the first time exchange unusual gifts, and as they talk the light fades behind the mist outside and the darkness creeps into the room, and Jessica again senses the loneliness of the man who will not move to switch on the light in case it reminds her that it is late and she should be leaving. But she does not stay because of his stories, she stays because of what he might know of the Selmos.

'Yes, I know the Selmos,' he says, when she finally asks if he has heard the name. 'What about them?'

He sits in shadow now and she cannot see his expression, but she senses the tension in him again.

'It's just that I'd heard they know quite a lot about the old myths and superstitions . . .'

'Urbain Selmo takes a class at the community centre in Abenaki culture. Yes, you should talk to him.'

140

'And there was a woman, I thought . . . Yvette.'

He watches her from the shadows of the room and she feels discomfited by the scrutiny, as if he is looking into her soul. At school all their teachers were nuns. Their encounters with priests were normally confined to the confessional or the Mass, where they were mysterious male figures of authority, distanced by ritual, ever associated in Jessica's mind with the smell of incense and whispered guilty secrets. She no longer calls them 'Father' and bows her head in respect as she did as a child, as she still sees older people do, but there is still enough of the child in her – enough of the Catholic? – to be shocked at her mendacity.

He heaves himself out of his chair and she thinks he has decided to bring the audience to an end. She is to be dismissed, unshriven. He switches on the light.

'I think we could safely say the sun was well over the mast,' he observes, looking over his shoulder to his mirrored image in the window. He heaves himself from his chair, levers a substantial volume from the shelf of books immediately to his left and removes from the space behind a half-full – or half-empty as he would doubtless perceive it – bottle of Jameson's.

'You will join me,' he says, 'in a small therapeutic glass.'

Jessica declines politely. He raises his own glass in a toast, without apparent irony, to 'the first of the day'.

'Now what was it you were saying?'

She wonders if this is a not very subtle way of instructing her to change the subject but, slightly astonished at her nerve, she persists.

'Yvette Selmo.'

'Ah yes. She has the reputation, locally, of being a bit of a *boheen*.'

The name means nothing to Jessica. It sounds Irish. But it isn't. It is Algonquin and it means a witch.

The Souriquois, he tells her, have an enduring belief in magic. For them it is an everyday thing, a matter-of-fact acceptance of the presence of another world, a parallel world of the spirits, invisible or only darkly glimpsed by most people but more readily accessible to those gifted with certain powers. The shaman is a medicine man, a healer, one who can commune with the spirits and seek their help in overcoming adversity. He uses his powers for the benefit of the tribe, in predicting future events, or in healing the afflicted, and when he cannot heal them he guides them on their journey into the world of the dead. But just as the benevolent spirits always have their opposites – the evil demons – so the shaman has his evil counterpart in the boheen, whose power is over the human spirit and who uses it to destroy any man or woman who crosses her.

'You will understand that these are a very simple, superstitious people,' the priest says. 'I don't mean in a racial sense but as many people who have lived all their lives in a fairly closed, rural community. As such, they are more susceptible to the spite of a neighbour, a casual slander, a campaign of whispers, what is called the evil eye. A psychologist would doubtless say that the boheen simply uses the power of suggestion to gain an ascendancy over susceptible minds – if this is ever a simple matter. However, the susceptible attribute to the boheen significant powers to do harm. They can cause mysterious diseases that defy all remedies. Bring bad luck on all your dealings. Pursue you in the form of an animal . . .'

'What kind of an animal?' The question is too quick, her tone too sharp. He considers her a moment, before he answers.

'The favoured form is, I believe, that of the bear.'

He perceives the look on Jessica's face, but interprets it as sceptical.

'I don't mean a literal transformation, of course, but if the victim believes the sorcerer has such power, that belief can achieve a great deal. The powers of the boheen are in using the mind against the body, in inducing a degree of terror that can, if unchecked, lead to physical decline, or injury.'

He pours more whiskey, more generously.

'There is a traditional belief among the Abenaki in what is called "shape-shifting". It's possible the boheen uses this to her advantage. The power of the imagination can be a terrible thing.'

'You think this might have to do with what happened to the church?'

She sees the careful look again.

'In what way would you be meaning?'

'To make people believe this can happen – and that even the church isn't safe.'

'Possibly. It might have been in the way of a warning, I suppose. I have been known to refer to the danger of certain superstitions and those who take advantage of them. But I'd better say no more about that. I've said more than enough already.'

A little drink might make him loquacious but there is clearly a point where it swings him toward the morose.

'Well, I seem to have walked into quite a complicated little set-up,' Jessica observes.

'At least you can choose to walk out again.' There is real bitterness in his voice now. 'Unlike the poor heathens of Nag-wind Cove and those of us who have so incurred the wrath of our superiors as to be sent to dwell among them.'

XVIII

Calhoun is not easy to convince.

'This priest, Father O'Neill, does he have any evidence against the Selmos?'

Jessica shakes her head. 'Not what *you* would call evidence.'

'And you're suggesting – what? There's some kind of connection here – between what happened in the church and what happened on the headland?'

'I think it's worth looking into, don't you?' His eyes appear to doubt this. 'There are precedents.'

'Precedents?'

There are people in remote parts of eastern Europe who think they are wolves. Jessica has met the doctors who treat them, she has even met some of their patients. The doctors call it lycanthropy. In extreme cases the victim howls like a wolf, runs on all fours and has a craving for raw flesh.

Before they would see her, or let her observe their patients, the doctors required to know the nature of Jessica's interest. She did not tell them she was a student of witchcraft. Experience had taught her that men of science are inclined to regard this as a frivolous pursuit. Possibly this is because of its association with women.

She told them she was an anthropologist. She told them of primitive peoples who dressed in the skin and mimicked the movements of the most dangerous predator they knew in the belief that this would give them its strength and cunning and speed. Its power. And that this was the origin of the witch cult.

The old religion, the worship of the Beast.

In eastern Europe it was the wolf, in India the tiger, in Africa the leopard, and in other places the bear.

There is a legend common to the great forests of Europe, to the

Auvergne in France and the Spessart in Germany and the Bernese Oberland, that tells of a woman who was raped by a bear and gave birth to a child. The child appeared to be human but he grew up to display many of the characteristics of his animal father. He loved to climb trees, had sudden violent impulses and was given to spending long periods in isolation when it was dangerous to disturb him. Animals were terrified of him. Eventually, he fell in love with a beautiful woman and they were married. But on the morning after their wedding the woman was found alone in the blood-soaked room with her throat and face slashed open as if by giant claws. Of her husband there was no sign. Search parties were sent out but could not find him.

A few days later, a bear was seen prowling around the village, roaring as if in great pain. The animal disappeared, but a few weeks later, the husband's frozen and emaciated body was found in the first snow of winter.

Tacitus wrote of a bear cult among the Germanic tribes whose members led them in battle against the Roman legions armed only with gloves made of the skin and claws of their guardian animal. They were blood mad and fearless with their power and were called 'berserkers'.

'I'm sorry,' says Calhoun, 'but if you're trying to say that a man can change into a bear . . .'

'I'm saying that a man might believe that he can, that he might seek to prove that he can by . . . by . . .'

'By dressing up as a bear?' He tries to make his voice gentle but there is an irritation directed as much at himself as at her – for is this not what he himself was trying to say to the ranger?

'The medical evidence is that your sister was killed by a blow – two blows – from a very large, very powerful animal. Not by a man – or a woman – with bearskin gloves on their hands.'

But something in her expression makes him relent. There is a bear in Jessica, too.

'I'll try and find out,' he says, 'if anything is known about the damage to the church.'

XIX

The reservation had its own police force of four men and two women. They dealt mainly with domestic incidents, street fights and drunks, and in between times they sat in their patrol cars just off the highway and swooped out on any motorist exceeding the speed limit. There was a 30-miles-an-hour restriction on the stretch of road bordering the reservation and the signs were discreet to the point of invisibility. They caught the occasional absent-minded local, but their real prey were the tourists who came hurtling down from Canada every season and fell like salmon into the net. The fines were a lucrative form of income for the community.

The chief of police was himself a Souriquois by the name of Frankie Lecoute, a powerfully built man in his fifties only a little run to flab. One of Calhoun's colleagues who knew him said you could bounce rocks off his head. Calhoun thought this was intended as a compliment.

He asked Calhoun what he could do for him.

'Heard you had a problem at the Catholic church here a couple of weeks back. Someone figured they'd try to brighten the place up a little.'

Lecoute regarded him for a moment while his brain computed what this had to do with the State police. 'We had a complaint,' he conceded.

'A statue drenched in red paint, like it was blood,' Calhoun reminded him. 'And the paw prints of a bear all over the walls and the floor.'

'Who said it was a bear?'

'I understand the priest did.'

'Not to me he didn't.'

'You saw them?'

Lecoute nodded. 'Could've been anything.'

'But an animal?'

'I guess that was the idea.'

'But you've no clue who did it?'

'One theory is the priest done it himself.'

'The priest? Why should the priest do it?'

A small shrug of the massive shoulders, like a buffalo shrugging off a fly. 'Guy's a drunk. Nobody goes to his church. Nobody never talks to him. Maybe he just wants some attention for himself.'

'I see.' Calhoun tried a different tack. 'You know a family called the Selmos?'

'What about them?'

'The woman who died out on Kitehawk Head was some kind of kin to them, apparently. Spent a fair bit of time with them. Guy called Joe Selmo worked with her on the dig out there. I just wondered what you knew about them.'

Urbain Selmo was a member of the council, Lecoute said. He did a lot of voluntary work, had a lot of respect. Joe Selmo was his boy. He didn't know too much about him. He'd been away a few years. Never in any trouble.

'And what about the sister, Yvette?'

Lecoute shook his head. She'd come back from Canada about a year ago. He didn't know much more about her than that.

'Apparently she has a reputation as a boheen,' Calhoun said. He watched Lecoute for a reaction. There wasn't one. 'I think that's some kind of a witch.'

Lecoute twitched at the fly again.

'The woman who died had a kid,' Calhoun said. 'Nine-year-old. Girl. Apparently Yvette Selmo used to tell her a lot of stories about bears.'

Lecoute rolled his eyes a little. 'She told her stories about bears?'

'About people who change into bears.'

'Like kind of Little Red Riding Hood?'

'No, that was a wolf, Frankie. The wolf changed into the grandmother.' No, that wasn't true. What was it? 'Or maybe it ate the grandmother and dressed up in her clothes. Anyway, apparently this is giving the kid nightmares.'

'This is a crime? You want me to arrest her?'

147

'No, it's not a crime,' Calhoun explained, 'but after what happened to the mother I thought it was worth checking out.'

'Thought you said it was the grandmother.'

'I mean the child's mother, Frankie. The one who died on Kitehawk Head. The one we think was killed by a bear.'

'You want to know if it's true – people change into bears?'

'I'd like to know if people think they can.'

'Well, it's not something I've discussed a lot, lately, but I'll ask around for you. Guess there's a few kids here could be under suspicion.'

It was as far as Calhoun was going to get. He left the office feeling a little like the rocks must feel.

The reservation community centre contained a museum of Souriquois native American culture. This was what the sign on the door said. Visitors by chance or appointment, entry free, donations welcome.

It was a good day for visitors. A very old woman sat at a desk in the foyer of the community centre, weaving a basket. Calhoun asked her if he could go in the museum and she said he was welcome and handed him a leaflet.

The museum consisted of one large room containing a birch-bark canoe, a tableau of waxwork models in traditional costume standing around a campfire with traditional Souriquois weapons and tools, a large wall map with the traditional lands of the Souriquois shaded in red and a number of grainy photographs of the people of the tribe in times past. They posed stiffly in their animal skins, gazing grimly at the camera. Craggy, much-lined faces. Log cabins in the background or trees covered in snow.

Calhoun inspected the map. The territory of the Souriquois seemed to extend across most of northern Maine to the coastline around Narragasco Bay. The accompanying blurb told him the tribe had once numbered over 50,000 people. Now it was less than 2,000, mostly living on the reservation which was marked, not as Nagwind Cove, but as *Muttanegwis*. And Kitehawk, he saw, was written as *Keytawkws* and marked with the symbol of a skull. Calhoun looked at the key at the bottom of the map and saw that this indicated an ancient burial ground. So Henry Savageau had been right about that, at least.

In the top corner, almost like a logo, there was a small picture of a young Indian woman sitting on a cliff looking out to sea where there was a strange kind of ship. It was an irregular shape, like an island, and instead of masts it had three pine trees and in the branches of the pines there were a number of men, covered in hair.

He was still staring at the map, though his thoughts had strayed to other things, when he heard the door open and he turned to see Urbain Selmo standing there. He was reminded momentarily of his meeting with the bear in the forest, not because they had anything physically in common – in fact the animal Urbain Selmo more closely resembled was a startled rabbit – but because the Selmos, like the bears, had been much in his mind of late and it was as if the appearance had been conjured up by the thought.

He had a feeling, though, that if he'd turned a moment or two later Selmo would not have been there. His hand was still on the door knob and he looked like he was about to step backwards out of the room rather than continue with his entrance.

Calhoun addressed him by name and reminded him of who he was in case there was any doubt that Selmo hadn't remembered him. 'Interesting map,' he remarked, as if he'd driven halfway across the county just to look at it, 'but I'm a little confused by the names.'

With obvious reluctance, Selmo came across to join him.

'This is Kitehawk Head, yes?' Calhoun indicated the place called *Keytawkws* on the map. 'But I guess this is the original name in Algonquin.'

Selmo nodded but said nothing.

'So what does it mean?'

There was a small but noticeable pause before Selmo replied, 'Ghosts. Or spirits. The place of ghosts.'

'Because of this?' Calhoun pointed to the skull on the opposite headland.

Selmo shook his head. 'Not that kind of ghost. *Keytawkws* are kind of . . . spirit creatures who bring warnings of death. They're heard in a storm, a scream followed by a long-drawn-out laugh. I guess to a fisherman caught in a sudden gale it was easy enough to believe, even if it was just the cry of some sea-bird in the wind.'

'And *Muttanegwis*?'

149

'This means a place where you leave things. I would say it was probably that certain stores were dumped here when the people went fishing. And now it is the people who have been left here, those of us that *are* left.'

He seemed to gather confidence as he spoke, at ease with the subject. He took a course of evening classes, he said, on the language and culture of the Souriquois. He was anxious, he told Calhoun, to give people an interest in their heritage.

He told Calhoun the story of the young woman who dreamed that she saw an island moving across the sea. The island was covered with trees and the trees were full of bears and when it came closer the bears began to leap ashore. The shamans could not divine the meaning of this dream until the first ship landed with the men from over the seas, men with white skins and hair on their faces who wore coats made of fur.

They had a madness for the skins of animals and would give anything for them. They brought wonderful presents: fishhooks made of steel instead of bone, pots and pans that did not break, weapons with a sharper edge than anything made of stone or wood, weapons that could kill at a great distance . . . and also syphilis, scurvy, smallpox, typhus, dropsy, pleurisy and consumption.

The first maps that were made of this coast in the late 1500s called it the place of many people, but very few of them survived the gifts the white men brought.

'The woman who died on Kitehawk Head,' said Calhoun. 'I believe she was very interested in her heritage.'

He was still looking at the map. After a moment he looked down at Selmo, who clearly needed time to think about this. He looked slightly hurt, as if he'd been tricked.

'Well, yes, she was curious – about her mother, and . . . yes, her people.'

'You saw a lot of her, I understand.'

'At first . . . not so much lately.'

'Think of any reason for that?'

Frowning, shaking his head.

'Nothing to do with your son, then?'

A look, then, that could have been of anger, quickly controlled.

'Why should it have had anything to do with my son?'

150

'Just something I heard. They worked together. I believe they dated a few times. I thought there may have been a falling out between them.'

Selmo knew nothing of this. Calhoun would have to speak to his son.

'He still works on the dig?'

A nod, gazing steadfastly at the map.

'That a particular interest of his, or is it just for the wages?'

'Again, you will have to ask him. He's twenty-one. He lives in my home, but at that age they are not always very communicative.'

'He share your interest in local history?'

'Some. He's only been back here a few months.'

'How long was he away?'

'Three years. He's doing a law degree at the university.' There was something almost challenging in the way he said this and the way he raised his chin to meet Calhoun's eyes.

'So what's he doing back here?'

His eyes slid back towards the map and his voice changed. 'He's taken some time off. He'll go back next year. I hope.'

'So – you've had quite a family homecoming in the last year. Your son. Miss Ross – if you can call her family. Your sister.'

He paused for comments, but Selmo just nodded without any change in his expression.

'I hear she also has an interest in this.' Calhoun looked over Selmo's head and around the room. 'Particularly in the folklore aspect, I believe. I guess you'd call it that.'

She did a fair bit of basket-weaving, Selmo said, if that's what he meant.

But Calhoun didn't mean basket-weaving.

'I understood it was something more in the spell-weaving line.'

He thought he'd feed it into the system, even though he knew he'd get nothing back. But for the first time since he had entered the room Selmo smiled.

'These are fairy tales, Detective,' he said. 'I don't know who's been telling them to you, but they are fairy tales.'

On his way out of the reservation Calhoun stopped off to see the priest. He hadn't warned him he was coming and there was no

151

answer when he called at the presbytery, although his car was there, or someone's car, with a crucifix hanging from the rear-view mirror. He walked over to the church thinking he might find him there. He wasn't sure why he was bothering. He was fast losing interest in what appeared to be a fool's errand.

These are fairy tales, Detective.

There was music coming from inside the church and the door wasn't locked. He saw the priest almost immediately, though for a moment, as his eyes adjusted to the gloom, he thought it was a large crucifix hanging down just in front of the altar. Then he saw the overturned chair in the centre aisle just below the dangling feet.

III. FROST AND FIRE

I

'Suicide is the worst sin a Catholic can commit. Worse even than murder.'

Jessica sits at what has become her usual table overlooking the bay. Framed against the pale light from the window, she reminds Calhoun of a Russian icon: an angel or a female saint, one of the tortured ones.

His mother's voice, ever practical, tells him she is not eating enough, not getting enough sleep.

'Worse than *murder?*'

'That's what Catholics believe. A suicide is denying the existence of Hope and therefore of God. The sin of despair – the worst there is. A priest would have known that – and to do it in his own church . . .'

'So what are you saying?'

Calhoun knows what she is saying, but one unexplained death is more than enough for Russell County and the autopsy report was unequivocal. *Death by asphyxia caused by strangulation. Advanced cyanosis of the skin and mucous membranes consistent with starvation of the oxygen supply to the brain . . .*

And a quantity of alcohol in the blood no doubt consistent with drinking a bottle and a half of Irish whiskey.

'His prints were on the chair,' he says, 'and on the CD that was playing.'

'You think he played a Requiem Mass and then hanged himself?'

'Why not?' It makes perfect sense to Calhoun, but then he is not a Catholic. Besides, there are reasons why he may have succumbed to the sin of despair. *He wasn't much liked in the community*, Frankie Lecoute had said. *He was a deal too friendly with the young ones, a deal too free with his hands.* This might

155

explain why his church was vandalised. But, then again, it might be a motive for more violent reprisals.

'There were no signs of any violence,' he tells Jessica. 'I don't suppose he'd have just stood there and let someone put a rope around his neck.'

'I only know he was frightened of something,' Jessica persists. 'And it was something to do with the Selmos.'

'You think *they* hanged him? Or just hexed him into hanging himself?'

Calhoun clings to the solid ground of reason like a man following a tricky path in a swamp and the siren voices beguiling him out of the mist. Moonshine visions of banshees and shamans and shape-shifters and paranoid priests and the pads of a bear on the walls of a church. And the only solidity in this shifting fog of myth and superstition the corpse of a woman lying on a headland with her face hacked off.

'All I'm saying is, if there is some kind of bear cult or something among the Souriquois, then it's worth checking on.'

'And where would you start checking?'

'Well, I'd be tempted to start with someone who works on the dig, lives on the reservation, and went out with my sister. But I'm not the detective.'

II

The bodies were in a single shallow grave where they had been thrown, one on top of the other, three centuries ago. Now they were a dog's dinner of bones, still half buried in the soft sandy soil among the roots of trees and the granite rocks that had been placed over them as a hasty marker, before their killers came back.

Calhoun felt like an intruder, someone from a different age.

'It's what we've been looking for,' said Kate Wendicott. 'It's what we've been hanging on for all these weeks.'

Her voice was tired but triumphal. She sat cross-legged on the damp earth with a skull at the conjoin of her shins, like a shaman performing some sacred rite, some communion with the dead, carefully stroking the dirt from the sockets of its eyes with a soft brush. A strand of hair had escaped from under the old tweed hat she wore and there was mud on her cheek. She looked exalted, Calhoun thought.

The entire team seemed to be here, mostly on their hands and knees in the dirt. Joe Selmo – who was the reason for Calhoun's visit but did not know it yet – was brushing soil from a rib-cage with a look of intense concentration. Innis was the only one on his feet, taking photographs.

'How many have you found?' Calhoun tried to sound as if he cared. To speak of a more recent death would doubtless be considered boorish.

'Five so far,' Kate told him. 'Five skulls, anyway.'

They were mostly in pieces except for the one that she was working on herself. Calhoun stooped down beside her, suddenly interested. There was a large hole in the top of the skull and another, smaller one just above the left eye socket.

'What caused the damage?' he said. 'Any idea?'

'Well, it could have been caused in the earth,' she said, 'they've

157

lain here long enough, but somehow I don't think so. I think this is the first evidence we've found of the massacre.'

'The massacre?'

'I told you, remember? There was a massacre here, in 1655, according to the records. But we couldn't find the bodies. I think this is them.'

Calhoun looked around, trying to work out the geography. They were in among the trees, about thirty yards or so from the nearest trench and about the same distance from where Madeleine Ross had been found.

'This was a grave, yes?'

'More of a shallow pit. They were worried about another attack. There was no time to bury them properly. They just threw the bodies in one on top of another and placed a few rocks over them as a marker . . .'

'They?'

'Russell and his men. When they came back.'

'Russell?' He had no idea what she was talking about.

'I'm sorry.' But she was frowning now and her voice was irritated. 'Do you really need to know all this?'

'It might help,' he said.

But he could not have said how.

He had to wait until they returned to the cannery before she would explain. They had been working from plans made by the French and British commanders in the 1600s. She waved a dismissive hand at the blow-ups pinned to the walls of her office. They showed a star-shaped perimeter of earth and timber surrounding a score of neatly labelled buildings arranged around a central courtyard or parade ground. But there was always a suspicion that these had been drawn up more to impress government officials in France and Britain, she said, than to reflect actual conditions on the ground.

It was Innis who found the map they now thought was more of an accurate portrayal.

He had been looking through some old books of his mother's and it was one of the illustrations – a copy of a rough sketch plan supposedly made by the surgeon of the fort in 1655. It showed a much less regular outline which straggled along the cliff edge and

158

there were several buildings outside the walls. One of these was marked as the infirmary.

Kate had seen this before and dismissed it as a fabrication, thinking the settlers would not have risked leaving their sick and disabled outside the perimeter walls, but Jarvis thought they might have feared the possibility of contagion more than the difficulty of defending them in the event of an attack. He persuaded her to have one last try at digging in the area marked on the surgeon's map, and she agreed to give it three days. On the second they found the pit of bones.

'Exactly where he'd marked the infirmary,' Kate said. She showed Calhoun in the book. He studied the map for a moment and then the cover as if to check its authenticity, though in truth he had no idea what he was looking for or why. It was leather-bound with raised bands along the spine and faded tooling in gold leaf. He opened it again and found the title page: *The English in Acadia*. Edited by T. Hinchcliffe with notes from the Journals of Captain Thomas Willard and Surgeon Isaac Trapham. Published by the Prince Society of Boston in the year 1878.

Calhoun knew the history of his country in fragments, snatches of song and speech, details from an epic mural. An uncompleted jigsaw composed of heroic figures in dramatic settings. Washington at Valley Forge, Lincoln at Gettysburg, Custer's last stand, Kennedy on the Berlin Wall: incidents in the lives of great men and, more rarely, women. He was only vaguely aware of another picture, darker, more primitive – cave daubings overlaid by the assured brush strokes of later artists – just as he was sometimes reminded of the wilderness that lay under the skin of concrete and glass, the neatly ordered lawns and parks of Boston. He had passed historic monuments without a backward glance only to be halted by the skeletal shape of a winter tree in an old-fashioned street light, the flight of a sea-bird across the waves of the harbour. Footprints of the city's past, recalled as if in some half-remembered dream.

He lifted the book to his face and thought it smelled of earth. Earth and apples.

He saw that Kate was watching him with an expression that was half puzzled, half irritated. He asked her if he could borrow it.

For a moment he thought she was going to refuse but then she said, 'It's not mine to lend.'

He turned to Innis who shrugged and said, 'Of course you can.'

Calhoun remembered why he'd come here. He looked around for Joe Selmo but he wasn't in the office. When he went outside, he saw his battered pickup had gone from the parking lot.

III

The Journal of Thomas Willard began in the summer of 1654, when he embarked from the port of Bristol as a captain in Cromwell's army, sent to the New World to fight the Dutch.

'For there is a Greete Passion among our Masters,' Willard wrote, 'to Seize upon the Profits of Trade and we the Poor Instrumentes of It.'

He was a blacksmith's son from the city of Ely in the Fens of East Anglia who had risen through the ranks to command a troop of dragoons.

'Give me a plain russet-coated captain,' Cromwell had told the Parliament, 'who knows what he fight for and loves what he knows than that which you call a gentleman and is nothing more.'

Willard was such a man. He had fought three great battles against the cavaliers of King Charles and three times put them to flight. But now the King was dead – beheaded outside his own royal palace of Whitehall – and the war was won and England was still ruled by gentlemen.

Willard had volunteered for service in America in the hope of settling there when the war was over, for he had heard it was a place where the son of a blacksmith had as much chance of honour as the son of an earl.

They arrived in Boston Bay in the last week of August. There was a haze upon the sea and the soldiers lining the rails could smell the shore long before they saw it. A smell that contained several distinct components, as Willard recalled, of rotting seaweed and smoke from pine-wood fires, of animal dung and pitch and the more elusive scent of crushed apples. The only sound he noted, that came to them across the still water, was the barking of a dog. Then, as darkness fell, they saw the lights of the settlements that had been established all around the bay.

It was barely three decades since the *Mayflower* had landed its 101 pilgrims at Plymouth Rock, two since John Winthrop had founded his commonwealth of Massachusetts Bay, but in those years a great exodus of English dissenters had followed them to the New World. By the time of Willard's arrival, there were some 15,000 settlers living along the shores and on the islands of Boston Bay, about a third of them on the narrow peninsula the Indians called Shawmut – *where there is a great going of boats.*

Governor Winthrop had aspired to build a new Jerusalem in America's green and pleasant land, an agricultural community bonded by shared values of brotherhood, freedom and equality. Now, twenty-three years later, his church upon a hill had become a hustling, bustling seaport, more like Bristol or Plymouth than any Puritan idyll of the Holy City, and with the same bawdy relish for vice.

The great majority of Bostonians were engaged in trades related in one way or another to the sea and the sins that sailed upon it. Crowding the wharves and shipyards of Town Cove and North End were the one-room cottages of coopers and carpenters, cordwainers, lighterers, shipwrights, sawyers, chandlers and sailmakers, while on the slopes above were the more substantial homes of merchants and brokers, ship's masters and owners who had begun by ferrying the surplus produce of the farms back to the Old World but since discovered there were greater fortunes to be made from slavery and privateering in the New. Most of the ships being fitted out under the cliffs of North End were bound for the Caribbean to prey on the commerce of England's rivals; others for West Africa to transport the slaves who worked their plantations – at a good price.

And the profits came back to Boston. The streets were not yet paved with gold; in fact, they were not paved at all – in the morning light Willard observed pigs and goats scavenging for slops on the waterfront and a great herd of dairy cows being driven along the high street to pasture on the town common. But the needs of the seafarers had funded a vast building programme, and the proud public amenities of the pilgrims – the fort, the meeting house and the schoolroom – were now supplemented by a score of taverns and an untold number of unlicensed premises such as that provided for the entertainment of the weak and the wicked by America's first lady of the night, Sister Temperance Sweete.

The soldiers were permitted ashore in batches to sample these unexpected pleasures or, if they were so inclined, to join in prayers of thanksgiving for their safe arrival. Willard had little choice in the matter. He was commanded to attend upon the Governor at the meeting house where he and his fellow officers learned that within a few days of their departure, God, in his infinite mercy, had bestowed the blessing of peace with the Dutch. The Governor had received the news by fast pinnace. After a few days of rest and recuperation, the troops were to return to England.

It soon became clear to Willard, however, that there was a feeling among the colony's ruling elite that God may have got it wrong on this occasion. They felt sorely squeezed between the Dutch to the south and the French to the north at a time when their own prospects for expansion had never been better.

All the Old World's bitter rivalries had been imported into a thin band of Atlantic seaboard and a few offshore islands. In a forest the size of all Europe, small groups of expatriates fought to corner the market in timber and the skins of wild animals. At the very edge of a wilderness that covered the distance from Murmansk to Madrid, Bristol to Baghdad, lines were drawn, forts were built, flags were flown, militias were exercised on patches of newly cleared land, unexplored rivers were declared to be international boundaries, cannon were fired. The French made Indian chiefs their *capitaines des sauvages* and sent them to war against the English. The English made them drunk and sent them to war against the French. Sagamores and shamans renowned among their people, wise men who knew the secrets of healing and the human psyche, who wrestled with spirits and communed with the dead, were confounded by the quarrel between Jesuit priests and Puritan divines, between men who believed that bread turned into the flesh and blood of Christ at the moment of communion and those who did not. The future of whole tribes turned upon this question, or upon the rivalry of court favourites in Paris and Madrid – upon who was in and who was out of a king's bed. But more important than any consideration of religion, sex or ambition, was the question of profit.

There were fortunes to be made in the fur trade but they were presently being made by the French settlers of Acadia. The Boston merchants wanted to end this unsatisfactory state of affairs and Cromwell's veterans from England gave them the means.

There was one small problem. France and England were not at war and any military incursion into Acadia would have to be without the official knowledge of the English government.

Soundings were taken and the following day Willard met with members of the Massachusetts Bay Company in Sam Cole's wine shop on the harbour. They wanted him to resign his commission and recruit fifty of his best men to build and garrison a fort in the region of the 45th parallel on the edge of French territory. They offered him three times what he was being paid as a captain in the English army and a share in future profits. He did not need to think it over.

As his second in command and guide, he was provided with a colonist called James Russell, who was a distant kinsman of the Earl of Bedford and an officer in the militia. Russell had fought in the Pequot War, spoke fluent French and a smattering of Algonquin. It was understood that his special concern would be arranging for the supply of furs by the Indian tribes of the north-east.

Early in the spring of 1654, the expedition set sail from Boston in a sixty-ton barque, the *Hope of Ipswich*, and, while cruising the densely wooded shores of Narragasco Bay, came upon the ruins of Fort Winter, abandoned by the French some fifty years earlier.

It was an attractive site, not least because it was in a particularly deep and sheltered anchorage where even quite large boats could moor without grounding on the extreme tides. And so Willard and his men disembarked and began to rebuild the walls of the derelict fort and to improve its defences.

A week or so after their landfall they made contact with a number of Indians who had come to the coast from the interior for what was apparently an annual event – the clam-fishing season. They spoke the Algonquin tongue and also some French, and Willard referred to them in his reports by the name the French had given them, the Souriquois. Relations between the two races were strained but not openly hostile. The soldiers continued to build their fort while the Indians fished for pollock and clams and indulged in giant beach barbecues which seemed to have some ceremonial significance for them.

By the end of May, work was sufficiently advanced on the fort for Willard to head back to Boston, where he was to pick up reinforcements recruited among the settlers themselves. Here he encountered his first major complication.

Despite the rapid expansion of the port, political control of the colony was still firmly in the grasp of its founding fathers, members of the First Church of Boston, who as staunch Calvinists believed they were predestined for salvation and were widely known, therefore, as the Saints. Newcomers who were not church members were known as 'sojourners', or 'strangers', and had no rights to vote in elections.

A number of these strangers were members of a new Puritan cult lately arrived from England, where its members had been subjected to intense persecution. They called themselves the Children of Light or the Friends of Truth, and were so truly amiable they insisted on addressing all folk by the familiar 'thee' and 'thou' regardless of their status in society, a custom that did not endear them to the righteous or the correct. They made no distinction of rank between men and women. They discarded all sacraments and all formal ministry, declined to swear oaths of allegiance and, most damnably of all, refused to make war. These were people who spoke as the spirit moved them – and were so moved they sometimes shook with the passion of their convictions, hence the name given them by their detractors, the 'Quakers'.

To the conservative, patriarchal authorities of New England, they were anathema – the Children of Satan.

So it was proposed to offer the opportunity of settlement in the new province to the Quakers. And should they should prove reluctant to expose themselves to the attacks of the French and their Indian allies, a bill was drawn up in the legislature to expel them from the colony.

It may have been that the board of the Massachusetts Bay Company considered that a short experience of life among the savages would soon disabuse the Friends of their pacifist sentiments. Either way, it would remove them from the vicinity of Boston where their presence was plainly insufferable to all honest men of God.

Willard at first raised objections. He needed men he could depend on in a fight, not holy martyrs. But the Saints were insistent, and Willard's own views appear to have been influenced by his initial contact with the Friends – in particular by a surgeon called Isaac Trapham and a wealthy widow called Eleanor Perry who were among the acknowledged leaders of the community. Both welcomed the opportunity to escape the growing persecution of the Boston Saints and to found a new colony according to their Quaker principles.

Widow Perry had been married to a cavalier – a captain in Prince Rupert's Horse who had died at Naseby – and she had become an early follower of George Fox, founder of the Friends, when he had preached against war. She had a daughter of nine called Margaret.

By the time they arrived at Fort Winter, Willard was halfway to becoming a Quaker himself. His lieutenant, Russell, was less enamoured. The two men had their first major disagreement, which was resolved only when Russell left with a dozen soldiers to make contact with the tribes of the interior and establish their credentials as fur traders.

Confidently, the settlers began to clear the forest from the area of the headland and to build a farm and a watermill outside the protective walls of the fort.

In the first week of September, a formal treaty was signed with the Souriquois.

The Indians had no concept of land ownership as the whites understood it, but all this determined activity along the coast, all this chopping down of trees and building of forts and farms and mills had made them jealous of their rights. Moreover, it appeared that the cove and its headland had some ancient and sacred significance to them.

It was at their feasts on the shore that the sagamores, and the wise men the French called *jongleurs*, made the annual decisions which most affected the tribe, allocating territory to the various hunting bands, sanctioning marriages and adjudicating in disputes. More importantly, it was where they told the great sagas and tribal myths, the endlessly repeated tales of heroism and hardship that were so vital for a people who had no written history, that gave them their cultural identity. This strip of sand and shingle between sea and cliff was more sacred to them even than the burial ground on the headland. This was where they renewed their collective soul.

The treaty was designed to calm their fears. Under its terms, the settlers recognised the entire coast of Narragasco Bay as Souriquois territory, but undertook to pay an annual rent in goods and produce to the value of fifty English pounds for the small area upon which they had already built and a greater area of uncleared forest to the south and east of the cove. They agreed to leave the rest of the headland untouched and to respect the Indians' fishing rights in the cove and on the foreshore.

Willard appended his signature to the treaty as representative of the Massachusetts Bay Company, and a copy was sent back to Boston in the ship that had brought the Friends north.

The evening it sailed, the settlers and the Souriquois celebrated their treaty of friendship at a feast under the granite cliffs which the Indians called *Keytawkws* and the settlers, Kitehawk Head. There was a magnificent sunset, Willard wrote in his journal, and as darkness fell, lamps were lit in the clam-shells and there was music and dancing to the fiddle and the flute . . . and then, as the moon rose over the sea, an unexpected guest came down from the cliffs to join them.

His presence was first announced by screams from the children who had been playing among the rocks, and the diners looked up from their feast to see a black bear, massive in the light of the moon.

There was brief concern among the settlers until the Indians calmed them, calling the bear 'Friend', which was naturally among the first English words they had learned. This was an emissary of *Memekwesiw*, the bear spirit, they explained, a great *jongleur* of the tribe who had changed himself into a bear and whose visits were occasions of great honour for the Souriquois. It was a good omen. It meant that *Memekwesiw* was pleased with the friendship between the People of the Dawn and the People who had come from the Sea. A selection of the best and biggest clams was placed at a respectful distance along the shore and the settlers watched with astonishment and growing delight as the bear sat himself down and joined in the feast. He stayed for a second helping, stood up to listen to the music, and then as the moon rose higher in the sky, ambled off into the night.

The next day, Russell returned to the fort with his hunting party supplemented by a number of Mohawk, or Maguas, as Willard called them in his journal. As allies of the French, Mohawk war parties had attacked a number of settlements in Connecticut and northern Massachusetts, and Russell was anxious to detach them from their allegiance. But they were also long-time enemies of the Souriquois and their presence caused considerable tension with the settlers' own Indian allies.

Willard and Trapham visited the Souriquois and assured them of their continued friendship. The Mohawk would leave, they said, before winter. They discussed plans for mutual aid and support when the snows came, which the Souriqouis said would be soon.

Then one day the bear came back.

In his journal, Willard recorded that he was working at the mill when a number of children came running to him in a state of great excitement and told him that 'they had killed the monster'.

He ran to the cliffs and looked down at the great black body lying on the shore below. It had been trapped by the incoming tide and killed with rocks thrown down from above as it tried to climb the cliffs. But it appeared to be the Mohawk, not the children, who had done the killing. When Willard arrived on the scene three or four of them were climbing down the cliffs to skin and butcher the corpse, before it was claimed by the sea.

With some difficulty and the help of other settlers, Willard drove them off, fearing that this was the beast held sacred by the Souriquois.

Their absence from the settlement that evening suggested that this was indeed the case. The following morning when the tide was out, Willard arranged for the corpse to be buried, with all solemnity, on the foreshore, but the Souriquois kept their distance.

A day or two later, Russell was dispatched for Boston with a quantity of furs in the only sea-going vessel belonging to the colony. He was to return before winter set in with much-needed supplies. The Mohawk left, too, but the Souriquois stayed away from the fort. The settlers had occasional sightings of them in the forest throughout the fall but they fled at any approach. On the sixth of October, it snowed.

It was a particularly severe winter, much worse than they had experienced some 300 miles south in Boston. By the first week in December the waters of the cove had frozen over and for several days the farm and the mill were cut off from each other and from the fort. When the storm passed, the settlers in both of these outposts reported hearing something like a scratching on their doors and the snuffling of an animal.

Such was their fear, that Willard took two members of the garrison into the forest to hunt for the creature. They never returned. A larger party sent out to search for them found the captain's mutilated corpse in the forest. Of his two companions there was no sign.

The final story of Fort Winter was told by Surgeon Trapham, in his own uncompleted journal.

They buried Captain Willard in the cemetery established fifty years earlier by the French for the victims of their own terrible winter. Like them, no one now dared to enter the forest. There was no sign of the promised ship from Boston, and shortly into the new year they began to suffer the first symptoms of the disease that had carried off so many of the French. *Mal de la terre.*

They now knew it by another name: scurvy. But they were no nearer than the French had been to divining the cause, or finding a cure.

'There is great suffering of this disease,' wrote the surgeon, 'being produced in the mouths of the victims great pieces of superfluous and drivelling flesh causing extensive putrefaction. Scarcely anything but liquid can be taken. The teeth become very loose and can be pulled out with the fingers without causing pain. The superfluous flesh was cut out causing them to eject much blood through the mouth. Afterwards a violent pain seized their arms and legs which remained swollen and very hard, all spotted as if with flea bites and they could not walk on account of the contraction of the muscles so that they are almost without strength and suffer intolerable pains. They experience pains also in the loins, stomach and bowels, have a very bad cough and short breath. In a word, they are in such a condition that the majority of them can not rise nor move and can not even be raised up on their feet without falling down in a swoon.'

By late March he recorded that thirty-two settlers and fourteen soldiers had died out of a total population of ninety-five. Of the remainder, all were afflicted, twelve so badly he did not expect them to live.

An editorial note recorded that the journal had been discovered in the deserted fort the following month by Russell and his men when they finally returned from the south. There was evidence of an attack by Indians. The fort had been stripped of its cannon and any objects of value, and part of it had been burned down. Then, in the ransacked infirmary, Russell and his men discovered the bodies of twelve men and women. All were emaciated and bore marks of scurvy, but their heads and upper bodies had been mutilated as if by the claws of a bear.

In his report to the Boston Assembly of Notables, Russell described a peculiar ceremony which he and his men had witnessed on Kitehawk Head where the Souriquois had set up their summer encampment. A young man had built himself a den out of brushwood on the edge of the village where he had lived for several days, isolated from the rest of the tribe. From time to time, they had seen him emerge, though he always remained within a few yards of the den, dressed in the skin of a bear and walking on all fours with the aid of two pronged sticks, not unlike garden rakes, which extended the length of his arms. He scratched around in the dirt with these artificial claws, apparently eating the grubs and insects he found. The soldiers called him the Bear-man. They thought he was mad, an outcast.

Then, about three or four days after his withdrawal from the village, a crowd of young men surrounded the den, shouting and waving spears, until he came out with a rush, running on all fours but rising up to strike at them with his claws, laying several of them out before he was finally overpowered and carried in triumph hanging head down from a horizontal pole. The soldiers thought he was dead but later they saw the same man, still in his bearskin, sitting outside the den with one of the village elders smoking a pipe which was passed from one to the other.

Later, Russell asked one of the sagamores who spoke some French to explain the significance of the ritual, and discovered it was one of the initiations that had to be observed by a young man before he was admitted into the elite Society of Bears. The initiate adopted the role of his spirit guide, enduring isolation, torment and a mock death, only to be reborn, just as the spirit of the bear itself was reborn if the proper rituals were observed in hunting.

When Russell asked what had happened to the young men who had been injured during the attack on the Bear-man, he was told that two of them had died. This was not considered excessive.

It was this ceremony that first alerted Russell to the existence of the bear cult that flourished among the Souriquois and to the shape-shifting that was reputedly practised by the shamans of the tribe. He concluded that in revenge for the death of the bear on the shore, the enraged members of the cult had first killed Captain Willard and then attacked the depleted settlement, leaving their gory signature on the bodies of the patients in the infirmary. If there were any survivors, they had been taken by the Souriquois into the forest and had vanished without trace.

IV

'You're asking me if people can change into bears?'

'No, Frankie,' said Calhoun. 'I'm asking if they *think* they can.'

'I guess a few people could be crazy that way. Boston's maybe full of them.'

This was the way you treated outsiders in Down East Maine, Calhoun recollected, especially when they asked damnfool questions. He'd probably done it himself when he was a kid, without even being aware of it. It was instinctive, a kind of defence mechanism. He was aware of it now, though, now it was happening to him on a regular basis. His father did it, Ranger Grainger did it . . . he could hardly have anticipated any better of Frankie Lecoute.

Calhoun spelled it out: 'It's a matter of historical record that the settlers on Kitehawk Head were killed by members of a Souriquois Bear Society. Now we have someone killed in the same place in exactly the same way . . .'

'Hold on there, hold on a second . . .' Frankie's face suddenly became animated. 'Who says this is "a matter of historical record"?'

'You're trying to tell me this didn't happen – that there wasn't any massacre on Kitehawk Head . . . ?'

'They dug up the fucking bodies. No evidence of any massacre, none at all. They did tests. They all died of scurvy.'

'Except they've just found some more,' Calhoun told him, 'with their skulls smashed in.'

It was the first time he had seen something approaching an expression on that slab of a face, but what was it? Disbelief and something else – apprehension?

'You're shitting me,' he said. 'When was this?'

'This morning. They'd found half a dozen when I left there. But there's probably more. Multiple injuries to the skull, much the same as those sustained by Madeleine Ross.'

This was a considerable exaggeration, if not outright distortion, of the facts but Calhoun wasn't in a court of law, not yet, and he was less interested in the facts than in the effect he was having.

'Jesus,' Frankie said. 'Jesus, this is really going to piss some people off.'

' *"Piss some people off"*? Excuse me?'

Frankie lifted his eyes up in mute appeal. He looked like a large, shaggy dog that has just lost its bone to something even larger and is begging for it back again.

'The land claim,' he said.

'The land claim? I'm sorry,' Calhoun said, 'I'm not with you, Frankie.'

'You don't know about the land claim? It was in the press – just after they found the bodies.'

'Well, it's news to me. Must have been before I came back here.'

Frankie nodded but Calhoun didn't think he'd taken it in. He was too absorbed with the apparent consequences of what he'd just heard.

'So tell me, Frankie,' he prompted him, 'what have I missed?'

There was a moment's hesitation – it probably went entirely against the grain of his character to be explicit. Finally Frankie said: 'Some time back in March, April maybe, the Council filed a land claim against the State of Massachusetts.'

'The Council?'

'The Souriqous Council. On behalf of the Souriquois nation. For land stolen from them by the State of Massachusetts.'

'What land?'

'Kitehawk Head. Most of the coast to the south, Bridport island . . . There was some kind of a treaty, way back, leasing the land to the settlers. But there was never any payment made. State claimed there was a massacre, the Souriquois broke the treaty . . . That was the justification for taking the land by force. I can't say I understand too much of it myself. But just after they dug up the bodies and found they all died of scurvy, the Council filed suit for compensation.'

'Compensation?' Calhoun seized on the one word in all of this that he entirely understood. 'How much compensation?'

'Three hundred million dollars.'

It looked like it hurt Frankie to say it.

'Are you serious? For something that happened 300 years ago?'

'Makes no difference. Still theft. There was no evidence of any massacre. Least, we didn't think there was until . . . what you just told me. The lawyers thought there was a good chance of winning a settlement. Don't look good fighting the Indian wars all over again in court. Not when they was so one-sided. Bad publicity, bad politics. There's been other cases. Government usually settles, one way or another.'

This might have been the longest speech Frankie Lecoute had ever made.

Calhoun said: 'And this claim is against the State of Massachusetts?'

'They were the legal authority, apparently. Them days, there was no State of Maine.'

'And who'd get the money – if you won?'

'The tribe.'

'The tribe?'

'All 2,341 of us.'

Us. Of course. Frankie was one of them. He'd have a share in this. No wonder he looked deflated.

'And in case you're trying to work it out,' he said, 'that's $150,000 for every man, woman and child on Nagwind Point. Not counting the land settlement.'

'Bridport?'

Frankie's laugh was like a bear grunting over a lost salmon and just as good-humoured. 'I guess we're resigned to the loss of Bridport – that's what the compensation's for. No. Kitehawk Head, where we used to bury our dead, make our laws, eat our clams. Sacred land, Detective. Intrinsic to the soul of the Souriquois.'

The irony was back in his voice but with a new bitterness.

'And you think now they've found evidence of a massacre . . . ?'

'I think,' said Frankie, 'I better give up the idea of early retirement.'

When Calhoun came out of his office there was a chill in the air and thin rags of fog drifting in from the sea and coiling around the street lamps. He drove through the reservation looking at the sad little cabins and the trailers and the junk in the yards – the old refrigerators, the rusting bedsteads, the clapped-out old cars – thinking of what Urbain Selmo had told him. *Muttanegwis*, the place where you dump thing . . .

Shamans, shape-shifters, bear cults, now money, and despite the fog, for the first time since they'd found the body of Madeleine Ross, Calhoun felt he'd caught a glimpse of clear blue sky.

V

The Graham House had been built in the decade after the Civil War by General Robert Russell Graham, and might have been modelled on one of the Palladian mansions he burned on Sherman's march through Georgia. Calhoun remembered how daunted he had been as a child by the white classical columns and the steps leading to the front door, though usually he would go round the back and one of the maids would let him in – after he'd carefully wiped his boots on the mat.

This time he went up the steps and it was Innis himself who answered the door. Calhoun told him there were one or two things he wanted to ask him about the dig. He looked puzzled, but invited him in.

Their footsteps echoed in the empty hallway and Calhoun had the impression the house had been shut up for the winter. He noticed paler patches on the walls where pictures might once have hung and the rooms he glanced in were strangely sparse of furniture.

It was far too big for his mother to live here alone, Innis said, with a trace of embarrassment, but he couldn't persuade her to move out.

'We're in the conservatory,' he said.

That was another marvel of the Graham House, Calhoun recalled from his childhood visits there: the conservatory. It ran the length of the house, overlooking the river, with wicker chairs and plants and pieces of ancient statuary, and a round table with a white cloth and a silver tea service. And Mrs Graham, with one of her friends, or more rarely, Mr Graham, pouring tea.

Calhoun half expected to find her there still, still pouring, but she wasn't. Jessica was.

She was reclining in one of the wicker chairs with a glass of wine and the look of a schoolgirl who has been caught playing hookey.

'I wanted to have a word in private,' Calhoun said to Innis after the first self-conscious exchange.

'That's OK.' Jessica levered herself up from the chair. 'I'll go and watch television for a bit with Freya.'

Calhoun felt a momentary relief that at least Freya was here, playing chaperone, but it didn't last.

'So what's on your mind, Michael?' Innis asked him when she'd gone.

The only thing on Calhoun's mind, now, was what Jessica was doing here. He tried to assemble his thoughts into some kind of order, but the fog was back in his head.

'The map you found . . .' he began.

'The map?'

'The sketch map, the plan in the book, showing the layout of the buildings . . . How long have you had it?'

'Well, I'm not sure – I'd have to ask my mother – years, probably, but . . .'

'Is your mother here?'

'Yes, but . . . she's in her room. She usually has a sleep about now. She hasn't been very well. I'd rather not disturb her, unless . . .'

Calhoun shook his head. 'It doesn't matter. But you found it yourself only a few days ago?'

'That's right. I think I saw it lying around on a chair in the library. She must have pulled it down off one of the shelves.'

'What's her interest in all of this?'

Innis rolled his eyes. 'My mother is completely obsessed with her own ancestry. Don't you remember? She must have talked to you about it. She talks to everyone else. Endlessly.'

Vaguely, now, Calhoun did remember. Or was it his own mother, who was impressed by such things, links with the past, claims to pedigree. One or other of them had told him, anyway. Something about English lords, robber barons, adventurers . . .

'Something about the Grahams and the Russells,' he said. 'There was a connection.'

'We go back a while,' said Innis, but his tone was sardonic. 'The Grahams came over with the first wave of Scottish im-

177

migrants in the 1700s. Mother claims they were lords, or lairds, or whatever they call them in Scotland – clan chiefs – but then she would. So far as I can make out they were cattle rustlers, not that I give a damn either way. They made a fortune in lumber and shipbuilding and married into the Russell family, who were the nearest thing to God in those days.'

'And this is the same family as the man who built the fort on Kitehawk Head?'

'According to my mother. He was supposed to be a distant relative of the Duke of Bedford and that's enough for her. She's like those people who believe in reincarnation, you know, they were never peasants, never nobodies, they were always Somebody. They always had a title.'

We're related to the Dukes of Bedford, you know.

It came back to him, through the ether. She was probably sitting at this same table, and she'd shown him a picture of a castle in one of her magazines, a castle or a stately home. It had meant little to him then, even less now, but it explained her interest in the fort. What was surprising was that she had no idea until a few months ago that it was there. No one had.

He said as much to Innis who shrugged and said, 'It was overgrown, no one ever went there . . .'

'But there were maps . . .'

'Plans – not maps. There were no bearings – they hadn't even invented longitude in 1650. Could have been anywhere. Anywhere within about a hundred miles, anyway. But what are you getting at, Michael?'

'I'm just wondering if anyone else could have known about this map of yours, that's all.'

'Well, sure, they could. I'm not claiming I discovered this or anything. They'd come across it in their research, only Kate reckoned it was a fake, or badly drawn or something. It was only a copy of the original. If there *was* an original.'

'But it turned out to be accurate.'

'In some respects. Not in others. The main thing was it marked a different position for the infirmary . . .'

'And that's what led you to the bodies.'

'Yes.' He looked puzzled, as well he might. Even Calhoun wasn't sure where this was taking him.

'Is there any possibility,' he said, 'that Madeleine Ross could have known they were there?'

Innis stared at him for a moment. 'I don't see how she could. I mean, she wasn't . . . the area she was given to dig, it was nowhere near there. Besides, if she had found them, she'd have told everybody.'

'Would she?'

'Well, why shouldn't she?'

'Because she didn't want anyone to know about the massacre.'

'Ah. I see what you're getting at. Because of her background. But the same goes for Joe Selmo. And two of the other field workers, they're from the reservation, too.'

'It's a theory,' said Calhoun.

'Sure. The only problem is – it took us two days to find them. Two days of constant digging. You think they could have done that, and no one notice? And if they had, why leave them there for someone else to find?'

But Calhoun had no answer to that.

Innis saw him to the door. There was no sign of Jessica, but he could hear the television from one of the rooms. Again, he had the feeling of emptiness. The house felt unlived in.

'You thinking of staying on here?' he asked.

'God forbid. No, I'm just trying to get a few things straight, that's all. My father left things in a bit of a state.'

'You wouldn't seriously think of selling this place?'

Innis looked at him, curiously. 'Why not?'

'The history, I guess. It's been in your family for . . . how many generations?'

'All the more reason to get rid of it, start again.'

There was a dismissive tone to his voice that surprised Calhoun. Perhaps because he had put such a high value on it himself when he was a child – the house, what it represented.

Ancestry, you can't buy that. That must have been *his* mother.

They were standing on the porch and Innis was still looking at him in that half-amused way.

'What is it, Michael – would you like to live in a mausoleum like this?'

'I guess not. But – I'm not a Graham.'

'A Graham. Jesus, you sound just like my mother.' Now, Innis didn't look at all amused. 'Look, it took – God knows how many generations to make the Grahams into whatever kind of people my mother thinks they are. It took my father about fifteen years to lose the lot. Believe me, a long line doesn't strengthen, it weakens. The only Graham I'd like to be is the first one – the first one who came to America – an adventurer with nothing except . . . whatever it took to make something of himself. That's all that matters, Michael. Who you are now, not that your great-great-gran'daddy was a Civil War general and his great-great-gran'daddy was second cousin to the Duke of . . . wherever.'

Calhoun drove back along the side of the small cove where Innis used to moor his little boat. He paused at the intersection with Route 1, wondering which way to go. He could turn right to Canada or left to Florida, it was his choice, the road went all the way.

But he sat there, with the engine idling, going nowhere.

Would you like a boat of your own, his mother had asked him once – maybe the summer he stopped going out in Innis Graham's – *because your father would make you one, you know, you only have to ask him.*

And Calhoun had politely declined the offer. Turning his back on the world that had rejected him? Or more likely, simply fearing the ridicule of sailing a scale model of the *USS Constitution* around Narragasco Bay.

It seemed more significant now, though. As if he'd known it could never be the same, never be as good as it had been, over those two or three summers sailing with Innis. Just as he'd known he could never be *like* Innis, that it was no use trying, because he didn't have the resources. *He was a home boy from the backwoods of Maine who didn't really want to go anywhere.*

His father had lived here all his life, apart from a short spell in the army. He came from old New England stock but he had no idea how far back they went or where they came from originally. He expressed no interest in the matter. His mother was more curious, of course – antiquity always intrigued her – but her own roots were obscure. So far as Calhoun was aware, there had never been any money in the family, no title. His only legacy was an ingrained Puritanism, a belief in the intrinsic value of hard

180

work, integrity, self-reliance . . . and on the downside, a degree of sexual inhibition which Calhoun had struggled with all his life. Sex was rude, sex was dirty, sex was Guilt. On the other hand, this could make sex quite exciting at times.

Not that there had been a great deal in recent months to feel excited – or guilty – about. Even fantasising was fraught with difficulties. His last affair had been erotic enough to keep him going for a lifetime, but other images would intrude – and a great sadness. He would have liked to fantasise about Jessica but somehow it didn't seem . . . respectful . . . in the circumstances. So lately, Kate Wendicott had begun to feature in his ruder thoughts.

It was for this reason, rather than anything to do with the death of Madeleine Ross, that he turned left at the end of the Graham drive, left towards Florida, and Kitehawk Head.

VI

Calhoun pulled up next to Madeleine Ross's VW, still parked where she had left it on the night of the killing. He wondered if Jessica would take it, or whether it would stay here until some of the kids from Bridport or the reservation came out here and set fire to it and did their bit to bring their crime figures more in line with Boston's.

He ran his hand over the patched sunroof, as if he was soothing it for the absence of its owner. It was the only thing she'd possessed worth more than a few bucks. Back in England she'd lived in a bus and Jessica reckoned she must have sold her share in it to raise the air fare. Most of what was left must have gone on the car. Unless she'd stolen it.

She had a criminal record of sorts. Two charges of obstructing the police and one for possession of drugs. If she hadn't had an American passport they probably wouldn't have let her into the country. They'd have saved her life.

For a while.

She was going nowhere, doing nothing.

Except . . . she had a cause, something she believed in. She was trying to save the planet. So why had she given it up to come here? Unless this was part of it.

There were lights on inside the cannery and he could hear music. While he was searching for the way in, a door opened and Jarvis almost walked into him. He let out a yell and jumped at least a foot.

'It's only me,' Calhoun said, 'I was looking for Dr Wendicott.'

'Shit,' Jarvis said. Calhoun let him calm down a little.

'She's in the lab,' he said. 'I'll take you through.'

Calhoun followed him down a barren corridor and through opaque plastic doors into what at first sight had the appearance of a film studio – a vast, hangar-like room with a small area near the door, furnished like a set and lit by two portable arclights.

Kate Wendicott sat at a table, inspecting a skull through a large magnifying glass.

'Visitor for you,' Jarvis said in his normal, sardonic tone.

Calhoun walked into a blast of hot air from an industrial heater and a cold frown from the face above the skull. He apologised for calling so late in the evening and said he was puzzled by 'one or two things'.

'I'll leave you to it, then,' said Jarvis. Neither of them acknowledged his departure.

'What are you doing?' Calhoun asked her.

'Trying to fit a few pieces together.' He couldn't tell if she meant it to sound ambiguous or not, but there was a tube of glue on the table and various bits of bone. Then, as he looked closer, he saw that the cranium had been more or less reassembled, leaving a crazy paving of cracks and three irregular-shaped holes, each about the size of a dollar.

'So Russell was right,' he said.

'Excuse me?'

' "Mutilated," ' he quoted, ' "as if by the claws of a bear." '

She continued her scrutiny of the skull and he wondered, for a moment, if it was to avoid meeting his eye.

'That's one explanation.'

'Can there be any other?'

'Maybe. That's what I'm *trying* to find out.'

But then she looked up at him, studied him for a moment as if she was trying to make up her mind about something, and then asked him if he would like a beer.

He was confused.

'Here?'

'Sure, we've got everything here.'

She peeled off her plastic gloves and walked away from him out of the circle of light. She wore flat-heeled shoes and loose overalls but she walked in a way that made him picture her naked – naked and aware of being watched, with a certain lazy shrug of the hips and the shoulders.

He looked at other things.

In the darker, uncarpeted area, there were bones and bits of skull laid out on plastic sheeting, like a troll's picnic, and a number of metal drums containing various chemicals, presumably used to clean and preserve them. Formic acid, he read, acetone, vinylite resin . . . Beyond them, receding into the gloom, there was more stuff – the muzzles of several cannon, pitted iron cannonballs, broken flintlocks, buttons and buckles, less identifiable objects which at first sight looked like pieces of rotting flesh but which turned out to be bits of leather belt, shoes and tattered fabric – all neatly laid out and labelled with numbers, like price tags in some particularly uninspiring flea market.

'We've got beer, wine or Scotch whisky.'

She had opened the door of a large refrigerator next to a trough of stainless steel sinks where he imagined they had once washed and gutted the fish. He said beer would be fine.

She brought two bottles over, one for each of them, and perched on the edge of a table, tilting her chin and drinking half the contents straight off in several large gulps. She wiped the back of her hand across her mouth, and belched softly. Calhoun drank in small, delicate sips watching her.

'You think it's the same thing that killed Maddie, don't you?' she said.

'Do I?' He held her gaze for a moment. 'How could it be?'

'It couldn't.' The merest pause before she added, 'but it won't stop some idiots thinking it. We'll be into the Curse of the Mummy's Tomb before we know what hit us.'

He gazed deliberately around at the artefacts spread across the floor.

'You didn't find any weapons in your excavations?'

'None capable of inflicting that kind of damage. And if we had you can be pretty damn sure it wouldn't have been in any condition to do much damage now. Is this why you came here – to ask me this?'

He smiled, but instead of answering, asked how long they were planning to stay on the site.

'We've got a truck coming tomorrow. We're aiming to load up over the weekend. Should be away by Monday.'

'So you're finished here?'

'For the time being. It's a bit late in the year for digging. We'll spend the winter cleaning up the artefacts, getting our notes up to date, and come back in the spring. If we can raise more funding.' She glanced down at the skulls. 'Now we've found these, it should make it a lot easier.'

'How come?'

'Because the people who pay for this kind of thing want value for money. Same as any other business. Pure scholarship's fine so far as it goes, but they like to know they're paying for something that will make people sit up and take notice. Publicity – the right kind, in the right papers. This isn't the Tomb of Tutankhamun. We're not going to find any priceless relics here, we're not going to get any dramatic revelations about the way people lived in the past. But this was . . . a unique experiment, in its way, and to tell the story, to make people *interested* in the story, we needed a dramatic ending, a tragic ending.'

'So this is why you stayed?'

'Why we stayed?' Now *she* was confused.

'After the death of Madeleine Ross.'

'Ah.' She nodded her head a few times. 'You think that was a little unfeeling of us?'

He said nothing.

'I suppose you think this is all hugely irrelevant, don't you?'

'I'm a little curious to know why it's so important to you,' he said carefully.

She considered him for a moment – in much the same way, he thought, as he had seen her inspecting the skull.

Then she said: 'You've probably noticed my scar.'

He stared at her, embarrassed, not knowing what to say, though you could hardly not notice it. She placed her hand under her chin and tilted her face to the light. At that angle it was more livid, the skin more puckered. Her upper lip looked as if it had been clamped.

'Some scars you can see,' she said. 'Others are deep inside. It's the same with nations. You have to dig for them.'

He looked away to the pieces of skull on the floor. Some of them were quite large, with discernible features like eye sockets or rows of grinning teeth; others no more than shards of bone.

'This was our Dark Age,' she said. 'The first hundred years of settlement. The French and Indian wars. We don't know how many were killed on either side. Well, we can make an estimate with the settlers. About fifty per cent – greater than the casualties we took in the Pacific during World War Two. And what they did to the Indians . . . It left scars. Scars on the soul.' He met her eyes again, trying not to look at the scar. 'Character-forming, though, don't you think.'

'Do you mean the American character?'

'Well, I don't mean mine.'

'I'd say the American character had more to do with the millions who came later,' Calhoun said. 'But I'm no historian.'

'No.' She regarded him thoughtfully. Then, 'Another beer?'

He nodded and watched that walk again.

She handed him the new bottle, standing unnecessarily close and pushing it at him like she was working the lever on a machine. He was disturbed by her closeness, by the thought of what she was or was not wearing under the buttoned-up overalls. The top of her head came up to his chin.

'What the hell are you doing here, Calhoun?' she said.

'Here?'

'Down East Maine. What do you do here?'

'I'm a detective.'

'I know that. Least I keep reminding myself. But what do you detect? Normally?'

'Not a lot.'

'I didn't think you did.'

There was a moment when they might have embraced, but he let it pass, and she retreated to her table, legs crossed at the ankle, studying him over her bottle in a way that disconcerted him. He rather thought that this was why she did it.

He said: 'What will happen here when you're gone?'

'You'll look after it for me?'

'Sure,' he said. 'Fuck all else to do.'

'It depends on the funding,' she said. 'But if we get the right kind of publicity . . .' It was the second time she'd used that expression – *the right kind*. It must be bothering her . . . 'There could be some kind of a centre here.'

He wasn't sure what she meant.

'A study centre. A culture centre. A reconstruction. That would be part of it but – it could be more than that. Something special happened here. Or didn't. It was the step we didn't take, the door we didn't open. Sure, there were all kinds of influences, all kinds of cultures, but those millions that came later, they had a role model, something to conform to. An idea of what an American *was*, and in case they missed it, there were plenty of people to tell them, and punish them for getting it wrong. All those frontier virtues, pilgrim virtues – self-reliance, honesty, hard work, co-operation . . . and greed. Mustn't forget greed in the scheme of things. When was it, d'you think, that greed became the dominant factor, or was it there from the start?'

'What has this got to do with Fort Winter?'

'Well, that's what we're trying to find out. Diet is my speciality, did you know? I guess you think that's irrelevant, too.'

He shook his head, more in irritation than denial.

'You ever think why all those pilgrims died of scurvy when the Indians didn't? There's a detective story for you. The Indians drank an infusion made from the needles of the white pine that contains large quantities of vitamin C. The Mohawk must have brewed it for Russell's men. No doubt the Souriquois would have given some to the settlers if they hadn't fallen out with them over the killing of the bear.

'There's a lesson in that, don't you think. Learn from your mistakes. Learn from each other. It's the only way we can survive.'

'You're talking about now or then?'

'Now *and* then. Past and present. That's why it's relevant.'

'What happened afterwards?' he asked her.

'Afterwards?'

'After the massacre?'

She shrugged. 'We're into the Dark Ages again – but I don't suppose they shed too many tears in Boston over what happened to the Quakers. And they could get on with treating the Indians like savages. Which suited them very well.'

'And what happened to Russell – and the survivors?'

'They came back to Boston. He led an expedition against the Souriquois and drove them into the arms of the French. This was French territory for the rest of the century. Part of French Acadia. Until the British kicked them out and they went to Louisiana. And the Indians – got what was coming to them. But you didn't come here for a history lesson, did you? I mean you must know all this.'

187

'I know fuck all about it,' he said.

She looked at him and he sensed her mood change.

'I wish you wouldn't keep saying fuck,' she said.

He could have said something dismissive – awkward, even – that would have diverted the moment, rendered it harmless. But he didn't. She pushed herself away from the table and walked over to him and kissed him on the mouth, and after they'd explored this area for a while he felt, with some small surprise and some larger concern for the circumstances, her fingers pulling at the buckle of his belt.

And he said: 'Here?'

'There are not a lot of alternatives,' she said. 'It's a bit chilly outside and we're all sharing the same camper. Why? Is it the fish?'

He said, no, it wasn't the fish.

He lifted her on to the table. It was the right height. The overalls slid off her shoulders and she sat, half unwrapped, with her arms around him.

They kissed with thoughtful pleasure as if taking bites out of some unfamiliar fruit. He put his finger inside her and then into his mouth.

'Eat it properly,' she said. 'There's a good boy.'

He felt like they were on a stage in the circle of light and there was an audience watching them from out there in the darkness and he wanted them to see her naked, so he pulled her pants down and stepped back to see for himself as she sat pink and exposed on the edge of the table.

This was fine while it was fantasy but a little later, when they were on the floor and she was astride him, he thought he heard the door open behind his head and he lay there, frozen with embarrassment, wincing up at her. But she was looking straight at the door and her expression did not change – except perhaps, it grew more seductive, more sensual, and she continued to move up and down on him without inhibition or shame.

She arched her back and threw back her head and he stared, lost now to all restraint, up the line of her throat to her jaw and her mouth and the scar on her upper lip and the blood throbbing there as if in a vein.

When it was over he dressed quickly, in case someone really

did come in. He was uneasy now, with the beginnings of guilt.

'Have you eaten?' he said. 'Do you want to go into Dover for some supper?'

She looked sideways at him. 'You don't have to pay for it,' she said.

He was hurt. 'I didn't mean it like that.'

'I know.' She patted his shoulder like an old pal and said: 'But I want to work a bit more.'

'OK.' He shrugged. 'I'll leave you to it, then.'

She nodded and moved her hand to his cheek. 'I've always wanted to fuck a detective, only I never found one that was fuckable.'

She linked her wrists around his neck and kissed him and said she didn't suppose she'd see him again.

'You never know,' he said, awkwardly. He felt dismissed.

When he stepped outside, the shock of the cold air was like an awakening, as if what had happened inside the building had been a dream or an enchantment. He held the door open, looking back down the corridor. She'd put the music on again. A classical piece he didn't recognise. He closed the door with a feeling that might have been guilt or sadness, or a mixture of both.

The temperature seemed to have dropped twenty degrees since he entered the building and the night was opaque with mist. When he looked up, there were no stars.

VII

Jessica drove east along the coast towards Bridport with Freya sleeping in back and the mist drifting out of the forest and shredding in the headlights. She kept her speed down in case one of the coiling wraiths formed into the solid shape of moose or deer, and slowed to a crawl on the strip of road that ran past the reservation. She passed the church of St Ann's and glimpsed the unlit patrol car outside, either to guard against further desecration or swoop out on a speeding motorist, probably both. A couple of hundred yards further on, without any clear thought in her head, she turned left and drove between the squat, ugly cabins of the village.

When she came to the Selmos' house she drove slowly past without stopping. There were no lights on.

She reached the end of the road with only the dark mass of sea and fog ahead of her and made a three-point turn, driving back into the centre of the reservation.

She stopped outside the community hall. A sign outside said it was Folk Night, and when she slid the window down she could hear the rhythmic beating of a drum and the fainter sound of the singers, though it was more chant than song. She listened for a minute or so, until she felt the freezing fog wrapping itself around her shoulders, and then she raised the window and drove on, puzzled by this small diversion, unable to explain why she had made it.

She crossed back on to the highway and continued her interrupted journey, but she was still conscious of the drumbeat, like a rhythm she couldn't get out of her head. She passed the sign welcoming the visitor to Bridport and knew she was approaching the narrow turning to Kitehawk Head, and the drumming was louder now, the keening more insistent and the wraiths of mist were like moving figures, moving in a wild dance and dispersing before her, making way for her but leading her on always to something that waited beyond, inside the circle of dancers, and then the last of them moved aside and she saw the dark, hunched figure, turning towards her out of the darkness.

The nearside wheels touched gravel and then something more substantial. The jolt sprang her out of whatever state she was in. She steered back on to the highway and then trod on the brake and stalled and sat in the sudden stillness and the silence – no more drums or chants – her hands gripping the wheel, shaken and angry with herself and with something or someone on the periphery of her mental vision. She felt that if she could only concentrate she would see it, but she was too frightened.

Then, through the mist, she saw the dark gap in the forest that was the road that led down to the cannery and the cove and the headland where her sister had died. And in the same instant she became aware of a movement behind her and turned to see Freya sit up, awake and alert, staring out of the window. She put her hands up to the glass, like an animal trapped in a cage.

'Mummy?' she said.

'It's all right, pet.'

Using the Scottish endearment like a comfort to keep out the cold – but scared, now, reaching for the ignition.

But Freya was already fumbling with the lock on the door.

'Freya.' Jessica spoke more sharply, turning in alarm, freeing her seat restraint, not knowing if the child lock was on, not wanting to drive off until she was sure it was, and then Freya had the door open and was out, running blindly across the road and into the mist.

Freya was a good runner but so was Jessica. She had run for her college, the 100-metre sprint, and she could run the pants off Freya with a head start and had done, many a day. But not today. She was afraid to let herself go in case she ran straight off the road and into a tree, and after a hundred yards or so she knew she had lost her. She paused, holding her ribs and fighting to still her breathing, listening for the sound of feet slapping on the wet surface of the road or blundering through the trees. There was nothing, only the silence of the forest. She called her again and again, her voice muffled by the fog. She felt tiny droplets falling silently from the trees, cold as ice on her face. She lost all sense of time. She might have stood there for less than a minute or an hour.

She heard the sound of a car coming down the track towards her and then the headlights were tearing a ragged hole in the mist.

The car stopped a few yards in front of her and she was pinned in the cold crossfire of the lights, hearing as if from a different world the mechanic alien clunk of the car door, the voice out of the void beyond calling her name, calling *her* name, and then the light had a hard black nucleus, an amoeba form which elongated, grew arms and legs and was standing in front of her, gripping her shoulders, gently shaking her, worming into her world. Calhoun.

It didn't occur to her to ask what he was doing here.

She told him what had happened.

He said: 'I didn't see her on the road so she must be in the trees.'

She had worked this out for herself and it didn't make her feel any better.

'She could be anywhere.' She heard the panic in her voice.

'She won't get very far through the trees, not at night.'

He fetched a flashlight from the car and they ran down opposite sides of the road, keeping to the edges and stopping every few seconds to probe the black silence and listen for the beat of its heart, the breathing of it. Jessica could barely see the hand in front of her face but she could sense the forest all around her, like some monstrous being, dank and dripping, and smell it, the sweet scent of the pine in the liquid air and the colder, sourer smell it masked, the breath of atrophy. And Freya lost in it, swallowed by it.

'She can't have come this far . . .' she began but was checked by his urgent *shush* as he turned, panning the light to the opposite side of the road, then holding it steady, spraying the wisps of fog that hung like breath in the dark throat of the forest.

And then Jessica heard it, too, though afterwards she would not be sure if it was a grunt or a sob.

'Stay here,' he said, 'in case she comes back on the road.'

And then he was gone, a diffused beam of light marking his progress through the trees until the mist closed around it and with the renewed darkness came the fear again, not the fear of losing Freya, but the less tangible, less rational fear that had gripped her in the car.

Then she heard a scream and a shout and Calhoun's voice calling her, more urgently, now, needing her, and she went in after him. Stumbling forward, arms outstretched, groping blindly through the trees like a child playing blind man's buff in a room full of giants.

She saw the light first, shining directly upwards into the branches of the trees – and then the face.

He was holding her from behind and the light directly under her chin made a harsh sculpture of her features, an angry, spitting goblin face twisted with rage and with fear, and the tortured mouth, shrieking at the trees.

And the trees now shocked into a real silence, shocked and still.

'It's all right, it's all right.' Jessica took her, feeling the tension in the thin arms, the panic and the anger threading, trembling, through her fingers.

'It's all right.'

Knowing it was not.

Calhoun carried her back to the car and Jessica stumbled along beside him, holding the flashlight with one hand and a part of Freya with the other – her wrist, her arm, even her ankle – stroking rather than holding, but feeling the wildness in her, knowing that if they were to let her go she would be off into the forest again and the fog. But when they got her into the car and fixed the seat belt around her, she drew up her legs and pushed her knuckle into her mouth, like a foetus wrapped around the umbilical cord, and began to whimper, as if they'd finally forced her into the inescapable trap of their world and she could no longer fight free of it.

Then Jessica heard the first words that made sense – or at least that were not part of an incoherent jabber – for in truth, they made no sense at all.

'Burning,' she said. 'It's all burning. They're burning all the children.'

Freya stayed in Calhoun's car for the drive into Bridport, while Jessica followed behind. When they pulled up outside the Old

Barrack House, he carried her in, asleep in his arms, and up the stairs to her bedroom, laying her gently down on her own bed. Her hands were stained with moss and lichen and she smelled of the forest but, astonishingly, she did not appear to have a scratch on her. Calhoun took her hands one by one, inspecting the palms and nails as if for dirt, and then looked into her face with a puzzled expression on his own as if he was looking for something specific but could not find it, and then he sighed and stroked her hair back from her forehead and said he would wait for Jessica downstairs.

When he'd gone Jessica cleaned her up a little with a warm sponge, stripped off her clothes and pulled a clean night-dress over her head, twisting and shoving the now pliable, if awkward, arms into the starch-washed sleeves. She mumbled once or twice, in a complaining tone, but did not wake.

Then, when Jessica finally left her, curled snugly into her bed, as if she'd stayed up too long watching television, she murmured a sleepy but clear, 'Night night.'

Jessica found Calhoun in the guest room, looking out of the window to where the cabins were, though he could not have seen them in the dark.

He turned when she came in and she gave him a small shrug that was half apologetic, half imploring and he nodded, watching her carefully. Then, tentatively, as if afraid to intrude into an area that was out of bounds to him, he said: 'I think you could use some professional help on this. There's a team of counsellors at the health centre in Bridport. Maybe if you . . .'

'But what can they tell me that I don't already know? She's suffering from post-traumatic stress. Her mother's just been killed by . . .' She felt she was going to lose it then. She hung on, fighting the tears. If he'd said something, moved towards her, they might have come, but he just stood there with his hands on his hips studying the painted wooden floor. Like a carpenter, she thought, working out an estimate.

'How long have we got to stay here?' she said. It sounded like she'd been running and had no breath to speak.

'You can go whenever you like.'

'Without my sister?' He said nothing but frowned, still looking at the floor. Smoky blue, it was, Shaker blue. The pictures on the walls were all of ships under full sail. She felt the floor move as if the house had suddenly tugged at its moorings. Perhaps it was the noise from the bar, the music from the bar, transmitted through the floorboards, loud and raw and raucous.

'It's been three weeks,' she said, 'and you still don't know how she died.'

'The medical evidence is confusing.' Still frowning, the carpenter, faced with a knotty problem. Then he looked at her and said, 'I'm sorry. I know.' And there was an expression now in his eyes, a pained helplessness that made her sorry, too. Sorry for thinking badly of him, for being accusatory, for thinking he had no feeling. 'I'll speak to the ME tomorrow, I'll try to get some . . . decision.'

'I need to bury her,' she said.

She wanted him to hold her then, hug her, but when he spoke it was in a different voice, his detective's voice, and his look was sharp, interrogative.

'Why did you stop – where you did?'

She sat down and thought about it but the only words that came to mind were disturbingly like the ones Maddie would have used.

Something *made* me, Maddie would have said.

It was like I just had to do it.

After some minor or major disaster, some new crisis in her life.

And Jessica so impatient, so angry with her.

'I don't know,' she said. 'I just – stopped. For a moment, that's all, I didn't mean to go . . . anywhere. But Freya . . . I thought she was asleep.'

She could hear the noise from the bar, distantly, through the closed door, the other world.

'What was it she said? Something about burning.'

'I don't know. It didn't make sense.'

Then he said: 'Why were you at the Graham house?'

She looked at him in surprise, alerted by a different tone – the tentative tone again, as if he was uncertain of his right to ask the question and was braced for the challenge to his authority, the rebuttal.

'Oh, because Freya wanted to say goodbye, that's all.'

That's all. She sounded anxious to reassure him. But of what?
'Goodbye?'

'Yes, he's leaving tomorrow. That is, he's taking his boat down the coast to somewhere . . . some place he leaves it for the winter. To winter moorings,' she said, more confidently, recalling the expression he had used. 'We didn't know if we'd be here when he came back and so Freya . . . wanted to say goodbye,' she repeated it, lamely, hearing the embarrassment in her voice. Remembering the embarrassment she had felt when she had seen him there, when *he* had seen *her*.

He nodded but, she thought, without understanding.

'Well, then,' he said. 'I'll be on my way.'

She did not register the awkward leave-taking and he was almost through the door when she stood up and moved towards him.

'Thank you for tonight.'

She reached out and touched his arm just above the elbow – the first time they had touched, and it felt like when she was a convent girl and had inadvertently touched one of the young priests, one of those who came to prepare them for confirmation – just to get his attention, to say something that had suddenly occurred to her.

Or was it more deliberate – more needy than that?

Either way, she felt the same tension, saw the same stiffening in his face, and drew back at once, mortified.

'What for?' he said.

'Well, just . . . just for being there and . . . and finding her.'

'No problem,' he said.

When he'd gone she stared at the closed door for a while, dealing with her embarrassment and wondering at her lack of perception, that she had entirely misread his interest in her. It was surprisingly depressing.

VIII

He feels like the ball in a pinball machine. Ping, bouncing off the electric contact, lighting up an image in his brain and then, before he can absorb it, deal with it . . . another and another . . . Irreconcilable images, flash frames, each with its accompanying shock of emotion – angst, guilt, excitement, self-loathing . . .

To meet the object of desire with your loins throbbing from sex with another, the smell of her on your hands . . . and the thought of *her* in your brain. Confused, mind-fucked.

Jessica. The first time she touched him, the arms reaching around him, the feel of her hair against his cheek. The warm, good feeling there should have been – and then the adrenalin shock . . . the sudden image like the lewd illustration on the electric panel, the naked body riding, riding, arch-backed and the heavy breasts pale in the light, so pale, the mouth and that livid scar, livid in the light, and the curve of her throat in the light, the yellow tungsten light of the gutting room . . .

The smell of fish.

He stood in the dim hallway between doors – the door he'd just closed, the door to the bar, the door to the street – and finally walked out into the fog.

He was a man who loved the idea of women, the fantasy of women, but the reality was sometimes a worry to him.

He loved to meet the eyes of a lovely woman across a room or in a train, in some public place, and see something there that aroused him – his curiosity, rather than his sexual appetite. It seemed to him that it was easier, far easier, to satisfy the appetite than the curiosity.

Have you eaten? Do you want to go into Dover for some supper?

It sounded so pathetic now – so *green* – especially in the light of her rejection, but he had meant it. He would have liked to have taken her to eat. He would have liked to satisfy his curiosity.

Sometimes, in the looks he got back, he would see something that made him smile, like making contact with aliens and finding them friendly. But all too often, when you moved to the next stage, or the one after that, there was a barrier of misunderstanding. Men and women, to have a successful relationship, need a translator. Instead, they have to make do with a phrase book, or sign language. It is so easy to get it wrong.

He met her at a party in Boston given by one of the people he'd met in the navy. One of the rich people. She was standing alone with her back against the wall and staring into a glass of wine as if there was a message in it, as if this was what you did at parties, read messages in glasses of wine.

She saw him looking at her and smiled.

It was not the most encouraging of smiles. It was more a kind of rueful grin, the kind you give someone who notices you standing alone at a party, apparently neglected and definitely bored. She wore a blue dress, a simple blue dress with buttons down the front, and canvas shoes laced up her ankles, and he wondered how anyone so beautiful could possibly be standing alone.

He'd just started to move towards her when an old girlfriend came up to him and introduced him to some man she had in tow. Ben Brandon. A lawyer he'd met once or twice in court – smoothly good-looking, impeccably dressed. He started talking to Calhoun about some big case that had just started and Calhoun half listened, his eyes straying over to the woman in the blue dress. Brandon stopped talking for a moment and looked in the same direction and jerked his head – just jerked his head, didn't say a word – and the woman came over and he said, 'This is Gemma, my wife.'

Afterwards, he always thought it was important that he'd seen her *before* he met Ben, that he'd fallen in love with her before he knew she was Ben's wife. But he knew, really, that this was as much a cheat as the rest of it.

It was Ben who made them friends, Ben who put the necessary effort into it from the start. At first it was the odd game of tennis or squash, and afterwards they'd have a few beers. Then Calhoun was going away with them for the weekend. Ben seemed to want his approval. For some reason the rich often did, the ones Calhoun was drawn to, anyway. And Calhoun, of course, had always been fatally attracted to the rich and the beautiful, ever since he'd met Innis Graham on the beach in Russell County.

Ben was a successful lawyer with political ambitions, and there was money in the family. Money in Gemma's family, too. Calhoun wasn't in love with her any more, of course. Ben was his friend and she was his friend's wife and that was that. They had two young children, Lucy, who was five and Jack, who was four.

One winter they all went ski-ing together, Ben's crowd, the special people he had collected and felt at ease among.

Calhoun was the worst skier in the party. He kept on getting his skis crossed. One day he took a bad fall on a steep slope and his skis came off and he started to slide. He relaxed and let himself go and hoped he'd hit something soft and what he hit was Gemma. She'd seen him sliding and skied across the slope to head him off. It was the first real physical contact they'd had.

By the time they'd sorted themselves out and found Calhoun's skis in the snow they seemed to be alone on the mountain. Visibility was down to a few yards and it was bitterly cold. They skied on, hoping to catch up with the others, but there was no sign of them.

It was Gemma who suggested they stop for a drink. It took two vino caldos to get some warmth back into them, and halfway through the third she told him Ben was having an affair with a secretary in his office.

'He thinks I don't know about it,' she said, 'but I do.'

Calhoun shook his head and said he just couldn't believe it.

'Really?' she said. 'So he hasn't told you?'

'God, no,' he said.

'Liar,' she said.

Ben had told him weeks ago after they'd been playing squash. He was besotted, he said. Calhoun was mystified. She was pretty enough – small and dark and plump – but not a patch on Gemma. Fantastic fuck, Ben said. And then he said that Gemma was just a bit too perfect for him. Great mother, great looker, but she didn't really turn him on. He liked to wallow in it, he said, and Gemma wasn't too keen on wallowing, wasn't that keen on sex, at all.

Calhoun had been thinking about this ever since, particularly the part about Gemma and sex.

He asked Gemma if she'd talked to Ben about it. She said she hadn't. She didn't see the point.

'What I should do,' she said, 'is have an affair.'

She was looking straight at him when she said it and after a moment he looked away, but not soon enough.

'Have I embarrassed you?' she said, when they were leaving. He shook his head, but outside the door she slipped on the ice and grabbed his arm and suddenly they were kissing. She held on to him for a moment, her head pressed into his shoulder. He might even have patted her on the back, pretending it was a brotherly kiss, but it didn't fool either of them.

He was soaking in the bath back in his room when he heard the outer door open and then she was standing there, still in her ski-suit.

'Do you want a towel?' she said. 'Or shall I get in with you?'

She was naked under the ski-suit. She had gone back to her room while Ben was getting drunk in the bar with the rest of them, and the two kids were with the nanny in the pool, and she'd taken off her clothes and put the ski-suit back on and walked along the corridor to his room in her bare feet. The thought of her doing this excited him at least as much as the sight of her body when she unzipped it.

When they made love she dug her nails into his scalp as if she was fighting him and he was later to think this of her: not that she wasn't that keen on sex, as Ben had said, but that she was afraid of it, afraid of letting herself go, as if it displayed a vulnerability that could be dangerous to her, like love itself.

But this was much later. At the time he was too confused about his own feelings to think much about hers at all. He thought it was probably a one-off and that afterwards it would be as if it had never happened, except that they'd be even more wary and awkward with each other, and riddled with guilt. But a couple of days after their return to Boston she phoned him and they met for lunch on his day off and then went back to his apartment. This became the ritual. First lunch, then sex, usually when he had a day off so they didn't have to rush things.

'I love you,' he told her, without caution or inhibition, and she would smile a little sadly and say nothing. She was afraid of believing him.

'You're a games player,' she told him once.

They were having lunch as usual and he'd said he would like to take her out to dinner for a change, to see what she looked like by candlelight.

But he didn't think he was playing games. He thought he just wanted to enjoy her. He wanted more than love in the afternoon.

In the whole of their loving they spent just one whole night together.

In the morning he woke before her and propped his head on his hand and watched the light on her hair until she opened her eyes and saw him. She looked surprised.

She had a problem with pleasure. He never saw her enjoying her food. This bothered him. He always associated the pleasure of eating with the pleasure of sex.

He kept on remembering what Ben had said about her.

The lunch before was a necessary part of the ritual for him. It annoyed him when she just picked at her food. Often she would just order a salad. He liked it even less when one day she suggested skipping the lunch entirely and coming straight round to his apartment for the sex. In the morning he shopped for an enormous picnic they would eat on the floor. They made love on the floor, too, and it was going fine when she said, 'Don't you dare come yet.'

It was what he called a cockcrinkler, but he forgave her. Unhappily his cock didn't. It went into an instant and prolonged sulk. 'I'm sorry,' he said, when this became apparent. 'I don't know what's wrong.' She didn't seem to mind. She just gave him a lazy smile and put on his dressing-gown. Calhoun decided to be philosophical. They had the whole afternoon before them. Also, he was hungry.

'Let's eat,' he said.

He laid out the picnic on the floor. Food from the Italian deli two doors down from his apartment. Cold chicken and olives, sun-dried tomatoes, anchovies in a mint sauce, bread rolls and several different cheeses, a bottle of wine . . . He wanted her to have a choice. She looked faint. 'My God,' she said. She nibbled at a bit of bread and cheese with her wine.

This depressed him more than the failed fuck.

He wanted to see her spread herself in a sensuous enjoyment of life, of sex, food, anything. He wanted to see her squat naked on the floor and stuff herself full of chicken and olives and belch like a peasant. But he loved her because she was not a peasant.

He took such pleasure in her appearance. Once she came to lunch wearing a red dress and a red hat. One of her friends had just had her baby christened. 'You wore that at a *christening*?' he said. He wanted her to wear it while they were fucking so he could take the dress off while she was sitting on him and just be wearing the hat. Annoyingly, she wouldn't play. He thought about her all week wearing the red dress and the red hat in many different situations and places and always ending up fucking in them.

He thought about her most of the time.

'I'd like to come back home to you,' he said.

'You only say that because you know you don't have to every day,' she told him.

He never asked her about her feelings for Ben, but once she told him he'd made love to her wearing a T-shirt of Calhoun's that had somehow found its way into his clothes drawer.

Calhoun was shocked.

'Deliberately?' he said.

She laughed.

'Not deliberately, you fool. He just happened to be wearing it at the time, but it was very strange for me – him wearing your T-shirt while we were making love.'

It was very strange for Calhoun, too, but what really disturbed him was the idea of her *telling* him about it. One of Ben's friends had told Calhoun she was a cockteaser. This was not a man he had ever liked and he liked him even less after this. But now he began to suspect that it was she who was playing games with him – and with Ben. Maybe the whole thing was just a way of getting back at her adulterous husband, cuckolding him with his best friend, destroying their friendship. And maybe he told her he loved her because it was the only possible justification for what they were doing.

He knew they weren't going anywhere. There was no question of her leaving Ben, they never even talked about it. All she ever said was that she didn't *belong* to him, that she was not his property.

But she liked being a married woman, even married to an adulterer. She had her own lover now, so it was all right, she had squared that, she was content with the arrangement. Arrangements were important to her. She was a woman who enjoyed the appearance of things. If he arrived in the restaurant later than she, as he often did, he would find her looking through a magazine on interiors or gardens. She loved the colour and texture of tasteful objects. He would see her trailing her hand along the back of a chair, or stroking the polished wood of a table, feeling the quality of a tablecloth, or sliding her finger and thumb along the leaf of a potted plant. She took pleasure in the names of which things were made. Maple, oak, pear . . . calico. The way she used the words made him think of a stately galleon sailing home with a rich cargo.

She moved in a different world from him. She had a different set of values.

His mother had often used this phrase – usually disparagingly – and although its general *application* was known to him he had never really considered its meaning. If he'd been asked to define it, he would probably have said it meant that someone valued possessions, for instance, more than friendship, success more than loyalty. With Gemma though, he saw that it meant an entirely different set of moral standards, a different way of judging things. To her a sense of order meant that everything was in its right place, he thought. To him it was a sense of right and wrong.

What he was doing offended his sense of order, even if it did not stop him.

He thought it was different for her, but he was wrong.

One day they were supposed to be meeting for lunch and she didn't turn up. He waited for her to phone him but she never did. He found out about it from one of Ben's friends at the squash club.

They'd been coming back from a weekend's ski-ing and Ben had pulled out at an intersection and hit a truck. He said later that he was distracted because he and his wife were having a row. The two children were in the back and bore the brunt of it. Lucy died in hospital two days later.

Calhoun saw Gemma once more at the funeral, but they didn't speak. They never spoke again. They moved away from Boston. He heard that Gemma wanted to. He heard they lived in Italy for a while. That was why he was so interested in Rome.

His drowning life sinks before him as he haunts the misted harbour, hearing his muffled footsteps on the wet duckboards and the softer tread of the unseen sea. Lights swimming in the waterlogged air and the boats gently nuzzling at their moorings like horses in a darkened stable. From far out in the bay the lonely boom of a passing ship. He thinks of the fishermen who first came here from Normandy and Spain, Bristol and La Rochelle, the bearded bear-men on their moving islands, who worked the cod banks, far from home off the coast of *Una-ma'kik*, the Land of Fog.

And finally, this giving him little comfort, he returns to the inn, where the ghosts are not so near, or will be lost in the crowd.

The bar is packed with the men off the dragger fleet – and women, too, in the regulation sweaters and jeans but less jewellery in their ears. Cajun music is pulsing out of the speakers, several couples dancing the two-step among the tables and half the room clapping and stamping and whistling them on. The other half shouting to be heard.

A fug of smoke as dense as the fog outside. Sweating, bearded faces, red mouths wet with drink.

'Qu'est que c'est qui sent le moule, eh maman?
Ton petit père veux le savoir.'

Sex and fish. Everything is sex and fish. The smell of it on his hands, up his nose. Sex and fish and something more chemical that reminds him of death.

'Ah, monsieur le detective. Bienvenue. Que buvez-vous?'

Little Raymond, in French mode, flamboyant and absurd in

starched white shirt with a red bow-tie, knee-length brown shorts and black ankle-socks with sandals. Sitting on the customers' side of the bar as if he is the proprietor, with three or four of his cronies from the local art establishment, crop-haired and tattooed in their sleeveless vests.

There are two women behind the bar and two more working the tables. No Hannah. Probably in the kitchen, sending forth the bowls of steaming gumbo. The waitresses snaking their slim hips between the men's shoulders.

That moment when he'd yanked the overalls down over her hips and the little gasp of rude pleasure. The shock of her sudden nakedness. The stomach-lurching swoop of the adrenalin ride. The rock-and-roller-coaster ride.

And Jessica.

Thank you for tonight.

Her hair smelled of flowers and pine needles after rain.

The way she had reached out to touch him, like a schoolgirl seeking reassurance. The face turned up to his with a slightly puzzled frown. He might have kissed her.

He wonders if she'll come through from the back room but he thinks not. It is too crowded, too noisy, and she will want to listen for any sounds of distress from Freya.

'You'll soon be the biggest employer in Bridport.' Calhoun shouting above the noise of the music and Raymond leaning his face forward. The sweet, acrid bite of his after-shave, the pressure of his plump hand on Calhoun's arm.

'You may not have noticed, dear heart, but there is not a lot of competition.

'And there'll be a lot fucking less when these sons of bitches leave town.' Thrown over the shoulder of a local fisherman, one of a surly huddle clinging to the bar like grimy sea-molluscs, resisting the unwelcome tide of newcomers with grim resolve, hanging on but helpless to turn it back. They hate this annual invasion of the scallop snatchers, the dragger fleet, ripping up their seabed with their great iron maws.

'Everything that's down there they drag it up, boy. It's under the legal limit you think they throw it back in? Fuck they do.'

'. . . One hundred an' fifty-seven draggers this year. Coves round here too small for that size of fleet.'

'You get a local man he throws them back in, gives them a chance for next season. Them offshore boats they take what they can to make the trip. We run out of scallops this place is fucked more'n it is already.'

Calhoun has heard it before but Raymond listens as if for the first time, while the girls at bar and tables rake in the dollars and his head moves from side to side with the music.

'Sent la mer ou l'oeuf pourri
Cette même chose me rend heureux, cherie'

And Calhoun's crotch itching like there's some kind of a fungus down there, activated by the warmth. His buttocks sore from the rough weave of the carpet in the gutting room. He needs to shower, failing which, a visit to the bathroom to splash a little water around. He half considers it but there is a constant stream of custom through the door . . .

And now here is someone else batting his ear with beery breath. A great looming presence with greasy black hair down to his shoulders and a face like a slab of red granite.

'Hello, Henry. How's hunting?'

Hunting is shit. Henry has been harvesting deer since the start of the season and shot himself one buck. Forest is full of damn fools falling over themselves to shoot something that ain't there.

'You mean the bear?'

Henry's eyes are glazed – from booze rather than the crossed sights of a rifle, Calhoun reckons, but a leery look comes into them now that is almost intelligent.

'They don't find that bear in no damn forest.'

Complacent, shuffling his mental pack of ghost stories, ready for the next deal, but Calhoun has had enough of games, enough of spirits. He wants something more substantial, more real.

'So where do they find it, Henry? The reservation?'

A wary, hunted look then from under the thicket of brow but something else too. A warning?

'You been down there, you speak to someone?'

'I spoke a little to Frankie Lecoute.'

A face like the beer is off.

206

'Frankie Lecoute don't know nothing. What he does know he ain't going to tell you.'

'No? Why's that, Henry?'

But Henry ain't going to tell him neither, hunched over the bar with his bottle of Bud in one massive paw. Brer Bear he ain't saying nuthin'.

'Come on, Henry, what's the big secret that Frankie Lecoute isn't going to tell me?'

A look then almost of anger.

'OK, because there's things happen no one going to believe. Think you still living in the forest, dancing round the totem pole. Only thing is . . .' Drilling at his thick log of a forehead with a hooked beak of a forefinger '. . . up here, some of them still is. This old woman, she don't like the girl her boy's running around with she takes some feathers, wraps them up in a little bundle and dips them in some tar. The girl tells everyone her whole body weighed down. She gets so she can't get out of bed, she so heavy, she got the sweats, the fevers, the doctors they can't do nothing for her . . . I seen this with my own eyes.'

Feathers, tar, fevers . . . ? Calhoun frowning his confusion.

'So what's that got to do with the bear?'

'I'm just telling you what kind of thing can happen – you don't see it you don't believe.'

'So who's the old woman?'

'There's no old woman, I'm just telling you . . .'

'I thought you might of meant the Selmo woman.'

The black olive eyes sliding away, the shutters slamming down. Calhoun can see his face in the big mirror behind the bar, but it's giving nothing away.

'You know the Selmos?' he prompts, but Henry shakes his head, takes a pull on his beer.

Calhoun waiting, then finally with a shrug: 'OK, Henry, I'll see you around.'

But then Henry turns half towards him along the bar, his face contorted in some private struggle, in the eyes an appeal.

'Lookit, place like this you can say things you might be sorry about later, when you're in the forest. You know what I'm saying?'

Calhoun nods but isn't sure if he means the forest outside or the forest in his head.

He has to get out of this place, the fug of smoke and bodies, the noise, the wild conviviality only impressing him with his own loneliness.

Outside the shock of the night air, a chill compress on his chest, tightening, and the mist all but dissipated, the moisture turned to ice, too heavy for the air to hold, forming a thin frost on road and roofs.

The harbour as jammed full of boats as the café is of people. You could step from deck to deck from shore to harbour arm. But Calhoun goes the long way, walking carefully for the rime on the wooden slats, letting the cold punish him, freeze the over-active machinery of his brain – and other parts. He stands at the end of the harbour looking out over the sea. There is still a haze of fog in the beam of the lighthouse on Pulpit Rock, but the night is clear enough to see the islands out in the bay and the red glow in the sky above Kitehawk Head.

It takes him a moment longer to realise what this is.

IX

By the time Calhoun arrived, the whole building was ablaze, a vast burning lung, drawing oxygen from the surrounding air and breathing it out as flame, a furnace. As soon as he opened the car door he heard its consuming roar, the crash of timbers, felt the heat.

The fire officers from Dover were there, but they'd given up trying to save the old cannery, if they'd even bothered to start, and they were aiming their hoses at the forest. He saw the tops of the trees bending towards the fire, then thrown back by the water. More trucks arrived, from over the border. They had the same enemy and it knew no frontiers. The sky was full of sparks. Calhoun saw them settling in a tree like a flock of fiery locusts.

He stumbled around the edge of the heat, shielding his face with his hands, looking for Kate.

He found Jarvis and the two students standing outside the camper, the bonfire glow on their faces. Jarvis saw him at the same time and ran towards him, his hands reaching up like claws, gripping his jacket, shouting: 'Is she with you?'

'With me?' Calhoun stared at him in total incomprehension. 'Why should she be . . .'

Then he turned back to the flames and started to run. He ran from one group to another until he found the fire chief from Dover. The man looked at him as if he was crazy.

'You want us to go in there? You think anyone could live in that?'

Calhoun watched the roof fall in. The flames rose up to the sky and smoke blacked out the stars. There were things burning on the sea.

He walked out along the headland, not knowing where he was going, just wanting to get away from the fire and the smell that was coming from it. And by the light of the flames he saw the skull.

It was fixed to a birch tree near where they had found the body of Madeleine Ross. A skull the shape of a large egg with four overlapping fangs at the end of the long jaw. And strange markings, like warpaint, daubed in blood between the black, empty sockets of its eyes.

He stayed there all night, sitting in one of the fire trucks, sometimes dozing. Just before dawn he went for a walk along the foreshore and watched the dirty grey light spreading in from over the sea, the colour of ashes. The air smelled of charred wood and something sharper, like tear gas, that caught in his throat and made his eyes itch. When he walked back up the cliff he saw the TV crews. They were filming the fire officers pumping water on the ruins, cooling them down. Then he saw another unit further along the headland filming the skull.

'You should have blocked the road,' Calhoun complained to Jensen, but he should have thought of it himself. They managed to clear them back just before they could film the body of Kate Wendicott being brought out from under a pile of debris that had fallen in from the roof.

They found her, the fire chief told him, from the body fat that had run out on to the concrete floor. Their boots had stuck to it.

IV. THE WAY BACK

I

When Freya woke in the morning it was clear to Jessica she was starting a cold.

'I think we'll keep you off school today.' Jessica sat on the edge of the bed and stroked Freya's hair back from the hot forehead. Jessica could remember when she had first held her, pushing her nose into the fine hair of the baby's scalp, a smell like fresh bread baked with meadow flowers.

'It's all that running around in the fog.' She watched Freya's face for a reaction.

'What fog?'

Jessica considered her carefully.

'Don't you remember anything about last night?'

She wasn't sure if it was wise to do this but she felt she had to know. Freya looked puzzled.

'We went to see Innis,' she said.

'And after that?'

'I can't remember. I think I fell asleep?' She was barely awake now, her face child-soft with sleep.

'You can't remember coming home?'

She shook her head, but Jessica thought she looked a bit frightened. She decided not to push it.

'I'll make you some hot lemon and honey,' she said.

Downstairs, she phoned the Medical Centre, and after some discussion with the receptionist and a lot of hanging on she was put through to one of the counsellors, a woman whose name sounded like Starlicker. Jessica told her about Freya's mother being killed and that she was having some disturbing nightmares. Ms Starlicker said this was only to be expected. How had her mother died, she asked? Jessica told her. She also told her about the incident last night. Another pause. Then, 'Maybe I could move things around a bit at the end of the morning.'

Jessica decided to put off telling Freya until the last minute, which just left the problem of what to do with her until then.

It was inevitable, she supposed, that Maddie's death should change the nature of their relationship. Being an aunt had been fine. It was like being a grown-up friend. She could give her treats, indulge her, be silly with her, be *honest* with her, up to a point. Being more like a mother was an altogether more tricky affair. She wondered, too, whether deep down she resented it, just as she had resented being responsible for Maddie all those years. She'd loved Maddie, but she didn't want to repeat their relationship with Freya.

As for the immediate problem, the easy thing would be to stick her in front of the TV for an hour or two, but the puritan in Jessica would not permit it. The child watched too much television. She should be out in the fresh air. Having a cold was irrelevant. If someone had a cold at Jessica's school the nuns made them wrap up warm and play hockey.

Hockey being out of the question, Jessica made her wear three layers under her coat and took her for a walk along the cliffs towards the harbour. It was not a popular decision but once they were out, Freya seemed resigned to it, if not precisely cheerful, and at least she stopped sniffing. It was another fine day, with a slight wind off the sea that brought with it a lingering smell of woodsmoke. The tide was in and the draggers were out, and as they both stood on the edge of the cliffs watching them plough their endless furrows a beautiful sail boat emerged from behind one of the islands in the bay, and Freya looked a little more animated and shouted that it was *Calliope*.

It was a moment before Jessica remembered that this was the name of Innis's boat. She would be on her way south to her winter moorings like a migrating bird. She looked like a bird – a white swan with her long neck stretched before her and her wings raised for flight. Watching her in the distance, growing smaller, Jessica saw another part of Maddie leaving. *Calliope* had been her last refuge, the last place she had found any human warmth and love, before she had gone out into the cold and whatever waited for her there.

She could be there now, on the deck, going south with Innis.

Jessica could well imagine her on such a boat and with such a man. Entirely at ease in such alien territory, in this exclusive fraternity of grown-up boys who raced around the world in the hardest way they could find and by the most difficult routes. But always with her secret smile, that hint of disdain, for Maddie had maintained an entirely vagabond approach to the perks of wealth and position. She had the scorn of the stray for the kept cat, though she didn't mind lapping up its cream from time to time. She would never turn down the offer of a free ride or a free lunch, but just so long as the people who were offering understood that it was *she* who was doing *them* the favour. She was the cat that walked alone.

But *Calliope* would appeal to the gypsy in her. It moved, it was not a house, it had style. It was seductive, like Innis himself, the irresistible eternal boy.

Jessica wondered if she would ever see him again. She thought probably not.

II

It was Stahlecker, not Starlicker – it said so on the door of her office. A woman probably not much older than Jessica, but with that look of somebody who has arrived where she is going and didn't want to be anywhere else. Jessica, with the sea still in her head, thought she looked *berthed* – at her winter moorings. Her brown hair was brushed firmly back from her forehead and tied at the neck so it would not be a nuisance, and she wore a blue cotton dress that did not veer dangerously from a uniform, a white cardigan thrown loosely over her shoulders in case there was a draught.

Jessica went in first, leaving Freya, sullen and resentful, with the receptionist.

She explained the family background. It sounded worse than she meant it to – worse, surely, than it was. Her father came over as cold and remote, a man who dumped his children in Dickensian boarding schools while he trotted the globe, and Maddie as a tart, a disturbed victim of her upbringing who got herself pregnant after a one-night stand and dragged her daughter from camp to camp, trailer to trailer, like a pair of homeless vagabonds.

Stahlecker made no comment until she had finished. Then she said: 'And you're worried about these nightmares?'

As if nightmares should be the least of her worries.

'It's the running off,' Jessica said. She hesitated, sensitive to ridicule – or, what was more likely, professional reassurance with that hint of the patronising. Then she said: 'I think she's convinced herself that she's changing into a bear.'

Jessica could not tell if this was a jolt or not. She remained berthed, gently nodding. After a moment she said: 'It's not so unusual for a child to identify with an animal. When I was a child I used to think I was Bagheera, the panther in *The Jungle Book*. I used to practise walking like a panther, growling, that kind of thing. I used to tell my mother: Lizzie's gone, I'm Panther.'

'I don't suppose a panther killed your mother,' Jessica said.

'No,' she said thoughtfully, as if that was a disappointment to her, or she couldn't be sure. Her voice when she resumed was more brisk. 'I suppose if she identified with a bear before the death of your sister, it could be an additional burden. Do you mind if I see her alone now?'

Jessica wasn't at all sure about Lizzie Stahlecker. She was half hoping Freya had seized the opportunity to run off again, but no, she was still sitting with her cross face in the reception room.

She marched past Jessica without looking at her and the door closed firmly behind her. Jessica felt shut out.

She couldn't sit still. She walked over to the window where there was a picture-postcard view of white clapboard houses and neat lawns leading down to the harbour, a white church with a white wooden steeple and a copper beech. It all looked so safe and secure and solid, as if nothing bad or untoward could ever happen in such a place. A few clouds – less white than they should have been – trailed a ragged hem into the distant sea and Jessica wondered about the storm Innis said was on the way. She felt she would welcome a storm, but instantly regretted the thought, thinking about him on the boat.

She read the notices on the board, not really taking them in, her mind on what was happening in the other room with Freya, reviewing what she herself had said and trying to gauge whether they had sounded hysterical or neurotic. After a morning when Freya had appeared perfectly normal, it was hard to imagine her any other way. Already the events of last night seemed like something Jessica had herself dreamed. But then she remembered the fog and the shapes in her own head and the panic.

After half-an-hour or so, Freya came out, and Stahlecker said she'd like to talk to Jessica again, alone.

'I understand she has not been able to see her mother since the accident,' she said.

Jessica pointed out that Freya's mother was hardly in a fit state to be seen by someone who had loved her.

'I appreciate that – and it's not what I'm suggesting – but it could make it that much harder for her to accept the fact of her death.'

Jessica said nothing.

'Have you talked to Freya about it?' Her tone was gentle, exuding sympathy and understanding, but Jessica took it as a criticism.

'I've tried to. She wasn't very responsive.'

'And have you talked to her at all about what is going to happen next?'

'Happen next?'

'To her mother. To her.'

'To her *mother*?' Jessica was confused. 'You mean – in the afterlife?'

'No, I didn't mean that, though it is something you might consider, but what I meant was the funeral – if there's going to be a funeral. And what will happen then – to Freya, I mean?'

'Well, it's been difficult – with the investigation going on – to think beyond that. I haven't been able to arrange anything definite. But Freya knows we're going back to England.'

'But not what will happen after that. Where she'll live, or anything?'

'Did she say that to you?' Jessica wished she did not sound so defensive.

'I'm afraid anything she said to me must remain confidential – but she's bound to be apprehensive, don't you think, as well as grieved? She'll be anxious about the future and very insecure.' She looked down at what were presumably notes – things Freya had told her? 'Will you be looking after her yourself, when you get back to England?'

'I don't know. There was no will. I'm not her legal guardian. I imagine the courts will be involved.'

'Can I ask – do you want to look after her?'

'Yes.' She said it without thinking but could she be sure? Did she really want the responsibility? 'Do you think Freya's worried about this?' she asked.

'I think any little girl would be, don't you?'

Jessica began to have more respect for Lizzie Stahlecker, and correspondingly less for herself.

'I know it must be terribly difficult for you, too. At a time of grieving. To make any kind of decision, to think about the future.'

'I can only think about Maddie,' Jessica said. 'I need to . . .' She couldn't finish. She was close to tears.

'I know.'

'I will talk to her. I'll try to . . . reassure her.'

'I think you should. Things are bound to be very difficult for a while, and I think you have to expect the nightmares to continue for quite some time. In the circumstances, I think anyone would have nightmares. She does know how her mother died.'

'And the running away?'

'I can't make any authoritative statement about that, not after such a short interview, but have you considered she might possibly have been looking for her mother?'

'It did occur to me, yes. I'd be less concerned about it, if it wasn't for this . . . obsession with bears.'

'Well, it is certainly a cause for concern, and I would say she would probably benefit from seeing someone when you get back to England. Possibly considering a course of therapy.'

'And in the meantime?'

'In the meantime, keep a close eye on her, of course. You don't want her running off into the forest again. But, if you do get this fantasy of the animal, don't be too alarmed by it, and don't deny it. Try to go along with it. If she's given space to express her fantasies they'll disappear over time, but don't deny them, don't deny her sense of reality. If you do, or try to make *her* deny it, it could turn out more damaging in the long term.'

They walked back to the Old Barrack House in a bleak silence. The clouds had moved in closer over Bridport and she felt the first specks of rain on her cheek.

'I'm sorry,' Jessica said eventually. 'I should have discussed it with you first.'

Nothing.

She stopped walking and gently restrained Freya by the shoulder. Freya stared straight ahead, still not looking at her.

'Freya, I was worried and I didn't know what else to do. I thought it might help, that's all, if you had someone you could talk to that you didn't know so well.'

Freya gave a small, dismissive shrug.

'But I should have asked you first, you're right.'

Was this the future? A one-sided dialogue with a closed door.

'Let's make a deal. In future, I will always ask you what you want to do, OK, even if we don't agree on it?'

'OK.' The lips scarcely departing from the horizontal, but OK was something.

'So.' They had the whole afternoon before them. A whole afternoon in Bridport, Maine, in November with rain on the way. 'What do you want to do now?'

An ice-cream in the Harbor Watch Café, another turn round the cliffs, even watch television, the possibilities were endless.

'Go and see Tante Yvette,' said Freya.

Her look was an open challenge.

'All right,' said Jessica. *Don't deny her*. Great. 'All right, we'll go and see Tante Yvette.'

III

The rain came before they left Bridport, lashing across the car windscreen from the sea, and the islands out in the bay were lost in a haze of cloud.

'I hope Innis will be OK,' said Freya, suddenly. They were the first words she had spoken for a while, the first that did not sound sulky or defiant.

Jessica glanced sideways at her as she drove.

'He seems to know what he's doing. He must have been in worse weather than this in his time. You like Innis, don't you?'

'He's all right.'

'Will you miss him then, when we go back to England?'

'A bit.' But a shrug in her voice.

'What about your friends at school?'

She did not ask if she would miss 'Tante' Yvette.

'Not really.'

Why did she go there, then, every day, when she didn't have to? To avoid spending much time with Jessica? Or was it something else, her way of trying to be normal? Jessica could at least understand that.

She took her hand off the wheel and gave her leg a reassuring squeeze.

You'll like Oxford, she almost said, but something held her back. It was partly the uncertainty over what would happen, partly the fear of commitment. She had not even begun to think about the practical problems of having Freya stay with her. Where they would live, where she would go to school. How she would cope for money.

The idea of being a single mother on a low income – of being like Maddie.

They drove on in a strained silence as they approached the turn-off for Kitehawk Head. There were vehicles pulled up on both sides of the highway, and she saw the TV scanners among them, and the impressive initials blazoned across the bodywork of the trucks – and the police patrol car from Bridport drawn up across the turn-off itself. She wondered what was going on down there, if it was something to do with Maddie, if they had maybe found the killer.

She pulled across the highway and wound her window down to ask one of the officers. The rain blew in her face.

'Keep moving, please,' he said. 'There's been a fire.'

Jessica kept moving.

Perhaps it was a forest fire. But there was no smoke in the air, and surely the trees were too wet to go up in flames. She remembered the dank, dripping silence of last night and glanced briefly at Freya, but she seemed to be in a world of her own.

The reservation looked bleaker than ever in the rain.

Jessica cruised between the uniform cabins, a little verse running through her head:

> I do not like thee, Dr Fell
> The reason why I cannot tell
> But I do not like thee, Dr Fell.

It was from a book of nursery rhymes she had read as a child, and she remembered the picture of the doctor all in black with his black doctor's bag, like a large rook arriving at the home of the afflicted, his beady eyes reading the measure of their days. And the two little girls waiting for him at the gate of the thatch-roofed cottage with its curtained rooms. She could remember it all so clearly, and the fear it had struck into her at the time, the thought of this dread visitor, death's courier. But it was the first time it had entered her mind since and could only have been suggested now, trawled up from her subconscious, by the thought of Yvette Selmo.

There was something about the woman that activated all of Jessica's defences. Something *practised* in the way she looked at her through those little granny glasses, the eyes that seemed to stare deep into her soul, as if she read things there that Jessica had spent a lifetime keeping secret, even from herself.

But was it *fear*? Her ego insisted on a prompt rejection. She

222

was not *afraid* of the woman; she thought her ridiculous, a poser, a sham.

But not a shaman?

She was, of course, a witch. *Shaman, boheen, ginap, jongleur,* whatever the local name for it. This was a less startling conclusion for Jessica than it might have been for someone without her academic background. In the course of her research Jessica had met a fair number of witches, and they all had one thing in common: they were all, to a varying degree, control freaks.

The cleverest were adept at divining vulnerability in others and using it against them. Less accomplished practitioners used a combination of threats and potions. Often, it was a fairly harmless dominance. No worse, at least, than that wielded by more conventional leaders of society. But there was a narrow dividing line between the control freak and the sociopath. Jessica suspected that, if crossed, Yvette Selmo could be vicious in her retribution.

She was sure that she and Maddie had quarrelled, perhaps over her nephew Joe, perhaps even over Freya. But it was one thing to believe her capable of causing harm, quite another to imagine how she could have contrived such a death.

Jessica has studied cases where humans have been drugged or hypnotised to perform ritual slayings in the guise of an animal. She has never heard of a case where an animal itself has been the means of retribution.

But it is not out of the question.

There is a colder part of Jessica that stands aside from these speculations with a critical, even incredulous, reserve and considers them a significant step in her decline from grief-driven obsession to psychosis. She has caught a fatal dose of the paranoia that afflicted the whiskey priest.

This more sceptical side of her nature reasserts itself as she approaches the Selmo house and braces herself for her interview with the shaman, the witch queen of Nagwind Point. But mockery is a thin shield for her apprehension.

The witch is at home. If she is surprised to see them, she hides it well. She hugs Freya, smiles at Jessica, invites them in. She makes coffee.

And Jessica makes conversation.

Drawing deep on her convent school training, she talks of the weather today, the weather yesterday, the weather for most of the time she has been here and the differences generally between the weather in England in autumn and the weather in Maine in fall. It is the kind of thing that, once she gets a roll on, she can keep up for as long as it takes to drink two cups of tea and eat a thin slice of lemon cake, and as a method of warding off more dangerous topics of conversation, if not the evil eye, it has a long and successful tradition.

Clearly, though, it is a strain on both parties.

From where she sits at the kitchen table, Jessica can see into the adjoining room where Freya sprawls on the floor under the supervision of one of Yvette's elderly acolytes happily plaiting sea-grass around the frame of a basket. Yvette, noting Jessica's frequent glances in this direction, seizes the opportunity for more meaningful dialogue.

'And how has the little one been?'

'Confused, frightened. In some ways I don't think it's quite hit her yet that her mother is dead.'

'Perhaps to Freya she isn't.'

Jessica makes a non-committal noise through her closed lips that might be agreement or thoughtful consideration, or simply an involuntary protest of the oesophagus at the bitter taste of the coffee.

'To some people the dead are as close as the living. Closer at times.'

Jessica makes the noise again, her eyes sliding around the room, as if she is admiring the decor.

'You don't agree?'

'I really haven't thought about it that much.' From the Book of Social Graces as taught by the Poor Sisters of Mary. Chapter One: Responses to Questions Regarding Sex, Politics or Religion.

'No? Are you so frightened by it?'

'Frightened? By what?' But she knows what.

'The world of the dead. The world of the spirits.'

'I spend a good part of my time studying it, I don't think I can be frightened by it. I'm just a bit wary of people who claim to have some kind of communion with the dead, that's all.'

224

'And why is this, do you think?'

'Because often it's based on deception, trickery. The desire to have power over others. To manipulate.'

Thin ice. Why has she followed her out on it?

Yvette inclines her head as if considering this, or acknowledging its truth. 'Well, isn't this the case in every profession? There are always the Tricksters. Even among the gods there are the Tricksters.'

Her voice gently mocking but an edge there, something in the way she says this one word – *Trickster* – that sounds to Jessica like a threat and stirs in her some indefinable fear.

Jessica knows something of these Trickster gods – the shadows on the wall of the cave that crept into the evolving brains of the species, but no superficial reading of Jung or Radin, no spurious rationalisation, can exorcise the primitive fear. And because she feels frightened, she responds with more aggression than she knows is wise.

'You are talking about power, control over people who are weaker than yourself.'

'Weaker?' She sees the anger in the woman now, and the naked power. 'A woman complains that her husband is beating up on her. What can she do? The man is stronger than her. She seeks the help of someone else who is strong in a different way. So then some leverage might be used, something to make her husband fear her – or fear the spirits that may be set to guard her. Men are sometimes very susceptible to this kind of leverage. They fear the darkness in women, the power that comes from the earth. As some women fear it in themselves.'

'You think I have this power – and I'm afraid of it?'

But she hears the fear in her voice and knows that Yvette can.

'Not very strong – you've spent so long denying it. It's much stronger in Freya. Freya is not afraid of the dead.' She sees the reaction in Jessica's eyes. 'Does that bother you, too?'

'Just leave her alone.' Her own anger overcoming the fear. 'She's been hurt enough.'

'Why should it hurt her? It's only a power of seeing. Things that others can't see. Why should that hurt her?'

'Because it frightens her – what she sees. Just let her be normal.'

'Like you are normal?'

She might have left then – started to leave, in fact – when the door opened and Joe Selmo came in. He looked at least as startled as Jessica felt.

Yvette introduced them.

'You are,' she said, 'distant cousins.'

He did not look particularly pleased at the relationship but at least this time he did not run back to his lobster boat. They shook hands. He was a good foot taller than Jessica, and ducked his head as if afraid of banging it on the ceiling. His long black hair was tied back in a ponytail which accentuated the angularity of his features, as if the skin, like the hair, had been pulled severely back over the framework of bone and muscle. There was a tension, too, in his manner, an agitation that expressed itself in his eyes and in the way he rubbed one large hand over the back of the other, the long, strong fingers extended as if in shock. But it had little to do with Jessica. He turned, almost at once, to Yvette.

'There's been a fire at the dig,' he said. 'They found a body.'

He did not know who it was or how she had died. He had driven there but the police had closed the road. He said it had been on the news.

He punched numbers on the remote until he found the channel. There were aerial pictures of the headland and the burned-out cannery, and then closer, more mystifying shots of a skull tied to a long pole.

Jessica saw the look that passed between Yvette and Joe an instant before the presenter reported that it was thought to be the skull of a bear, but before she could consider it, and what it meant, an image of Maddie appeared on the screen, a still photograph from when she was working on the dig – and the report speculated on a possible link between the two deaths, a link they described with the inevitable journalistic licence as the Curse of Kitehawk Head.

At the first sight of Maddie, Jessica had glanced sharply at Freya to see how she was taking it. For once she was not looking at the television at all, but appeared engrossed with plaiting the sea-grass around the reed frame of the basket.

'I think we'd better be going back . . .' Jessica began, but now there was someone else she recognised – the man called Henry who played in Little Raymond's Cajun band. He was being interviewed against a backdrop of forest and sea, and he was talking about an Abenaki tradition of lashing the skull, ears and muzzle of a slain bear to a pole in order to pacify the spirit of the dead animal. This protected the hunter and his tribe, he said, from the bear's revenge.

Jessica did not see how Freya was reacting until she heard the noise, as if there was a scream trapped in the back of her throat.

It was Joe who reached her first, scooping her up in his arms and carrying her quickly through into the kitchen with Jessica trailing in his wake. She stood watching, confused and miserable, unwilling or unable to take her from him while he murmured gentle words of consolation and reassurance, and when Freya was quiet he looked up at Jessica and said: 'Do you have your car keys? I'll carry her out for you.'

She looked back as she turned the corner at the end of the street and saw him standing there in the doorway, and Yvette in the shadows behind him.

IV

'I'd like you to look at something,' the deputy medical examiner said, and Calhoun, wits dulled by his sleepless night, realised too late what the 'thing' was.

He turned abruptly away, retching, and his mouth filled with the taste of chemicals, an acid burning in his throat.

'OK?' A hint of laconic satisfaction betraying the pretence of concern.

'What is it?'

'There's an interesting injury here, see, on the forehead, just above the left eye . . .'

Calhoun looked directly now at what he had only glimpsed before, wiping the back of his hand across his mouth, trying not to think of it as Kate Wendicott but as the burned-out carcass of some animal. But there were parts of her that were devastatingly human.

The fire chief had explained it to him as they were bringing her out in the bodybag. She had been found lying face down on the concrete floor under a pile of debris and the whole of her back had been burned away, right down to the bone, but the front had been more or less preserved. 'Boiled, rather than charred,' as the chief had put it. There was still flesh on her features, flayed and horribly raw, but he could see the dent in her temple where the ME was pointing and the broken skin around it.

'Couldn't that have happened in the fire?'

'It's possible, but the way she was lying you'd expect it to damage the back of her skull. Besides, this looks like it was caused by something fairly narrow.'

'You're saying someone hit her.'

'I'm saying it's a possibility.'

'If she fell . . . ?'

'She'd have to fall from a hell of a height to cause that kind of a fracture.'

'A weapon, some kind of a club or . . .' He almost said claw.

'You're rushing me. This is just speculation.'

'Could you tell any more from an autopsy?'

'Well, I'll be sure and let you know.'

They zipped her back in the bodybag.

Calhoun sought out the fire chief and told him about the injury to the skull.

'Makes sense,' he said. 'Otherwise why didn't she get out? She was on the ground floor a few feet from the door.'

'Perhaps there was an explosion – threw her to the floor . . .'

But he was shaking his head.

'If it was that big, folks here would have heard it.'

The fire investigation officer already had men sifting through the debris. He said he'd have to send off samples to the lab and it could be two or three weeks before they got a result. They stood side by side for a moment considering the ruin. 'All these chemicals around,' he said. 'It could have been an accident but – you want an instant opinion – I'd say it was deliberate.'

'Why?'

'Why? Because it looks to me like it didn't start in one place. Looks to me like something was splashed around – the acetone, most likely. And also – because she didn't get out.'

Calhoun walked away from the laager of vehicles and out along the cliff edge where the reception was better for his mobile. Down below, a thick scum of ashes floated on the tide like dead skin, the living muscle rippling beneath. But the sea was retreating, shedding it bit by bit on the shore.

Calhoun felt as if his own skin was polluted with this film of ash. It was in his hair, his mouth, clogging the capillaries of his mind, the fine, ground-up bones of all the dead who had ever died on Kitehawk Head. He made a conscious effort to cast off this sense of desolation, of the atrophy he felt in his soul. He lifted his face up towards the clouds, closed his eyes and felt the chill rain sting his cheeks, imagined it trickling in small rivulets through the ashes. He stood like this for a minute or two like some primitive tribesman propitiating the gods, or offering himself in sacrifice. Then he put through the call to headquarters in Augusta.

When he'd finished, he saw Jensen walking up the headland towards him. He waited for him, still taking some masochistic satisfaction from the rain on his face.

'We're getting a lot of pressure from the media,' Jensen said.

'Fuck the media,' said Calhoun but he did not fuck the media, they fucked him. They already had.

The Curse of Fort Winter, the Curse of the Cliff of Bones, all Kate Wendicott had feared. And now he had the Lieutenant flying up here with a team from homicide, eager to be in the spotlight of media attention.

He told Jensen they were on their way – the Lieutenant could give a press conference as soon as he arrived. He'd like that.

V

Calhoun stood in the rain at the edge of the runway waiting for the plane that was bringing the Lieutenant and his team up from Augusta. He could have waited more comfortably in his car, or even in the frontier shack that served as the departure lounge on the infrequent occasions when there *was* a departure from Bridport municipal airport. But the rain was a comfort in itself. It was something physical and familiar, and served the more practical function of keeping him awake, if not precisely alert.

He looked out over the sea towards the dim, distant shape of Kitehawk Head, almost lost now in the murk of cloud and rain and descending darkness. There were no buildings, no lights to fix it in the present and it was not difficult to imagine himself back in the past, seeing it as the pilgrims from Boston had when they approached it from the sea in the spring of 1655, scared refugees trying to find some place where people would leave them alone, clinging to the edge of a wilderness.

An unseen hand threw a switch and a twin row of lights appeared in the earth at Calhoun's feet, pointing out towards the sea. His timeless landscape was instantly transformed into a landing strip for aliens. He stood, momentarily dazzled, disorientated by this sudden projection into the future present. Then his imagination shrank into the darkness of its long exile and he squinted into the driving rain until he could make out the lights of the plane from Augusta dropping through the low, scudding clouds above the bay.

Beckman had a cold and his rheumy eyes considered Calhoun with a look Calhoun remembered from his time at headquarters in Augusta. The Lieutenant's dislike had always been apparent, the reason for it more of a mystery. There were times when

Calhoun had wondered if Beckman, a man of puritan inclination, had somehow discovered the real reason for his return to Maine. He had learned that some months previously Beckman's own wife had left him for another man, a trauma which might well have reinforced his rigid moral code. On the other hand, it might simply be that he had interpreted Calhoun's withdrawn manner at that time as an expression of superiority based on his years of experience with a big city force.

Either way, the Lieutenant was not a man to count on for commendation, and Calhoun had considered himself fortunate to have escaped to the obscurity of K troop way up on the Canada border where his antipathy was at least not a daily infliction. Now he felt a familiar discomfort, and rising irritation, as he endured that sour-faced scrutiny and attempted to summarise what he knew about the Souriquois land claim.

Beckman, at the best of times, was not an easy man to inform. He had a low tolerance for exposition and an acid tongue which he exercised at every hesitation, everything he considered an irrelevance. And this was not the best of times. It had been a rough flight up from Augusta, his stomach was unsettled by turbulence, and this was not a simple story to digest. He sat across the low coffee table, fidgeting in his chair, sighing and sniffing and flicking the occasional hooded glance at Detectives Milic and Colby who'd flown up from Augusta with him.

'OK, I got all that,' he said, when Calhoun tried to emphasise some point about the massacre and the state of the skulls. 'But let's forget what happened 300 years ago, let's concentrate on what happened last night . . .'

It was useless for Calhoun to protest that the two were quite possibly related. He curbed his frustration and composed his features into what he hoped was an expression of attentive deference.

'The woman's working alone in the building. You leave her at what time?'

'About eight-thirty.'

And who else is around – that we know about, forgetting any Indians that might be hiding in the trees?'

'Her three colleagues on the site – Dr Jarvis and the two students . . .'

'Who say they're together in the RV from the time you arrive until they give the alarm at . . . when is it?'

'Eleven forty,' said Detective Milic.

'So, as far as we know, you're the last person to see her alive.'

'Apart from the killer.'

'Apart from the killer.'

There was something in the way Beckman repeated the phrase that Calhoun did not like, but then there was so much about the Lieutenant he did not like it was hard to be specific in his objection. However, he thought he detected something in the air that was more than the usual animosity.

'Tell me, what was the precise reason for your . . . visit? At this particular time?'

'I wanted to talk to her about the skulls she'd found.'

'What about the skulls?'

'About the way they were damaged . . .' Calhoun saw the trap ahead of him, but there was no way of avoiding it now. 'I was curious about the wounds,' he said.

'Curious? You mean in a, what, a medical sense or, or what?'

'They seemed to me to be remarkably similar to the wounds that were inflicted on Madeleine Ross.'

The eyes flickered again to one of the detectives sitting beside but slightly behind Calhoun.

'Inflicted? As in inflicted by the same person or the same animal?'

'The same weapon. The same kind of weapon.'

'I see. So you were following a line of inquiry?'

'I know it might seem slightly bizarre . . .'

'Bizarre? You tell me what's bizarre, Calhoun. You see, we had a call from Dr Pete Jarvis a while back. Just before we left Augusta, in fact. He says he took you in to see Dr Wendicott at around eight o'clock and half an hour or so later, just about the time you say you were leaving, he looks in again and you seem to be having a bit of a party in there. Or to be specific, he sees the pair of you stark naked, fucking on the floor. Has he got a vivid imagination, a dirty mind or what?'

VI

They left him alone for the best part of two hours in the interview room at the State police barracks in Dover – *his* interview room. They were possibly checking out his alibi, but he knew the Lieutenant would have said: 'Let him sweat a while.' It was the kind of thing the Lieutenant would say.

It was a room designed to make you sweat. There were no windows but the overhead lighting was very bright, and running almost the entire length of one wall was a one-way mirror which permitted observation from the corridor outside.

Calhoun felt like a specimen in a jar, a bug in a collecting box.

But a bug would have run around in circles. Calhoun sat still and impassive at the table in the centre of the room with his elbows resting on the arms of the chair, his hands clasped against his chest, his chin propped on two joined fingers. For the most part he kept his eyes closed, some of the time he even dozed, waking with a start and momentarily wondering where he was before his features assumed their expression of bland detachment. Only his thoughts ran around in circles.

Calhoun's sexual fantasies were largely focused on the idea of watching and being watched. He was attracted to women who showed a tendency to exhibitionism, who liked, or might be coaxed, into parading naked around his apartment with the light on and the blinds raised. Or who would venture with him into restaurants or bars, even supermarkets, wearing a coat and a pair of shoes and nothing else. He played fantasy games where he imagined making love in public places. His favourite locations for these fantasies were an empty railway carriage on a moving train or an almost empty cinema in the afternoon – sitting near the back and exciting his lover to such a frenzy she was incapable of stopping when he removed her clothes, exposing her to the full view of anyone who turned a head.

But they remained fantasies. He had enough restraint, or inhibition, to know that no matter how exciting the experience might be at the time, he would be devastated if somebody actually witnessed it. Devastated for the woman, and for himself. And so it was now.

It was clear, though, that Kate had seen Jarvis in the open doorway and did not share Calhoun's inhibitions but had enjoyed performing to this silent, solitary audience.

Calhoun regretted making love to Kate Wendicott for a number of reasons, but to be *seen* making love to her, and in such circumstances, made him feel cheapened, shoddy, vulnerable. To be caught with his pants down by Jarvis, the white rat, and thereby exposed to the censure, the derision, of such a man as Lieutenant Oscar Beckman . . .

Calhoun felt that he had let himself down, betrayed his own precarious sense of worth. Just as he had done in Boston.

Calhoun had been known as a man without slyness or deceit. In a sense, his integrity was the coinage he traded against the more material assets of his richer friends. And of course he knew how to behave, he would not embarrass them in public.

But there was something more than that which Calhoun only vaguely appreciated until he lost it. There was something in him which made these people seek his approval, want him to be their friend. Calhoun's apparent affection enhanced their own self-esteem. He could not be bought, he did not flatter to deceive, and so they desired his approbation.

'You are an officer and a gentleman, sir,' Ben had once said to him, meaning it as an absurd comment but, at the same time, meaning it. For Ben, like most of his circle, liked to feel they retained certain ancestral values.

No matter that their ancestors had, in reality, included more than their fair share of cheats and liars, thieves and scoundrels, they had succeeded in creating a myth, a mystique, of honourable conduct – conduct becoming an officer and a gentleman – which, though they might ridicule it in public and constantly betray it in private, they valued as something of merit, something they had inherited beside money, something which raised them above the merely rich.

When he made love to Ben's wife, Calhoun lost his own good

opinion of himself and gradually he lost his friends. Unable to face up to his own deceit, he retreated from their company, though strangely, he never lost *their* good opinion, right up to the time he left Boston, possibly even after. He had become one of their myths.

But now he had been found out. He was in the pillory, exposed in his own mind at least, not only for his indiscretion with Kate Wendicott, but for his illicit affair with Gemma, his betrayal of Ben and Ben's circle. They were all there, out beyond the one-way mirror, seeing him now for what he was and not what he pretended to be. And he knew, even though he might escape with one of the Lieutenant's famous rebukes, he would never forgive himself for putting himself in this position, for being in Beckman's power to hurt.

Shortly after eight Colby, one of the detectives Beckman had brought up from Augusta, came in and told him he was in the clear.

His manner was guardedly friendly.

Calhoun asked him if they'd spoken to Jessica Ross. He was worried about what they'd told her.

'She someone else you laid?' He recoiled from the look in Calhoun's eyes. 'OK, OK, she confirms she saw you shortly after nine o'clock and the barman at the Old Barrack House says you were there up to the time the fire started.'

'I could have killed her before nine and left some kind of timing device.'

'Get the fuck out of here, Calhoun.'

'Just making sure you've thought it all through. I'd hate to be picked up again when you got round to it in a couple of weeks' time.'

'Yeah, well, it so happens we did. Only there's a guy at the university in Orana says the DOA called him at home just before eleven o'clock. He was about half an hour talking to her on the phone. So she was still alive when you were in the bar. The Lieutenant's real pissed off.'

'So what happens now?'

'You got any sense, you take what leave that's owing you before the Lieutenant gets back from the reservation.'

'What's he doing at the reservation?'

'Picking up your friend Joe Selmo, with any luck. Seems he's not so smart at standing up alibis as you are.

'We checked him out. He said he got home just after nine-thirty. But the reservation police saw him driving past from the direction of Kitehawk Head about two hours later, just before they heard the fire alert.'

VII

Jessica was sitting at her usual table in the Old Barrack House when Calhoun came in. This time he didn't do his usual trick of peering in every corner. He came straight over and sat down.

'I hear you had to vouch for me,' he said. 'Thanks.'

'Don't mention it,' she said. 'What were you supposed to have done?'

'Killed Kate Wendicott and burned the body,' he said. He gazed around the room. 'Quiet tonight.' Raymond was looking at him from behind the bar and Calhoun raised a hand and pointed a finger at him in some kind of ironic acknowledgement.

'You're not serious,' she said.

He looked directly at her. 'You don't think I could?'

'What are you talking about?' She began to feel annoyed with him.

'I was with her not long before she died.'

'But you're a policeman.'

This seemed to amuse him. 'You'd be amazed what *policemen* can do,' he said.

She looked at him curiously, puzzled by his manner. What was it? He had always been careful with her, perhaps too careful. He treated her like she was bone china that would break in his hands. Now there was a negligence about him, almost a slovenliness, that she found puzzling, though, on the whole, she thought she might prefer it. He was not so buttoned-up.

One of the girls came over and he ordered a beer for himself and asked her what she would like. She had been drinking mineral water but now she ordered a wine.

She told him he looked tired.

'I was up all night.' He sat forward over the table so his face was closer to hers. His eyes were bloodshot and he hadn't shaved for a while. 'Listen,' he said. 'There's something else I have to tell you. They've arrested Joe Selmo.'

He told her the story, keeping his voice low so no one else would hear.

'We checked out all the people who worked on the site. Joe's alibi was confirmed by his father and his aunt. He said he was with them and some other people at the community centre on the reservation until about nine-thirty. Then they went home together and he stayed there all night. But then Frankie Lecoute – he's the chief over at the reservation . . .' he almost smiled . . . 'the chief of *police*, that is. He said Selmo had been seen by two of his officers in a patrol car outside the church of St Ann's just after ten. He was leaving the village in his pickup and heading in the direction of Bridport – and Kitehawk Head. An hour and a half later they saw him coming back.'

'We pulled him in, took his prints and got a match on the ones we found on the bear skull that was left out there.'

For all her suspicions about Joe Selmo, she found it hard to believe they had been so directly confirmed. Perhaps it was the image of him when she had last seen him, whispering words of comfort and consolation to Freya.

'What does he say?'

'He admits he planted the totem. But he says he didn't kill anyone and he didn't start any fire.'

'But why did he leave this . . . totem?'

'He says it's supposed to ward off evil spirits. The spirit of the bear. Apparently there was some kind of ceremony last night at the community centre. They made this thing and he volunteered to take it out to Kitehawk Head.'

His tone was sceptical.

'You don't believe him?'

'Oh, I believe that part.'

'I meant about the fire – and the woman.'

'Well, he had motive, opportunity . . . All we have to do is find the means.'

'What was the motive?'

He told her about the land claim.

'So the theory is he was trying to destroy evidence of the massacre?'

'I'm not sure about trying. He seems to have succeeded.'

'But other people must have seen these skulls, apart from this woman. You saw them, you know what state they were in.'

'It's not the same as producing them as evidence in court. Besides, even Kate didn't seem too sure. She said they had to do some tests on them . . .' His voice tailed off as if he was thinking about something else.

So was Jessica.

'Could he have killed Maddie?'

'I don't know.' He sighed heavily. 'There's no motive that we know of.'

'Except they were probably . . .' she could not say 'lovers', hesitated over 'fucking'.

But he knew what she meant.

'Yes.' He half smiled again, as at some private joke, except there was no laughter in his eyes. 'If that's a motive.'

She said: 'There *was* some kind of ceremony last night at the community centre.' She told him about driving there on her way back from the Graham House.

He looked at her sharply. 'Why did you do that?'

'I don't know. Why did I stop at the road leading to Kitehawk Head?'

His expression might have been cautious or simply weary. Then he said: 'Where's Freya?'

'Watching television with Hannah. I'll take her up to bed soon.'

'I'll maybe see Hannah about staying the night,' he said. 'Can't face the drive back.'

Then, unexpectedly, he said: 'What is it you call *policemen* in England? What is it – *Bobbies*? *Bobbies on bicycles*. Why do you call them *Bobbies*?'

'Because the man who invented them was called Robert,' she said. 'Sir Robert Peel.'

'Get out of here. The man who *invented* them?'

'Not many people call them Bobbies,' she said. 'Not any more.'

She was still thinking about Joe Selmo.

'What else d'you call them?'

She searched her vocabulary. It was not something she thought about a lot. Maddie, who had had more dealings with the police, called them many things, invariably impolite. She was a little perplexed by this sudden interest. More than a little perplexed by the change in him.

'It kind of varies with the region. In London we call them the Bill.' She couldn't remember why. 'In Manchester it's the Dibble, after PC Dibble who's a kind of cartoon character. The one I like best is from Liverpool – the Bizzies. Because they're always busy-busy, busying around.'

'Yeah. I like that. The Bizzies. Beckman's a Bizzy.'

'Who's Beckman?'

'The Lieutenant. He's taken over the investigation.'

'Where does that leave you?'

'We haven't discussed that yet. Kind of sidelined, I would say.'

'Does that bother you?'

'I'm thinking of quitting.'

'Oh.' She knew now why they were talking about the police. 'I'm sorry,' she said.

'Nothing to be sorry about. In fact, in a way it's a relief. I wasn't very convincing at being a Bizzy, only . . .' He paused, frowning.

'What?'

'I think I'd like to go out on a high note.'

He had watched the tall Indian through the one-way glass of the interview room, sitting in the chair he himself had so recently vacated. He was being questioned by Beckman and Milic. He sat very straight, his face impassive. When he looked directly at them he turned the whole of his head, quite slowly. Watching him from the corridor, Calhoun thought he looked *controlled*.

He stuck rigidly to his story. He had been surprised when the dig uncovered evidence of a massacre but he had not thought to destroy it. He had planted the totem on the headland, near the spot where Madeleine Ross had died. He had not killed Kate Wendicott. He had not set fire to the cannery.

When they asked him why he had planted the totem he said it was a form of atonement for the evil that had been done there, an appeasement of the spirits.

Beckman said: 'You're an educated man, a law student, you expect us to believe that?'

For the first time there was expression in his features, the hint of a smile.

'No,' he said.

241

VIII

Freya is speaking urgently to her but there is no meaning in her words, none that Jessica can understand. What is the language of dreams? Freya is in her dream, her lips moving, the message clearly important. And now Maddie is there.

She has not appeared so clearly before in Jessica's dreams, only as a shadow on the edge of a greater darkness. But now she walks towards her and the features are indistinct. It is as if Jessica cannot focus on them for fear of what she might see. And Maddie, too, is trying to tell her something, but speaking in the language of dreams.

Well, of course, even in her dream, Jessica knows this is a projection of her own thoughts. So why then, can she not understand them? Her brain is thinking through this dream, trying to work it out. Is it something in her subconscious, something she has forgotten? What is her subconscious trying to communicate, and why through an image of Maddie?

And with the memory she wakes, startled, sitting upright in the soft light of the bedroom. Freya is still sleeping, her breathing deep and reassuring. Jessica looks at her watch. It is just after three.

She gets out of bed and pulls on her jeans, puts on her coat, fastening it over the man's T-shirt she wears as a night-dress. She carries her boots in her hand.

She finds the flashlight plugged into the battery charger in the kitchen and the keys are on the hook on the wall.

It has stopped raining but the sky is overcast and there is a chill wind off the sea, carrying a hint of snow. The wind moves the trees against the sky with a noise like someone blowing across the neck of a bottle.

She opens the door of Maddie's cabin, and her light finds the papers where she left them on the table. A moment later, the wind pushes past her and sweeps them away like a giant hand, hurling them about the room. She closes the door and starts to pick them up.

The first one she looks at contains a drawing of a man in a bearskin crawling on all fours with what look like grappling hooks or rakes attached to his hands. The others are as she remembers them: notes in Maddie's barely discernible scrawl, or pages photocopied from a book. It seems strange to her now, that she did not see the drawing of the Bear-man when she first looked at them, but then she remembers she was interrupted by Innis Graham.

She begins to read. It is hard work reading what Maddie has written, and often painful. She is not aware of the time. She has closed her mind to the buffeting of the wind but a part of it has remained alert for any other sound, and at the first faint scratching at the door she switches off the light and moves swiftly away from the table, crouching on the floor in the far corner of the room.

She is momentarily blinded by the sudden darkness and does not see the door open but she feels the wind, gusting into the room and swirling the papers in the air. One of them flies into her face like a bat and she almost screams.

Now her eyes are adjusting to the gloom and she can see the patch of paler darkness that marks the open door. There is no one there, no one she can see. Perhaps the wind blew the door open. But still she crouches in the corner, close to the floor, listening for something else in the room beside the wind. She has to tell herself that this is not a continuation of her dream, that this is far more dangerous than a dream. After a while, she crawls on all fours towards the oblong of night sky, keeping close to the wall and moving very slowly, easing her weight on to her outstretched fingers and then bringing her feet forward one after the other. She has the strong, almost paralysing, sense of something else crawling in the far corner of the room, in the shadows to the left of the door, but she does not look at that, she keeps her eyes firmly on the opening, and when she is level with the end of the table and there is nothing in the way, she takes off like a sprinter from the starting block.

It rises from the floor, blocking the light, dark as a shadow but more solid, the weight driving the wind from her lungs and bearing her backwards against something hard and painful. She grabs hold of a clump of hair, tugs viciously and hears a savage, animal grunt of pain. But it is human hair and as the head jerks back and the weight eases slightly, she brings her knee up between his legs. But not quite far enough, not enough to cripple, and so she brings her heel down, raking his shin, grinding into his instep, crying out now in fear and frustration, as she feels his hand tighten on her wrist . . .

'Jessica?' he says.

It is Calhoun.

He puts on the main light by the door and they stare at each other for a moment in some embarrassment. She puts her head down, struggling for breath.

'You could have knocked,' she says. There is not enough air in her lungs, it comes out as a thin, plaintive whine.

'I saw the light. I thought it was an intruder. Why didn't you say something?'

She concedes that she is probably more at fault than he.

'I'm sorry,' she says. 'I was frightened.'

He sits down on one of the chairs by the table and takes his instep in both hands where she stamped on it and begins to rock his leg backwards and forwards with his eyes closed. There is a piece of skin missing from his forehead and a trickle of blood down the side of his face. Perhaps a little more than a trickle. Her nail must have caught him when she pulled his hair.

Her hip feels bruised where she hit the sink but she thinks she will not mention this.

'Did you learn how to fight like that,' he says, 'or does it come natural?'

'I did a course,' she says, 'in Rome – called Surviving the Streets.'

He looks wonderingly at her. 'Are the streets that dangerous in Rome?'

'They can be.' Why are they talking about Rome? 'I'm sorry,' she says again.

The papers are blowing about the floor, and he bends down to pick one of them up.

'What's this?'

'Something Maddie was doing. Some research.'

She closes the door and scrambles around on the floor for the others.

He reads aloud: 'The sworn testimony of William Meadows made before the committee of the House of Notables in Boston, September 15th, 1656 . . .'

She shivers, hunched in her coat, suddenly aware of how cold it is in the cabin. Her breath, now she has it back, a ruffled feather in the air.

'Can we go back into the house,' she says.

It is warmer in the house but she is still shivering. He takes down a brandy from the shelf behind the bar and pours for them both. They sit in the big Shaker chairs on each side of the fireplace and she remembers sitting here with him once before and talking about fairy tales and magic, a frog that can turn into a prince. She has a different story for him now.

There were still a few Quakers left in Boston to grieve for the lost colony on Kitehawk Head, and in the fall of 1656 they began to question Captain James Russell's account of how the colonists had died.

It appeared that some of his men had talked unguardedly in the Boston taverns and from their drunken, semi-articulate expressions of remorse, an alternative picture began to emerge. One of them, his conscience clearly troubled by the events on Kitehawk Head, was persuaded by the Quakers to sign a statement. His name was William Meadows.

Meadows stated that there had been a serious rift between Russell and Willard over the purpose of the settlement. Russell was interested solely in establishing a base against the French and a trading post for furs. Willard seemed to favour the Quakers' dream of a model farming community built on land legitimately purchased from the Souriquois.

Meadows and some of the other soldiers had taken Russell's part and, instead of sailing to Boston for supplies, had joined up with the Mohawk to scare the settlers into abandoning the fort.

But then Willard had been killed.

Meadows suspected that Russell and his Mohawk had murdered him and mutilated his body so that it looked as if he had been mauled by a bear. But by now, he said, they were too afraid of the Mohawk to protest.

Shortly afterwards Russell led them into the interior to hunt and trade for furs.

They returned to the coast in the spring hoping to find the fort abandoned. Instead they found a handful of survivors being nursed by Surgeon Trapham in the infirmary. The rest had died of scurvy.

Trapham had enough strength and spirit in him to curse Russell for deserting them.

Meadows claimed that he and some others went to fetch water from the well. When they returned the infirmary was ablaze. Whether the fire was started deliberately he could not say, but Russell forced them to uphold the fiction of massacre by the Souriquois. He said that otherwise they would be blamed for abandoning the settlers. When they returned to Boston, he even produced an edited version of Willard and Trapham's journal as evidence of the bear cult among the Abenaki.

But there were a number of inconsistencies in Meadows's story and none of his comrades could be persuaded to corroborate it in public. The case against Russell collapsed. Opinion had by now swung violently against the Quakers. They were banished from the colony. When four of them returned the following year, they were hanged.

The treaty Willard had signed with the Souriquois was held to have been broken by the Indians and a punitive expedition was sent against them, under Russell's command. It drove them into the arms of the French and they proved such a menace, the British issued a proclamation.

'Given at the council chamber in Boston, this 3rd day of October, 1716, in the 3rd year of the reign of our sovereign lord, George I, by the grace of God, of Great Britain, France, Ireland, King defender of the Faith . . .'

Jessica read the document aloud, trying to convey in the coldness of her delivery and in the words themselves, some measure of her own outrage.

'Whereas the tribe of Narragasco Bay Indians (also called the Souriquois) have repeatedly in a perfidious manner acted contrary to their solemn submission unto his Majesty, the General Council of the Province have voted that a bounty be granted and paid out of the Province Treasury, the premiums being agreed as following:
For every scalp of a male Indian brought in as evidence of their being killed, Forty pounds.
For every scalp of such female Indian or male Indian under the age of twelve years that shall be killed and brought in as evidence of their being killed, Twenty pounds.'

Jessica looked up from the document to where Calhoun sat, his hands cupped around the brandy glass, his face partly in shadow. He nodded slowly to himself.

'Under the age of twelve,' she repeated. 'Twenty pounds.'

'Yes.' He was looking curiously at her now. 'I'm sorry, but this is not some great revelation. Don't they teach you what we did to the Indians? Or is it the fact that it was done under the British?'

She looked at the document again. 'I suppose it's just seeing it written down like this, the language like . . . some kind of – Nazi.'

'In the name of King George.'

'It's not that, not only that. It's . . . the enormity of the crime. The fact that they got away with it.' She held the papers in her hand, as if she had the evidence, all written down, and no one to give it to, no one to indict, no one to sit in judgement.

'What if it's true – the man's statement – that there *was* no massacre? At least, not by the Indians.'

'But there was. They found the bodies. In the grave where Russell and his men buried them.'

He stood up and picked her empty glass up from the floor and went over to the bar and she watched him as if she expected something else of him, as if she thought there was something he could do. He turned and saw her looking at him.

'It doesn't . . . justify what happened afterwards. But they *were* killed and pretty much the way Russell described. I saw the bones. I saw the holes in the skulls.'

IX

They stood in a group down on the harbour, stamping their feet and sometimes turning their backs on the wind that came in from the sea. Three of them Calhoun remembered from that first day of snow on the headland when they had found the body of Madeleine Ross. There was snow in the wind now, thin, gritty flakes, so light they whirled up in the air again before they could settle, and worse on the way according to the forecast. Most of the draggers had been out all night getting in the harvest while they still could.

He was relieved when they finally picked her out among the whitecaps, a graceless pig of a boat, butting her snout into the troughs and pitching the spray over her rust-red back. The *Charlotte Rose*, she was called, out of Portland. She came reeling round the harbour arm and swung in towards where they were standing, and they could see the black bag among the nets and tackle on the deck, an ordinary black plastic bag, the kind you put the garbage in.

It had been torn when it came up in the drag off Kitehawk Head and the skipper had told Jensen what was in it, but there was a surprise when Calhoun tipped it out on to the plastic sheet in the harbourmaster's office. Wrapped inside the bundle of blood-soaked clothing there was an implement like a short garden rake with five curved prongs four or five inches long. It was the kind of rake that you normally used for weeding between rows, one of Jensen's men said, but usually the prongs weren't filed down to such a sharp point. There was dried blood on them, and a small but recognisable piece of human scalp.

'I thought I told you to take some leave,' Colby said, when Calhoun tracked him down at Dover headquarters.

Calhoun wondered if somewhere in his brain Colby thought he was God. He decided to humour him.

248

'I thought I'd wait for warmer weather,' he said.

Colby told him it was warm in Florida.

'Just give me the name of the man Kate Wendicott talked to in Orana,' Calhoun said, less humorously now.

Colby asked him why he wanted to know.

Calhoun rejected the first reply that came to mind. 'Because I want to ask him what it was she wanted to discuss with him so urgently that she called him at eleven o'clock at night. Unless you asked him already.'

He knew that Colby hadn't from the short silence on the phone.

'Decker,' said Colby. 'Dr John Decker. But the Lieutenant says you're off the case.'

He didn't think he was God, then, only God's deputy. Calhoun cleared him off the air waves and called the university at Orana. Decker wasn't there. The faculty secretary said he had driven up to the site with other members of staff. She also told him that Decker's subject was forensic archaeology.

X

The Lieutenant had given his interview, the media had taken all the shots they wanted and the only people left on the headland now were from the university: five of them standing outside the RV, warming their hands on steaming mugs of coffee and staring bleakly at the charred skeleton of the cannery. The wind picked up the ashes and blew them in the air to join the swirling snow. It was heavier now, and beginning to form drifts against the banked-up earth of the dig. The trees were already dusted down one side.

Calhoun walked towards them, head down against the wind. When he looked up he saw Jarvis, gazing into space, deliberately avoiding his eye. He told them who he was and that he'd like to speak to Dr Decker. He saw Jarvis look at him then with sharp inquiry, but he took Decker aside and walked him to the edge of the trees where they could talk privately out of the worst of the wind.

Calhoun had already guessed what Kate had wanted to talk to him about.

'She wasn't happy about the skulls,' Decker told him. 'She wanted to check out one or two things with me.'

He was a man of about fifty or sixty with a greying beard and an air of gentle solidity, the kind of man you want as your therapist or your accountant. He wore a black overcoat with a scarf knotted at the neck and a Russian-style fur hat. Calhoun remembered that Kate had worn one too when he had first met her. He wondered if they'd been close. His eyes were moist, though that could be from the wind.

Calhoun asked what exactly it was that seemed to be bothering her.

'Well, the way she described them to me, they'd been fractured in a number of places as if with something sharp and pointed.' He looked at Calhoun as if to confirm this, and Calhoun nodded. 'Well, she was a little puzzled by the way the skulls had shattered with the impact. And a number of them seemed to have cracked along a suture line. This is unlikely to happen if the skull is held together by facial tissue. There would be a fracture, of course, but not quite to the same extent.'

'Couldn't it have happened when they were in the ground?'

'Skulls in the ground tend to be quite remarkably preserved, even after thousands of years. Unless there's some significant disturbance, like an earthquake, of course. But more curiously, the breaks themselves were quite rough, jagged even, at the edges.'

'If they were struck by a sharp weapon – or a claw – surely they *would* be quite jagged . . .'

But Decker was shaking his head.

'Not after three centuries in the ground. The point of impact would have been worn smooth by the action of water in the soil.'

'So you're saying they were fractured much more recently?'

'Well, we'd have had to examine them to be sure about that. It's hard for me to say anything now.'

Calhoun was silent for a moment, trying to think it through. It seemed easier to think aloud.

'If they were damaged recently, it has to be because someone wants to fake the evidence of a massacre.'

'I imagine,' said Decker. 'But – why?'

'I don't know.' He looked at him directly. 'Who could possibly gain from it?'

Unless it was the archaeologists themselves, he was thinking. What was it Kate had said – something about funding and the 'right kind of publicity'?

We needed a dramatic ending, a tragic ending.

'And where would they have got the skulls from?' he said.

Jarvis led them along the path that skirted the edge of the cliff beyond the cleared area of the dig. The tide was in and they could hear its muscular rhythm on the rocks below, and sometimes a deeper, hollow drumming where it surged into the caves and crannies at the foot of the granite cliffs. Calhoun could see the waves breaking over the end of the jetty where Innis had moored his boat, and tasted salt spray on his lips along with the melting snow. It was thicker and softer now, the path slippery beneath his feet.

Beyond the steps that led down to the jetty the path veered inland a little and they were sheltered by a belt of white pine and spruce. Calhoun saw evidence of digging here and there among the trees, though not recently, judging from the pine needles that already formed a thin, patchy carpet over the disturbed earth. About fifty or sixty yards back from the cliff there was a log cabin with a sloping roof in the Swiss style reaching almost to the ground. It was like something out of a fairy tale – the woodcutter's hut in the middle of the forest – except for the simple wooden cross on the roof and the padlocked chain on the door.

The key had been kept in Kate Wendicott's desk at the cannery and Jarvis had brought a screwdriver and a pair of pliers to force the lock, but it was too tough for them, and in the end, feeling foolish and a little sacrilegious, Calhoun told everyone to stand well back and placed the barrel of his police revolver against it. Even then it took two shots. It was the first time he had used it outside of the range.

His first impression when he opened the door was of a row of pale faces and dark eyes staring at him out of the gloom like prisoners, he thought, who have been locked up for a very long time. Then, as his own eyes adjusted to the dim light, the flesh seemed to fade from the bones and the eyes became empty sockets. He stepped inside, sensing the others crowding at his back, presumably more accustomed to this intrusion into the world of the dead.

The walls on both sides of the hut were lined with deep shelves, almost like bunks, and they were neatly stacked with piles of bones, each marked by an individual skull, as if, Calhoun thought, the imprisoned sleepers had died where they lay and slowly rotted. The smell was of damp earth and new pine-wood shelving.

These were the mortal remains of all the bodies they had dug up in the cemetery outside the fort, all those French and English colonists who had died of scurvy and malnutrition in those two terrible winters. Many of the graves had contained more than

252

one body, and thirty-two of them had been found in a shallow pit under a heap of stones that might once have been a chapel or charnel house. The ground would have been too hard, the survivors too weak to have buried them properly, Jarvis said. Kate had hoped that some day there might be a proper ossuary built of granite as a lasting monument.

Under each of the skulls there was a label attached to the shelf with a number on it and sometimes, but not often, a name. Calhoun walked along the narrow passage between the shelves. Some of the skulls were quite small, and here and there in the darkness behind them he could see the tiny bones of a child's fingers or toes. A million particles of dust moved through the light from the open door, a private galaxy in this closed, secret universe of the dead. He had the odd impression that the skulls were singing, a song like a long-drawn-out sigh, rippling along the length of the shelves. But then he realised it was the wind in the pine trees.

Decker, clearly less moved by sentiment, had lifted one of the skulls down from the shelves and was examining it with some interest. He showed it now to Calhoun.

There were four holes in the top of the skull, in a more or less straight line ending in the left eye socket.

'See this – where it's been fractured – see how smooth and worn the edges are. Run your finger along it – it's not rough at all, or jagged. That's what happens when it's been in the soil a few centuries. And the holes in the skull are quite distinct, neat almost. The cranium isn't at all shattered like the ones Kate described.'

But Calhoun was interested for another reason.

'I thought there was no sign of any injuries,' he said, almost accusingly, to Jarvis. 'Not in the bodies you found in the cemetery.'

'This was the only one,' Jarvis told him. 'It's Willard. We found part of his uniform and the remains of his sword with his initials on the hilt.' He pointed to the name on the shelf where the skull had been. There were two others beside it, one of them clearly that of a child. Calhoun read the names: Eleanor and Margaret Perry. Jarvis said that all three had been found in the same grave.

A map pinned to the back of the door showed the position in the cemetery where all the bodies had been found. There were eighty-six in all, Jarvis said. There were no obvious gaps to show that any were missing. But when Calhoun counted the skulls there were only seventy-four.

XI

Jessica woke with her head full of cold, but Freya seemed to have shrugged off hers, and was perversely keen on going back to school. She wanted to say goodbye to everyone, she said, if they were going back to England. Hannah offered to drive her in. She was spending most of the day there, she said, helping prepare for an inspection.

Jessica was glad enough to crawl back into bed. She drifted in and out of sleep almost until lunch.

She sat at her usual table in the window watching the snow and the whitecaps out over the bay, a grey-white world of sea and sky all mixed up and floating about like a paperweight that someone has just shaken. It felt a bit like that in her head.

Raymond was hanging up decorations over the bar – arrangements of squashes and corn cobs and pine cones, as if for a harvest festival – and when she asked him what it was 'in aid of' he said it was Thanksgiving on Thursday.

She was startled by this reminder of how long she'd been here. She was becoming a fixture. She could hardly imagine a world any different now, from this panorama of sea and sky that had once made her feel so lost and disorientated. Rome, Oxford, they were remote memories. In a kind of panic she rang her father in Scotland, and got Virginia instead. Her father was having a nap, she said, and she didn't want to wake him. Jessica told her she'd decided to come back at the end of the week, whatever happened. There was a funeral director, she said, who would ship Maddie home to them.

'And what about Freya?' Virginia asked, almost as if she thought the funeral director might take care of her, too.

Jessica told her she imagined she would take her back to Oxford, but there were some legal formalities to be observed, as Maddie hadn't left a will. Freya would probably have to be a ward of court.

There was a small silence on the line, and then Virginia said that her father had talked about having Freya with them, and how would Jessica feel about that?

Jessica's first feeling was of relief, followed by instant guilt.

'He thought she might like to be with the boys,' Virginia said in quite a small voice.

It would be like putting a feral cat in with a pair of puppies, Jessica thought, and there was satisfaction in that, also. Sometimes she was not a very nice person, she concluded. It was probably the strain of all those years of being a 'nice' child.

When they'd finished, Jessica put her coat on and went out to Maddie's little cabin in the trees. She wanted to make sure she'd packed everything. She was particularly concerned not to leave any books behind. It would be like leaving a part of *her* behind – and the only part that Jessica was still able to keep. Except Freya, of course.

Most of the titles on the shelves were the kind of blockbusters people bought to read on vacation and had probably been left there by previous visitors, but there were a few children's books that might belong to Freya – several Roald Dahls and Dick King-Smiths, and Saint-Exupéry's *The Little Prince* with an inscription inside in French from a man called Jim. And on the top shelf, in one corner, there was a wedge of verse, thin enough to pull out with the span of fingers and thumb, that were more characteristic of Maddie, or at least the Maddie that had sometimes emerged through the storm clouds.

Jessica read the titles: *Dancing the Tightrope – New Love Poems by Women*, Carol Ann Duffy's *Mean Time*, *The Love Poems of John Donne* . . . then, with a shock of recollection and grief, one that she herself had given her a couple of birthdays ago. *Anna Akhmatova: Selected Poems*, translated by D.M. Thomas.

She turned to the poem called 'In Memory of Mikhail Bulgakov' whose novel *The Master and Margarita* was among her own favourite works of fiction, and read:

This, not graveyard roses, is my gift,
And I won't burn sticks of incense:
You died as unflinchingly as you lived,
With magnificent defiance.

Drank wine and joked – were still the wittiest,
Choked on the stifling air,
You yourself let in the terrible guest.

There was little of Maddie in this and everything of a drunken
Russian novelist raging into his last goodnight, but something in
the final line checked Jessica, as if it held some significance for
her. She rejected the thought as morbidly imaginative and was
diverted by the discovery of a book with her own name inside the
cover: Eliot's *Collected Poems*, the one she had taken into the
hospital when Maddie was having Freya. A blade of sea-grass
had been used as a bookmark and the smell reminded her of
Yvette Selmo, or at least her house – sea-grass was the material
she used to make the baskets and those little toy animals that
hung on her walls. The poem it marked was 'The Dry Salvages'
which, according to a note in parenthesis, referred to a small
group of rocks – presumably a corruption of the French *les trois
sauvages* – off the north-east coast of Cape Ann in Massachusetts. Jessica turned the page, recalling the familiar lines:

Where is there an end to the drifting wreckage,
The prayer of the bone on the beach, the unprayable
Prayer at the calamitous annunciation?

Again there was the sense of some hidden significance, or
warning. Again, she rejected it – there were enough hidden
meanings in Eliot to keep you guessing for several lifetimes –
and took down the final two books: *The Virago Book of Love
Poetry* and a thin volume by Alice Walker, *Horses Make a
Landscape Look More Beautiful*. The former was inscribed
'To Madeleine, Happy Birthday, Love, Jim.' Jim again. She
remembered the name now. He was the man she had met in
Newbury, the one Jessica had liked. She closed it, fighting back
the tears, and glanced instead at the Alice Walker. It had a
drawing of a dappled blue pony on the cover, the kind of thing
you might find on the wall of a cave, or the side of a wigwam, and
inside was a quote from someone called Lame Deer, Seeker of
Visions:

We had no word for the strange animal we got from the white man – the horse. So we called it sunka wakan, 'holy dog'. For bringing us the horse we could almost forgive you for bringing us whiskey. Horses make a landscape look more beautiful.

The author had dedicated the book to two of her ancestors, a woman, Tallulah, who was part Cherokee, and a white man, possibly Anglo-Irish, who had raped and impregnated her great-great-grandmother when she was just ten.

The final verse read:

Rest. In peace
in me
the meaning
of our lives
is still
unfolding.
Rest.

Then the tears came.

She was clearing the books from the bottom shelf when she noticed the single sheet of paper on the floor at the bottom of the bookcase. She slid it out and turned it over, thinking it must be one of the papers scattered by the wind when she was here in the early hours of the morning. It was. An illustration of a map. Sketch map of Fort Winter, the caption read, made by Dr Isaac Trapham, in the summer of 1655.

Jessica sat on the floor, staring at the map and thinking of what Calhoun had told her.

It bothered her that Maddie had a copy of the map that had directed them to the bodies. It bothered her that Maddie's own body had been found so close to the grave.

She tried to remember what Calhoun had told her.

The map was in a book that belonged to Mrs Graham. Innis had found it a few days ago.

So when had Maddie found it?

Was it the same book, or another one?

And why had she made a copy?

There was only one person who could tell her, and she wasn't the kind of person you could call with questions like that.

But before she left, she rang Hannah at the school and asked her if she'd mind bringing Freya home at the end of the day in case she was late getting back.

The snow was a little heavier when she went out, but it hadn't started to settle yet on the wet roads.

XII

Calhoun found Hannah in the school gym watching a basketball game. She was clapping and shouting like an overgrown school-girl, but she stopped when she saw him and he thought her face lost a little colour.

'What's happened?' she said.

'We might have found the weapon that killed Madeleine Ross,' he told her. He asked if there was somewhere they could talk in private, and she took him into the administrator's office. Through the window he could see the snow sweeping in across the play-ground. It was almost dark but she didn't switch the light on.

He told her instead about the skulls that were missing from the ossuary.

'I think it's a fair bet they're the same skulls that were found in the grave,' he said and then, after a moment for her to think about it, worry about it, 'and that they were put there to provide evidence of a massacre. So, I've been thinking who was going to lose out if the Souriquois won this case of theirs?'

She watched him carefully, her eyes very big in the pale moon face.

He said: 'Obviously the State of Massachusetts, but I can't see them being that concerned about the taxpayer's money, can you?

'So then I started wondering who the landowners were. They'd get compensation, of course, but maybe there was some reason they wanted to hold on to the land, something they couldn't claim for, something we didn't know about. D'you find gold there, Hannah? Or what?'

Still she didn't answer. She looked away from him out of the window at the snow.

'I got the name from the university – a company called Russell Estates, registered in St John. I've just checked them out with the Chamber of Commerce. There were only two directors – Innis

Graham and yourself. And the company secretary was Raymond Pellet. That's Little Raymond, I guess?'

The silence lengthened and he thought he might have to suggest a trip down to the State police barracks in Dover – but then she started.

It had begun more than two years ago with the collapse of the Graham business empire and the death of Innis's father, Richard. The Graham lumber and paper mills in Bridport had been the last major employers in Bridport, and government had finally come up with a rescue plan. It included building a large marina with berths for more than a hundred boats, summer cabins, shops, restaurants . . . a massive investment in tourism.

'I came back from the council meeting and told Raymond about it. I told him it was all very confidential, but he talked to Innis, and Innis said with the kind of tides you get on this coast, the only place to site a marina that big was Deepwater Cove. Apparently it's the only anchorage for about a hundred miles that isn't drained at low tide. Otherwise, he said, we'd have to spend millions building a new harbour.

'The Grahams still owned the land on Kitehawk Head, but they were going to have to sell it to pay off their creditors, and there was a chance they'd lose everything – the house, even his precious schooner. So what Innis proposed was that he sell the land to me at a knock-down price to stop it going to the creditors, and make him co-owner. Then, if the marina plan came off, we could sell it at a premium and share the profit.

'Raymond said I couldn't lose. If the marina didn't happen I could sell the land for what I paid for it. If it did, I'd make a killing.'

It was an unfortunate word to use and she was silent for a moment. Calhoun sat very still, watching her face in profile against the fading light in the window, as if it would be a mistake to remind her that he was there. After a moment or two she picked up the story:

'I raised a mortgage on the inn, capitalised all my savings, borrowed as much as I could . . . Raymond did all the business for me. There was nothing illegal about it, but if the council members found out I was involved they'd think I pulled a fast one – and they'd be right, I guess.

'Well, then they found the graves. The university wanted to excavate. Innis said we should turn them down, but there didn't seem to be any reason, and I was scared the local press would get on to it and find out who the owners were. So they dug up the bodies and found they'd all died of scurvy, and the Indians slapped in their land claim.

'There was still no movement on the marina. If the Indians won their case, all we'd get was the money we'd paid for it. *I'd* paid. Maybe I'd have settled for that, I don't know, but Innis was . . . it was like something personal for him. It was *his* land. His ancestors' land. He was going to be cheated out of his inheritance, all he had left.

'He offered to help with the dig. Moved his schooner into Deepwater Cove. I didn't figure it out at first – who would have? But then Raymond started spending more time with him. Sometimes he'd come back in the middle of the night and he'd always have a shower before he came to bed . . .'

It was the first indication she'd given that she and Raymond had more than a strictly professional relationship. She turned to look at Calhoun directly and he saw there were tears in her eyes.

'Raymond's bisexual, I guess you know that? Well, it sounds crazy – it *was* crazy – but I was jealous, they were so thick together. I thought him and Innis . . .' She shook her head. 'Sad, stupid old woman. But I challenged him with it and he told me what they were up to. Pleased with himself, like a big kid. They were taking the bodies they'd already dug up, smashing the skulls and burying them again in a different place, in amongst the trees. They could only manage one or two at a time, covering the ground with pine needles afterwards so no one would notice.

'I couldn't believe it. They had to be out of their minds. I went to see Innis next morning and told him that was it, I was having nothing more to do with it. He said I didn't have to have anything to do with it, all I had to do was keep my mouth shut. I'd not seen this side of him before, he was always such a charmer. He was like a gangster. "I was in too deep to pull out now", that kind of thing.

'I fell out with Raymond over it. But . . . I did keep my mouth shut.' She nodded to herself a few times as if accepting the responsibility for that. It was hard to know if she accepted the responsibility for anything else.

Calhoun said: 'The night Madeleine Ross was killed – was that one of the nights Raymond was out there planting bodies?'

She shook her head but she wouldn't meet his eyes. 'I don't know. We'd stopped . . . spending the night together. But I know he was in the bar until way past eleven.'

Then she looked up and there was a desperate appeal in her eyes.

'I thought it was a bear. Everyone did.'

'It must have crossed your mind that she saw something,' he said, 'and that one of them killed her.'

She put her hand up to her face and held it there as if she was holding herself together. He waited for her to say something but she didn't. Perhaps there was nothing else for her *to* say.

XIII

Jessica emerged from the tunnel of pines into a vast monochrome world of sky and sea and whirling snow. She felt as if her eyes had retreated back into her skull with the sudden shock of the encounter, and it was a moment before they focused on the house on the edge of the cove. For all its substance there was something almost ethereal about it, something hopelessly out of place. It might have been a film set, a shot in a black-and-white movie, the temple of the lost tribe, glimpsed through a sandstorm in the desert.

There were no lights in the windows.

When she opened the car door, the wind whipped the snow into her face as if moved by some personal animosity. Bowing her head, she hurried up the steps to the front door and rang the bell. As she waited she watched the snow being blown, almost horizontally now, across the inlet. It had covered the surrounding pines and the little wooden jetty, and when she looked back up the drive she saw the tracks of her car were almost erased.

She turned away, almost with relief, after the third ring and was halfway down the steps when she heard the door open. A woman stood there, huddled against the cold, her eyes wincing as if from a hard light.

'I'm sorry,' Jessica began, 'but I wondered if Mrs Graham was in.'

'I'm Lindy Graham,' said the woman.

She had appeared too young for Innis's mother, but as Jessica looked more carefully she saw the lines at the corner of the rheumy eyes, the threads of grey in the long brown hair. She wore Levi's tucked into cowboy boots and a baggy sweater.

Jessica tried to explain who she was and why she'd come. The woman watched her without enlightenment or welcome, but when Jessica finished, she asked her if she'd like a glass of wine. Jessica thought she'd probably had a few already.

She followed her through the darkened house towards a wedge of light from a half-open door.

'Is Innis not back?' Jessica called after her, but there was no indication that she had heard.

The light came from the kitchen which Lindy Graham had clearly made into her refuge, or den. There was an armchair pulled close to the cooker with a blanket and some magazines on the floor beside it – and several dirty cups and glasses. There were dirty dishes everywhere, in fact, and the remains of a meal on the table with two or three open bottles of wine.

Lindy inspected them one after another, as if she was wondering how they came to be empty. She opened a cupboard.

'Must have some somewhere,' she said.

Jessica sat at the table and moved a plate of congealed food out of her direct vision.

'Maybe in the refrigerator,' she said, more out of embarrassment for the increasingly desperate Lindy than because she herself needed a drink. In fact a drink in this place was the last thing she needed.

'No, there won't be any there,' Lindy said, and she gave the refrigerator a brief, bitter glance as if it was a fair-weather friend who had let her down badly in the past. She opened it, all the same. From the glimpse Jessica had, it looked almost empty. She wondered if they were really this broke, or whether it was just a measure of Lindy's dottiness that there was no food in the house. Either way, she thought Innis might have made sure she had enough to keep her going while he was away.

Lindy gazed vaguely around the room, perhaps, and as if for the first time, noticing the state it was in.

'You can't get the servants these days,' she said. Jessica smiled, thinking it was an old joke, but from the expression on Lindy's face she wasn't at all sure that it was.

'I better not stay,' she said, 'or I'll be snowed in. I was just wondering about this.'

She opened her purse and unfolded the page with the map. Lindy put on the glasses that she wore on a ribbon around her neck.

'I found it in Maddie's room,' Jessica said. 'I think it's from a book of yours.'

Lindy inspected it briefly and then gave it back. 'Could be,' she said. 'I know she borrowed one of my books for a while.'

'When was this?'

'Oh, I don't know, months ago, I don't remember.' Her eyes continued their restless search across the chaos of the kitchen. 'I only remember her taking it because Innis got so mad about it when he found it was gone.'

'*Innis* got mad about it?' What was the woman talking about?

'Oh yes, you should see him when he's mad. You all think he's so charming, but I'm his mother. He may not like to think so but . . .'

'But I thought Innis only found this book a few days ago.'

'Well, if that's what he wants to tell everybody. All I know is, I gave it him when he first came back here, before he ever started working up there. I told her when she phoned.'

'When who phoned?'

'Kate Wendicott. And it's no use him pretending he never read it. I saw him. I told her, he's known about that map for six months or more . . .'

'I'm sorry . . .' Jessica tried to slow her down. 'But when did you have this conversation with Dr Wendicott?'

'What day is today?'

Jessica told her.

'Must have been Wednesday, then.'

'You mean the night of the fire?'

Lindy looked blank. 'What fire?' she said.

'It doesn't matter. About what time was this phone call?'

'Oh, I don't know. It was late, I know that. I was in bed, reading. I remember thinking, I wonder where *he's* off to, this time of night?'

'What do you mean?' Jessica felt as if the blood had drained from her face. 'You mean *Innis went out* – after he spoke to Kate Wendicott?'

'I heard the car,' Lindy's voice was petulant. 'There was no one else here.'

But there was something in her eyes besides irritation, something that made Jessica suddenly very cautious. A glimpse of intelligence, more than that, what was it? Something catlike, something cunning.

The sound of the phone made Jessica jump. Lindy picked it up.

'Jessica?' she said. 'There's no one here called Jessica, you must have the wrong number.'

'That's me,' Jessica said hastily. She took the phone from her before she could cut the caller off.

It was Hannah. Immediately Jessica heard the tone of her voice she knew Freya had done another runner.

'It completely went out of my mind,' Hannah said. She sounded close to hysterical. 'I got there within minutes of the end of classes, but she'd already gone. I've driven all the way back to the inn, but she's not here.'

'But where could she have gone? It's practically a blizzard.'

'The only thing I can think of is the bus.'

'What bus?'

'The school bus. It does a tour of the town and then drops off the kids who live on the mainland. I've been trying to get through to the bus driver, but her mobile can't be working in the snow . . .'

'The mainland? Hannah – does it go anywhere near Kitehawk Head?'

'The last stop is about half a mile away. I'm just going to call the families of the kids who get off there, but maybe I should drive out . . .'

'No, you make the calls. I'll drive out there.'

'Something wrong?' Lindy asked when she put the phone down.

'I have to go,' Jessica said.

But when she opened the outside door and saw the snow she hesitated for a second and turned back . . .

'I have to drive out to Kitehawk Head,' she told Lindy. 'My little girl's missing, and I think that's where she's gone, only I don't have four-wheel drive. You don't happen to have a truck or a jeep I could borrow . . . ?'

But she could see from Lindy's face that she might as well have asked if there was any food in the refrigerator.

'Why should she have gone to Kitehawk Head?' she heard her say but she was already out the door.

The wheels spun a bit when she started, but once she had the car moving it wasn't so bad. Then, about fifty yards or so from the end of the drive, a pickup turned off the highway and came barrelling towards her, spraying snow. She trod on the brake and felt the back of the car slide away from her into the trees. There was a crunch as it hit one of the pines and she was temporarily blinded by the fall of snow on the windscreen. When the wipers cleared it she saw the pickup had stopped and Innis was getting out.

The engine had stalled, and when she started it again the wheels were spinning hopelessly in the deep snow at the edge of the drive. She saw Innis shouting something at her but couldn't hear him for the sound of the engine. She revved violently, and then just as he reached the far side of the car, the wheels gripped and it lurched forward into the drive. She swung the wheel, slewed wildly, and somehow shot through the gap between the pickup and the trees. Seconds later she was skidding across the highway.

XIV

'Let me tell you the theory,' Calhoun suggests to Beckman. A part of him is surprised at the arrogance in his voice. The other part ploughs on regardless, quite enjoying it, the sense of power. More surprisingly, there is silence on the other end of the phone. Beckman is apparently listening.

'There was snow forecast for the night of October 30th. Graham knew he had to get the last of the bodies planted before they packed up for the winter and this was the perfect night for it. The snow would cover up the evidence that someone had been digging among the trees. But then Madeleine Ross turns up. He has to get rid of her. They quarrel and she stalks off and Graham, he heads straight for the ossuary. But when she gets to the car she finds she's left her keys behind. Halfway along the cliff she runs into him with an armful of bones. Or maybe he's already smashing the skulls with that fake bear's paw he made.'

'So he makes a few holes in her instead.'

Calhoun cannot tell from the Lieutenant's voice if this is meant to be ironic or not. He does not particularly care either way.

'He probably thought he didn't have much choice, if he thought about it at all. More likely he just took a swing at her.'

'And what's your theory about the other one, your Doctor Kate? He takes all this trouble to provide evidence of a massacre – then sets fire to it?'

'He had photographs. He took them himself when they came out of the ground. Plenty of witnesses. He probably reckoned that was enough. But, again, she forced his hand. Maybe she said something so he knew she hadn't fallen for it. And if she finds out about the scam it throws a whole new light on the death of Madeleine Ross. It's easy enough to start a fire with all those chemicals. What he doesn't figure is on running into Kate . . .'

'Runs into a lot of women, your old buddy.'

'Maybe he meant to kill her. Who knows? But he had the motive and the opportunity, and in a little while forensic are going to tell us he had the weapon.'

'You hope.'

But Calhoun has more than hope.

'The garbage bag was dragged up just a few hundred yards out from Deepwater Cove where Innis kept his boat. On his own admission he had been out to check his lobster pots. We've got the weapon, the clothes – and the boots. And we already know they're a size too small for Joe Selmo.'

'Maybe his feet have grown.'

'You're not serious.'

'No, I'm just in the mood for a few laughs, Calhoun. I'm that kind of guy. The bastard's already confessed to fucking up the church.'

'What? Him personally?'

'Not him personally but some kids he put up to it. Says he thought they went a bit far with the statue.'

'We haven't established any connection,' Calhoun points out, 'between what happened at the church and what happened on the headland. And I'm pretty damn sure there isn't one.'

'Well, let's wait for the analysis from forensics, shall we, before we're pretty damn sure about anything. You already picked up Graham once and let him go.'

'The hell with that,' Calhoun says aloud to the phone, a moment after the Lieutenant has hung up.

'Excuse me?' Jensen, ears flapping across the room.

'I need to talk to Innis Graham. You got a jeep can get us out to his place?'

Jensen looks out of the window in mock horror. 'In this? You'd need a fucking snow plough.'

Jensen does not normally swear. He takes his lead from those he looks up to. Calhoun's mother would have said he should set a good example.

'Well, then get us a fucking snow plough.'

But in the end they went in the jeep.

XV

And so finally she took the turning she could not take and came to the place where her sister had died, to the place of the bear dreamers and her own nightmares.

It was darker now and the wind hurled the snow into her face like grit. But she could make out a shape here and there that jolted her with the shock of recognition, either from the pictures on television or her own dark imaginings: the black girders of the burned-out cannery and the ragged fringe of pines along the edge of the cliff.

She stumbled towards them through the snow, turning frequently as if batted by the wind's paw, hands held up above her head to peer through this scattered jigsaw of a world searching for one small, darker shape among the flying pieces.

She passed the banks of snow-covered earth that marked the dig and skirted the stand of birch trees where Maddie had died, looking more carefully here, searching the ground itself for the child-sized shadow that might be kneeling in prayer or, more likely, crouched in a grieving huddle, curled up in foetal submission to the mother's womb, as if begging the earth to let her in.

But it was surely more than grief that brought her here. It was as if something *called* to the child, something beyond Jessica's understanding but not quite beyond her own power to sense, if not to see. She could sense it now, as she struggled up the cliff path, and it terrified her.

A light came on, high above her head, so unexpected she almost lost her footing on the path, and in its gleam she saw the snow, falling far heavier and faster even than she had imagined, and then the steps leading down the side of the cliff and far below the waves breaking over the pier where Innis had left his boat. And in the wind she heard the whistling buoy somewhere out in the dark turbulence beyond the headland and the crashing waves, the sea voices . . .

. . . *the sea howl and the sea yelp, and the wailing warning* . . .

Warnings. She was assailed by warnings – warnings in the verse she had read in Maddie's cabin, warnings in her own dreams – and had ignored them all. And now she was moving away from the cliff and into the forest, and her flashlight showed her the graves where the bones had been buried and the charnel house where now they lay – and the dark shadow that moved towards her through the trees beyond it.

But not the shadow she sought, too big for that, too black for that, and she fled away from it, back towards the cliff and the light.

And in the light she saw Innis.

She knew it was Innis despite the mask he wore, the black woollen mask that terrorists and bank robbers wore, that the nuns in a more innocent age had called a Balaclava and that now seemed so like the face of a bear. And even in her terror she remembered the theme of the Oxford lecture – a snatch of memory from a distant world – that masks are worn not for disguise but for resolve, to enable the wearer to act a part, to break his own taboos and play the Devil.

He moved towards her but she was faster, moving the only way she could which was down, down the steps to the sea. Too fast. There was ice beneath the snow and her right leg shot from under her and she fell, twisting in the air and landing heavily on her side at the very edge of the cliff, a terrible pain in elbow and hip. She took the first kick in her head and then he stamped on her hand and she felt the bones crack against the ice-sealed granite.

He heard, or sensed, something before she did, for even in her shock and pain she saw him turn, raising an arm above his head. It came out of the darkness and the snow and she could not be sure if there was a blow, but he was falling across her shoulders, almost taking her with him, and she heard an exhalation of breath, a deeper note of the wind, that could have been him or the animal itself.

That there was an animal she was never in any doubt, though she saw it for a mere fraction of time against the light on the top of the steps before it moved away into the forest and the snow.

There was no exchange of glances.

Above and beyond the pain of her body and the confusion of her soul she heard the whistling buoy, the calamitous annunciation.

There was a theory that he had slipped – and certainly the steps were icy enough – and there was little enough of his face after a night of pounding against the rocks to give any certitude to pathology.

Calhoun, when he came, found Freya in the ossuary where she had gone to shelter from the wind. She did not seem unduly bothered by the skulls. The children had stayed with her, she said, in case she got scared. When they asked her what children, she said the children who saw them kill the bear, and they guessed she meant the children of the Quaker settlers that were long dead.

But Freya was not afraid of the dead.

XVI

With those other, grimmer associations of her childhood – sex and guilt, love and pain, pleasure and remorse – there was one more cheering. Sickness and comfort.

It would have been different, she supposed, if she had been seriously ill, but one of the rare treats of Jessica's schooldays was to be confined in the convent infirmary in the care of Mother Martha.

The infirmary was a sanctuary of calm and order, unchilled by the rigorous disciplines that prevailed elsewhere in that stoic institute of virtue and strength through suffering. Jessica remembered the smooth, cool sheets and the plump pillows, the red nightlight burning under the statue of Our Lady, the sharp smell of medication, so welcome after the ubiquitous odour of candle wax, beeswax and incense – and most of all the consoling presence of Mother Martha herself, clean and starched as the sheets and smelling like them of lavender and the linen cupboard.

When she understood the meaning of the word – as much as she ever would – Jessica would consider it ironic that the nuns at her school were called Mother, not Sister. Sister, she felt, would have been more appropriate to their strict supervision, their fear of unrestrained affection, their abiding concern to send their charges armoured into the world. (Was this where she had learned her own concept of sisterhood, she wondered, and defined her relationship with Maddie – or was it there before, laid down by the genes of her father, who had his own problems with love and pain?) But the guardian angel of the infirmary was the one Mother deserving the name, the one who did not hold back from affection, who was not afraid of warmth in case it weakened them against the cold.

Mother Martha, as Jessica remembered her, was neither young nor old. Her face was unlined, her complexion blooming, but there was a maturity in her expression, a gravitas that made you think she was older. She was also American, and began another lifelong association in Jessica's mind – of a certain type of American accent with kindness and composure. After her amah, Selma Kuresh, she was the nearest Jessica had to a real mother.

It was surprising that she was not sick more often, but then the route to Mother Martha was well guarded for fear of indulgence and the cracks it opened in the armour plating of the soul.

She was detained for observation, they said, mainly on account of the blow to the head, though when she arrived it was the only part of her that did not hurt. She had a cracked rib, three fingers broken in her left hand, and a wondrous bruise from hip to thigh. She slept better than she had for any night since she had learned of Maddie's death. They said it was the painkillers.

Freya was also *detained for observation*, in another part of the hospital, though her physical condition, they assured Jessica, gave no cause for concern. They dodged the question of her mental state. No one spoke of the potential effect of the hours she had spent in the charnel house on the headland. No one spoke of the bear. Not, at least, to Jessica. Not then.

In the morning Calhoun came and told her about Innis, and how they had found his body on the rocks at the foot of the cliffs where it had been left by the retreating tide. He had just been to see his mother.

'How did she take it?' Jessica asked.

She saw that he had to think about this and even then he had trouble finding the words.

'I can't say I was ever too sure what goes on in that lady's head.'

'A lot more than people think,' Jessica said, more sharply than she had intended, and he looked at her as if he was wondering how much to tell her, or how much she already knew.

'She's always used a lot of cover,' he said, 'and now it's the drink.'

'She told me enough to put him away for life – as if she had no idea what she was doing.'

'Maybe she didn't – and if she did, he did kill two women.'

'I don't think that had a lot to do with it, do you? I think it had a lot more to do with the fact that he kept her on short rations. "*I remember thinking I wonder where he's off to, this time of night. . .*"' Jessica mimed the little girl voice with its discontented whine . . . 'And then she told him exactly what she'd told me and exactly where he could find me. Malicious old bat.'

He said: 'She can hardly have known he was going to come back in time to catch you there.'

'He probably phoned her to say he was on his way . . .' But already she was starting to feel sorry for the woman, guilt for blaming her. 'Oh, I don't know. I don't suppose she figures things out that rationally. I think she just likes people to suffer for her own pain, or whatever it is . . . Discontent. I suspect that's why Innis was . . . partly the way he was, but . . .'

'What?' he said, watching her carefully.

She shrugged. 'I'm just surprised he thought he could get away with it.'

But it was not what she had meant to say. She had meant to say she still could not believe he had tried to kill her, that it was his body they had found at the foot of the cliffs.

'They always have,' Calhoun said. 'Haven't they?'

And she looked at him sharply, startled by the bitterness in his own voice, but his expression seemed more sad than sour.

'Besides,' he said. 'He nearly did. If we hadn't found the weapon we'd have been trying to hang it on Joe Selmo, still.'

Selmo had been released in the early hours of the morning. It was doubtful, Calhoun said, if he would be charged with vandalising the church. Given the allegations against the priest, they'd never find a local jury that would convict him.

Calhoun had talked with him shortly after his release and he'd told him about the falling out between Yvette and Maddie.

'Joe was in love with her, or thought he was, and Yvette . . . well, I guess she thought Maddie was fooling around with him. The older woman, *femme fatale* . . .' It was difficult for Jessica to think of Maddie as an older woman, perhaps not as the *femme fatale*. 'They're very protective over that boy. They've got a lot of hope pinned on him.'

'Will they get the land?'

'I don't think there's much doubt about that. Not with the publicity they're going to get over this. The land and the money. They were cheated 300 years ago – Innis Graham tried to cheat them now – you can just see the headlines if some smart State lawyer tries to cheat them in court. He wants to come and see you, by the way.'

It was a moment before she realised who he meant.

'Joe?'

'I think all three of them. Do you have any objection?'

Surprisingly, she found that she did not.

She would never warm to Yvette Selmo, but she knew her dislike, her hostility, had less to do with the woman herself than the fear she evoked, fear of something in Jessica herself. Of *the backward half-look, Over the shoulder into the primitive terror.*

Avoiding that – trying not to look – had been a guiding principle of Jessica's life. But for Yvette – and for Freya, too – the primitive held few terrors; the dead, the living and the world of the spirits were bound together by one continuous, reassuring thread.

It was something Jessica faintly remembered, from her own childhood, a part of that dreamy little girl who had watched the kites flying with her mother from the roofs of Lahore but had got lost somewhere on the route to adulthood.

She focused her mind on Calhoun again. He was saying the police would want her to make a statement about the death of Innis Graham – and probably Freya, too.

'But she wasn't there,' she protested, instantly protective. Then, qualifying this: 'Not so that she could have seen anything. What could she tell you?'

He nodded to himself, but not in such a way that she thought he was agreeing with her.

Then he said: 'We haven't been able to find any traces of the bear.'

She said nothing.

'We'll keep looking, but . . .' he shrugged as if he had no expectation of success – and perhaps did not care, either way.

Jessica did not want to talk about the bear, or whatever it was that had saved her on the headland of the *Keytawkws*. She was glad enough to be saved. Let the bear rest in peace. Pray that it would.

'And now will I be able to bury my sister?' she said.

But it was Freya who made the decisions, who chose the way of it.

And it was not so different from the way Jessica would have chosen – except for the place.

They walked together, hand in hand, out on to the headland, the Selmos and Calhoun a few steps behind and the ashes in their little wooden casket.

The bear totem was back, or another just like it, near the place where Maddie had died. No one challenged its right to be there.

The Souriquois Council had plans to build a permanent monument – a learning centre along the lines proposed by Kate Wendicott, to commemorate the dead and instruct the living. It would be a memorial to her and Maddie and all those who had died on Kitehawk Head. A place to keep the bones.

Urbain Selmo had asked Jessica if she would help to set it up, to be a consultant. She had been touched by the thought, but had declined. It was Freya who chose the pattern of their life now, and Freya thought they should live in Oxford until Jessica finished her doctorate.

'And how do you feel about that?' Calhoun had asked Jessica.

'We need to get away from this place,' she said. 'At least for a while.'

'I meant more . . . about having Freya with you,' he said.

'Good. I feel good about it,' she said. 'I think I was a bit scared of being a mother, scared that I'd fail, but it's better than not trying.'

His own plans seemed less defined. He had said nothing more to her about resigning from the police, but he talked vaguely of 'travelling'.

He said: 'One of the navy doctors – the only one I had any time for – said I just didn't want to destroy my illusions. That I'd been everywhere – up here . . .' he tapped a finger against the side of his head '. . . by the time I was thirteen. I'd done the Caribbean, the South Sea islands, the Med, and we never left the bay . . .' She knew then he was talking about Innis and his boat '. . . He thought that deep down I was scared of doing them for real in case I was disappointed.'

'And what if you are?' she asked him.

'I don't know,' he said, the failed fisherman considering his sad nets, but then he smiled and quoted her own expression back at her: 'Perhaps it's better than not trying.'

'Well, if you do, don't miss Oxford,' she told him. It was the thinnest of threads but she cast it carefully, like a spell, and hoped that it would bind him.

They walked in single file up the cliff path with Freya determinedly leading the way, past the place where Innis had moored his boat and where he had died on the rocks. Past the place of bones, out on to the headland proper and the place of the *Keytawkws*.

The wind was blowing from the north-west and it carried the ashes clear of the cliff and out beyond the rocks to the now-quieted and properly sombre sea.

Jessica had brought a rose, a late rose she had found filled with snow in Calhoun's mother's garden, and Freya had made a doll from sea-grass, though it might have been a bear, Jessica did not like to ask. They watched them fall through the still air in the lea of the cliff and float together on the redeeming tide.

A NOTE ON THE AUTHOR

Paul Bryers was born in Liverpool and was a history
teacher before working as a journalist and film maker.
He has written many novels and screenplays. He now
lives in London.